DARK WINGS
DESCENDING

By the Author

Truth Behind the Mask

Playing Passion's Game

Dark Wings Descending

Visit us at www.boldstrokesbooks.com

DARK WINGS
DESCENDING

by

Lesley Davis

2012

DARK WINGS DESCENDING
© 2012 By Lesley Davis. All Rights Reserved.

ISBN 13: 978-1-60282-660-1

This Trade Paperback Original Is Published By
Bold Strokes Books, Inc.
P.O. Box 249
Valley Falls, NY 12185

First Edition: May 2012

CREDITS
EDITORS: CINDY CRESAP AND STACIA SEAMAN
PRODUCTION DESIGN: STACIA SEAMAN
COVER DESIGN BY SHERI (GRAPHICARTIST2020@HOTMAIL.COM)

Acknowledgments

Thank you, Radclyffe, for your untiring support and fantastic encouragement always.

To the Bold Strokes family of writers and staff that bind us all together stronger than any Force I know!

For Cindy Cresap, who constantly has to tread through the mine field of Brit speak and does so with such grace, and amazingly, very little swearing! I appreciate everything you do for me and the care you take with my writing. You truly rock.

Thank you, Stacia Seaman, for making sure that nothing sneaks past on your watch! You are a great companion on this writer's journey!

Thank you, Sheri, for another amazing cover that just blows my tiny mind! You're fantastic!

For Wayne Beckett, for always supporting me in all I endeavor to do.

For Jacky Hart and Jane Morrison for never ceasing to offer support, friendship, and gentle hints for me to put my controller down and get back to writing for them!! Thanks guys!!

And for Cindy Pfannenstiel, with much love and thanks to you always. xx

To the ones who watch over us and keep us safe from harm.

CHAPTER ONE

The dead woman was laid out in the alley like a grotesque mannequin, half-naked and fixed in pose. She lay on her back with one arm reaching up above her head while the other lay at her side. Her blond head was tilted as if to follow where her arm was pointing, her sightless eyes fixed on a point somewhere down the dark alley. A dark red stain spread underneath her from waist to shoulders. The blood fanned out, glistening like an oil spill framing her upper torso. Clouds shifted across the pale moon, and for a brief moment, the horror of what lay in the alley disappeared from view. Lost to the dark that blanketed the city. Dead to the night.

Ashley Scott leaned a little further out over the fire escape railing. The flashes from her camera lit up the alley like bolts of lightning. She stepped back into shadow as she heard the familiar wail of sirens racing to the scene she had just anonymously called in. She checked her watch. "Three minutes. Guess three murders in just over a month will make you skip a few red lights." Carefully, she picked her way down the fire escape steps, then settled herself out of sight in a doorway well out of light's reach. She watched the police cars draw up and scanned the faces of the officers who began to secure the scene. She didn't spot the forensic team's black SUV and strained to hear the conversations of the busy police as they cordoned off the area until the team's arrival. She garnered the exact piece of information she needed from their chatter and furtively cast a look around. "Where's a telephone booth when you need one?" she muttered, then stepped out of the doorway and strode purposefully toward the crime scene tape.

Ashley nodded at the policewoman guarding the alley entrance. "Evening, Officer Atkinson."

"Hi, Jim," Officer Atkinson replied and lifted up the crime scene tape for Ashley to slip under. Ashley headed straight for the body, snapping off photographs on her way to document the whole scene from close quarters. She took as many photos as she could, aware that the medical examiner was standing nearby.

"Evening, Jim," Dr. Joseph Alan greeted her absently, patiently waiting for her to finish so he could get back to his own work. "Third dead woman we've been called out to looking like this. I hate to say it, but I'm beginning to see a pattern emerging." He looked at the sky. "There's not some strange planetary alignment going on that we don't know about, is there?"

Ashley edged closer to the body, clicking her camera the entire time. She carefully stepped around the spreading blood. "I think Jupiter is right where it should be, Dr. Alan. Some people don't need their stars aligned to kill."

He shook his head. "What is the world coming to when a killer can't leave a calling card so we can identify him from the rest of the crazies?"

"There was still nothing left on the body at all?" Ashley was aware of the previous victims. She'd been at the last one's final resting place too. She steeled herself to stand over the woman and her eyes swept down the posed body. She couldn't prevent the shiver of horror that chilled her to the bone at the look of abject terror frozen on the dead woman's face. "She took a nasty blow to the head this time."

Ashley's camera flashed to document the injuries. She noticed how the woman's hair had been swept out of its natural parting to hide the wound. Did the killer regret what he'd done and had made some attempt to make her beautiful once more? Ashley found herself unable to look away from the woman's face. What had once been a pretty visage was now a contorted mask of fear. "Nasty neck wound too." Ashley saw the deep slash that had slit the woman's throat wide open. *Hope it was quick.* She made her way down the posed body, noticing how the woman's clothes had been ripped to shreds. "I can't get my head around this one, Doc. The killer rips open their jackets and shirts and pulls down their skirts or pants, but there is no sign of a sexual assault." She took a few more pictures, frowning at the state the clothing had been left in. "The clothes are cut off strangely," she said to herself. "Almost like they were just in the way. As if leaving the body unclothed wasn't to defile them, it was just a simple act of moving the cloth out of the way so he could get to what he wanted." She took a step back and called the medical examiner forward. "Care to do the honors, please?" She moved around so that the doctor could ease the body over for her.

Ashley grimaced as she saw the familiar trait of this particular killer. "And again with the ripping open of the back." She took her photos, making sure to capture the horrendous wounds. The skin had been cut right through to the bone, exposing the spine itself. Jagged cuts ran from the base of the neck down to the hips. The skin was pulled back and everything else had been hacked at to reveal the bones inside. "Why would you kill someone just so you could rip open their body to expose their backbone?"

"Maybe he's searching for one of his own?" Dr. Alan said as he placed the woman back on the ground reverently once Ashley signaled she was finished.

Ashley spared him a look. "He doesn't even take a piece of disc with him. You'd think if he was cutting someone open to get to their spine he'd want something specific from it." She watched as he got back to his feet with a groan. "You okay there?"

"I'm too old to be dragged out of bed to come to yet another dead woman in an alley," he grumbled.

Ashley looked him over, seeing a balding, slightly overweight man in his late fifties who had seen death in all its forms for way too many years. "I'd say you still have plenty of years left, Doc. Then you can retire on that yacht of yours with Mary and kiss Chicago good-bye." She looked at him over the top of her camera. "You've got grandbabies to bounce on your knee one day before you even think about getting too old."

"I hope you're right. I'd rather deal with them than any more of these." He stared down at the body. "I estimate time of death at being barely an hour ago."

Ashley nodded, knowing that was roughly the time she'd been informed that another body had been left. "And no one saw or heard anything again, I bet." She looked up at the surrounding apartment buildings that crowded the alley like protective monoliths.

"This killer strikes so fast they don't have time to make a sound." Dr. Alan pointed at the victim's neck wound. "He comes up behind them and cuts their throats open, very effectively silencing them."

"He's got to be covered in blood," Ashley said, looking at her feet. She had been making sure her boots didn't touch any of the blood that stained the ground. "Yet there are never any partial prints left behind."

"He's clean and efficient all right. It's like the devil himself slips in and brings his own hell on earth."

Ashley's whole body tensed at his words. She forced herself not to react and just continued taking photos. She looked at the dead woman, her sightless eyes wide open and her last terrifying moments etched permanently on her face. Her mouth was left open in an endless silent scream as she lay posed reaching for…what? Ashley shook her head. *Salvation maybe? Someone who could stop the madman?* "I think the devil's been here all along, Doc, but only a few of us recognize his handiwork."

Dr. Alan slapped her gently on her shoulder. "Finish up your job, son, and I'll get this lady taken away from here."

Ashley nodded distractedly as she heard more cars pulling up. Taking this as her cue, she faked looking at her camera in dismay. "Oh Christ, Doc, I'm sorry. I've been running on empty. The damn camera has no memory card in it." She stepped back from the body. "What a stupid amateur mistake. The boss will have my head if he finds out. I'll be back in just a second. I need to go get one from my case." She watched from the corner of her eye as Dr. Alan just sighed and stared back up at the stars.

Ashley left the crime scene and dodged under the tape. There was a growing crowd of officers all huddled together keeping the fast-arriving press and interested onlookers back from the alley. She spotted Detective Stephanie Powell gathering people together. Ashley let her eyes linger just a second longer than usual. *Please tell me you're not in charge now that a third murder makes this a serial case and headline news at ten every night.* She saw another detective rush past Powell, a man who appeared to be in his late thirties, quite tall and boyishly handsome. He seemed to be making a path for the detective who was following him with a much slower gait. Ashley's curiosity got the better of her and she stopped to see who this other detective was. It was a woman, at least five feet eight, making her easily as tall as her male counterpart. She was slender but broad-shouldered. Ashley was surprised to note she looked oddly frail as she walked past. Her handsome face was also strangely mottled under the moon's waning light. A woolen beanie hat embroidered with a police shield was pulled down over her head, hiding any clue to her hair color. Ashley grinned as the male reached out a hand to the woman only to receive a withering glare in response.

"Just show me the damn body, Dean, and quit with the nursemaid attitude."

Ashley liked the deep quality to her voice, even colored by the exasperation audible in it. She wondered at the story behind his solicitude. Aware she needed to leave, Ashley disappeared into the crowd, cradling her camera protectively to her as she passed Crime Scene Photographer Jim Pope as he headed toward the scene. She heard Officer Atkinson remark, "How many more pictures are you taking tonight?" but never heard his reply as he set about doing his job. Ashley slipped through the cars that lined the alley and crossed the road.

Out of sight of prying eyes she *shifted*; a glimmering, sparkling, golden tone colored her world for a moment and then dissipated. Ashley watched her reflection in a small window as she lost the appearance of a young man with short cropped hair and a height of at least six feet dressed in his CSI uniform. Left behind was a much shorter woman, sporting tousled blond hair and wearing a long black jacket over her black shirt and jeans. She stared at the reflection looking back at her. "Still a neat trick," she told herself and headed for home.

Entering her apartment building, Ashley chuckled quietly at the boy who sat sprawled in his chair, supposedly keeping watch. His head was back, his mouth wide open as he slept.

"Nice to know you're keeping the building safe, Jeffrey," Ashley whispered, electing to take the stairs to her second-floor apartment so as not to disturb him with the elevator's noisy arrival. The building was silent. Everyone else was apparently asleep as she walked down the corridor to her door. She opened it and reached in to switch the lights on. She studiously ignored the drabness of her hastily rented apartment, trying once again to quell the desire for a home of her own. She didn't even flinch when a voice spoke from her living room.

"Was it the same pattern as the others?"

Ashley locked the door behind her and just stared at the man in the room. He was incredibly tall and impossibly slender, his hair a blond that was almost gold. His attention was fixed squarely on the photos attached to a board resting on an easel.

"Good morning to you too, Eli. Please, do make yourself at home." Ashley tossed her keys onto the small table by the door and wandered into the room. She had to physically nudge Eli out of her way to switch her laptop on. "You need to scoot over, Eli. You're in my way. Stop hogging the death board." He stepped back absently, his attention never wavering as she puttered around him. Ashley watched with satisfaction as the laptop booted up. "If you see anything, any kind of signature to what this guy is doing, please don't hesitate to speak up. I could do with the help." She removed the memory card from her camera and popped it into her laptop's SD slot. Eli crowded in behind her and peered over her shoulder. "What the hell has gotten into you? You're quieter than usual, which isn't saying much, I know, but you're beginning to creep me out!"

Eli stepped back but his eyes flicked between the laptop screen and the board. "There is something very wrong about these deaths."

Pulling up the new photos on her screen, Ashley cut Eli an incredulous look. "They are incredibly violent, gruesome, bloody deaths." She straightened to look at him. "Wrong doesn't even begin to cover it." She set the photographs to run as a slideshow. She and Eli watched the tableau of shots flash by one after another as the scene was captured in its vile testament to evil. Ashley watched each photo with a growing sense of unease.

"Eli, I don't think this guy is going to stop any time soon." She was barely able to suppress a shudder as a photo flashed up of the woman's terrified face, twisted and contorted in her final moments.

Eli craned his neck for a look at one particularly graphic close-up. "I'd say he's just gotten started." He straightened again, then turned his attention to the easel behind him. "You're going to need a bigger board," he pointed out drolly.

Ashley couldn't help but laugh at Eli's comment, glad for the slight lightening of the mood. She headed for the small kitchen just off the main room, opened up the fridge, and removed a bottle of beer. She twisted off the lid and drank deeply. "I think it's time I go find out what the police investigation has managed to find out about these women."

"Yes, now that *you're* here..."

"Yes, now that I am here I can go do my magic trick and walk into the Chicago Police Department. I can gather intel and walk right back out again." Ashley took another long drink from her bottle, not thirsty anymore but needing the bitter taste to sharpen her senses. "I got here in time to see body number two." She gestured to the board littered with the photographs of the second victim. "And tonight I've got body number three to add to the wall. I need to gather information on the first woman killed and see if their autopsy reports have something we just can't see by looking at the body via Kodak."

"Do you know who the lead detective is?"

"I couldn't tell, but they had the press darling Stephanie Powell courting the news crews again."

Eli looked less than impressed. "They need a better lead to run this case."

"I think she's just the camera fodder. Three deaths, all with their backs opened up and their spines on display. They're going to need more than the hotshot poster girl for the Chicago Police Department to solve this." Ashley remembered the leggy chief of detectives, her long black hair pulled back from her face, makeup skillfully applied. Her brand of femininity would settle best in front of the cameras to assure the public that there was nothing to fear in their fair city. Ashley grinned to herself. *Pretty, yes, but so not my kind of woman.* Her mind drifted to the other detectives she'd seen on scene. "I saw two other detectives there. I think they're the ones on the case."

"I hear they have assigned a secret task force," Eli said as his long fingers flicked over the laptop keyboard to set the slideshow off again.

"And where did you hear that?" Ashley asked, knowing all too well.

"The same place that told me I needed to call you in on these cases."

"You and your secret missions, Eli. It's enough to turn a girl's head."

"It got you a trip to Chicago."

Ashley stared around the shabby apartment she was now calling home. "Yeah, whoop dee freakin' doo. Three women savagely killed. It's not exactly something that you want in the tourist brochure for the Windy City, is it?" She carried her bottle away with her toward the bedroom at the rear of the apartment. "I'll leave you to it. I'm going to try and sleep before I go face that task force you mentioned earlier."

"The DDU," Eli said.

"DDU? And what does that stand for?"

"Deviant Data Unit."

"What?" Ashley made a face. "Catchy title, if a little weird. Do you have to be a deviant to join that squad?"

"Be sure to ask them," he said.

"I might just do that. Maybe they'll have a spot free for me."

CHAPTER TWO

Detective Rafe Douglas rested back against the wall of the elevator as her partner, Detective Dean Jackson, pressed the button for their new floor. He turned to her with a big grin creasing his face.

"Geez, I'm off work for a little while and they've already moved my desk," Rafe grumbled good-naturedly as the elevator took them up to the third floor instead of their regular first-floor office.

"We got moved to a bigger office more fitting for the DDU, Rafe. You'll find the view much more pleasant from this height, I assure you." Dean gestured for Rafe to precede him.

Rafe slowly walked down the corridor to her new office trying not to be obvious that she was favoring her left side. She'd been a part of the Deviant Data Unit for a few months now, and its importance among the other task forces was finally paying off. Other Deviant Data Units had been set up around the country for her to access and compare information. The data streaming in was vast, and every team assigned to the units was kept busy following leads and chasing down suspects. Rafe gritted her teeth as each step pulled at her still-healing side. *Guess I'll be leaving the chasing to others for a while,* she mourned and watched as Dean hurried before her to open the door.

"I can still press elevator buttons and open doors all by myself, Detective." She was frustrated by his need to look after her.

"Stop bitching and come see our new digs," Dean said, ignoring her mood as always. He gestured to the door. "Welcome to the new DDU."

Rafe dutifully noted the crisp lettering on the door announcing the unit and its officers. She waited until Dean opened the door for her and stopped abruptly with just one foot through. "Christ, they emptied the whole of Best Buy."

"Detective Douglas, I'm so glad to see you back." Officer Alona Wilson got to her feet and went to Rafe's side. "We missed you here." The young African-American officer's eyes searched Rafe's battered face as Rafe removed her beanie hat and revealed her seriously shorn hair. Rafe knew the stitches across her skull showed up starkly against the dark brown stubble left on her head. "Well, you've looked better."

Rafe bit back a smile. "You should see the other guy." She looked around the room at all the hardware lined up on desks and on the walls. "You're our resident tech geek. How cool a haul is in this room?"

Alona's answering grin said it all. "We have a tech geek's wet dream here. I oversaw the installations myself, and everything has been up and running for a week without a glitch. I can go through the basics with you and you'll be up to speed in no time."

"Yeah, it's that easy," Dean said, rolling his eyes.

Alona cut him a look. "For those of us who know how to turn on our computers correctly, this is child's play." She gestured around the room. "We have various computers gathering data, all with easy access. The search engines are so simple even Detective Jackson here can't mess it up." She added under her breath, "Even though he's tried, many times." She pointed to a new widescreen monitor. "This is my baby." She reverently ran her hand along the side of the huge screen that dominated the back wall. "Watch." She tapped in a few keystrokes on her keyboard and brought up a picture. She then seemingly swiped the picture from her screen and Rafe watched as it appeared on the big screen behind her. Alona reached out and enlarged the photo with her hands, moving the picture across the screen as if she were physically handling something real and not just an image. "How cool is that?"

Rafe was impressed. "Seriously cool."

Alona manipulated the photo again and then with a flick of her hand sent it back to the other computer. Rafe shared a conspiratorial look with Alona. "How long was this installed before Dean asked if he could bring his Xbox in?"

"Twenty-five minutes exactly," Alona said. "I timed him."

Dean spluttered behind them. "Hey! I resent that!"

Alona just laughed at him. "She knows you too well, Detective, as do I."

Dean shrugged off their amusement. "So what if I feel a screen that large would be better served in a rousing gun battle online with my pals than it is in here used to display the deviants from which we get our unit name?"

Rafe couldn't argue his point. "Just don't even think of sneaking that console in here." She barely registered the sound of him nudging his messenger bag further under his desk to hide it. She was too busy staring around the office in wonder at the screens sifting through endless streams of data. She caught one screen flashing up photographs of people. She cocked her head at Alona. "You know how all of these work?"

"Every single one."

"You need to teach me ASAP."

"That will be no problem. You'll pick it up easily. It's just a matter of knowing what to look for in the endless data threading through."

"So when do we get more staff to help man these threads and make up our team?" Rafe looked about the large room occupied by just the three of them.

Dean shrugged. "They paid for all the equipment first. I guess when the budgets are back in the black they can help us out by giving us more man—" He shot a look at them both. "Or woman power."

"The early stages of any new unit is a trial," Alona said. "We're just a small task force compared to some of the units being built now."

Rafe nodded and padded over to the window for a moment. She looked down at the city inhabitants going about their business as usual.

"Impressive view, isn't it?" Dean said. He rested his forehead on the glass. "And look, from here you can see if there's a line at the hot dog stand."

"Always good to know." Rafe's stomach rolled a little at the mention of food, and sweat began to break out on her forehead. She swiped at it in annoyance. "Which desk is mine so I can sit down a minute to take all this in?" Dean directed her to a seat and Rafe sat as gently as she could, trying desperately not to show how every movement hurt her. She knew she was fooling no one.

"You sure the doctors said you were well enough to come back to work?" Dean ignored the sharp look he received.

"I was declared fit for sitting at a desk and doing light duties, so here I am. Stop fussing and go find me a bottle of water." She reached inside her jacket for a bottle of pills. Looking up, she found Dean still hovering over her solicitously. "Please, I need to take these damn horse pills and can't swallow them dry." She watched him rush from the office and knew Alona was now standing over her just as closely. "How much were you told?" Rafe asked.

"That you were stabbed by some lowlife and got beaten pretty badly. But I can see most of that still emblazoned on your face."

Rafe reached up to her forehead where the purpling bruises were still vivid and painful to the touch. "Never let a hulking quarterback head-butt you," she said wryly.

"I'm just glad you're back. The DDU needs its leader and we'd only just gotten started before..." Alona trailed off, obviously uncomfortable.

"Before I played face ball with the Quarterback of Quaaludes." Rafe sat back in her seat. "Still, while I was away you did the office up nice."

Alona agreed. "I was so excited when they said we were getting new office space and high-tech equipment. It shows we mean business."

Rafe ran her hand over her new keyboard. "All this tech had to have cost a small fortune."

"It's all state-of-the-art. Big-boy toys."

"You promise to still do police work in between playing with all these buttons?"

Alona laughed at her. "I promise. But, Detective, there are just so many buttons to try!"

Rafe pulled her keyboard forward and typed in her password. She was relieved the screen accepted it. "Thank God I remembered that."

"Guess the blow to the head didn't shake everything out, eh, Detective?" Alona teased her.

Rafe stared at her screen blindly, counting herself lucky that the bruises and the hairline fractures were all the damage her head had sustained from the attack. She was chillingly aware she should never have left that alley alive.

The cold night air burned Rafe's lungs as she sucked it in greedily. She ran, gun drawn, chasing down a killer in the alley. Ahead of her she could hear the familiar sound of someone else running, the perpetrator of the brutal stabbing they'd been called in to deal with. The owner of Castello's Bar and Grill had just been killed for a few hundred dollars. Had the perp waited until the night had ended, he could have made off with the entire night's take, which would have been a more substantial heist. Instead, he had tackled the owner mid-evening. Once he'd gotten his money, he had then stabbed the man to death in plain view of his young son. The child had run to call the police, begging them to come save his papa from the crazy man with the knife.

Seven years old, *Rafe thought as she ran,* what a sight to have to witness for so young a pair of eyes. *She cursed under her breath as she banged her hip on a pile of boxes haphazardly stacked. She heard them topple over and whatever had been inside smash to the ground. The sound of things shattering echoed down the alley. Rafe hoped the boxes wouldn't cause too much of a hassle for Dean to clamber over. He was supposed to be right behind her, but she'd taken off first when he'd pulled up and she'd left him to radio their location in.*

Rafe skirted around a Dumpster, furious at the garbage strewn all along the alley. The alley was so poorly lit she could barely make out the rotting obstacles in her way. She slipped on a piece of something and swore out loud. I'm going to kill myself out here. Cause of death: rotten vegetables that missed their destiny with the Dumpster. *Her only comfort came from hearing the guy running ahead of her pinballing his bulk off the endless line of Dumpsters crushed together behind the restaurants that ran the length of the street front. The dull thuds easily reached Rafe's ears and his grunts of pain only served to make her smile as she continued to chase him.*

Suddenly, one by one, what little light was available in the alley fizzled out. Rafe slid to a halt as she watched each lamp pop and the lights inside die. "What the hell?" she muttered breathlessly as the alley plunged into darkness. She paused for barely a moment to try to get her bearings, then took off again, praying she didn't break her neck in the pitch-black. Not even the moon cooperated as it slipped behind a cloud and left Rafe blind. The sounds ahead suddenly ceased. Rafe stopped in her tracks just as an arm slashed out in front of her. The knife caught in her jacket, slicing through the leather and snagging in the material. She just managed to escape the blade from plunging into her gut and clubbed the guy with the butt of her gun. He turned to her, barely dazed by the blow, and Rafe got to look directly into his eyes. Shit, a crackhead, *she thought just before he head-butted her soundly in the forehead, rocking her back on her feet. In the tussle he freed his knife and brandished it at her. Rafe clutched at her forehead. The pain was excruciating. She managed to raise her gun and pointed it at him.* "Freeze!"

He just laughed at her and took a step forward. The bullet that hit him didn't even seem to register. He stormed at Rafe and stabbed her. The knife plunged into her side, the force behind it doubling her over. Slowly, he withdrew the blade, twisting it in the wound. He seemed to enjoy the howl of pain that escaped Rafe's lips. He meticulously wiped the bloodied blade on Rafe's pants and readied it again.

Rafe tried desperately to stop the flow of blood from her side. She staggered backward and raised her gun again. "I'm warning you, you bastard. Put the knife down now." *She could faintly hear the sound of running from behind her and could make out Dean's voice yelling for her. Her head pounded from the concussion she knew she was suffering. Her side felt like it was on fire and the man just stood there laughing at her. He stuck his neck out, his foul breath hitting her in the face.*

"Fuck you, bitch," *he growled as he lunged for her again.*

The second shot knocked him back but still didn't take him down. He righted himself, looking down almost comically at his T-shirt where holes were pouring out blood. He switched his knife to his left hand and lashed out with his fist. He caught the side of Rafe's head and knocked her off her feet. She was almost rendered unconscious from the force of the two blows she had received and the loss of blood she couldn't stem. Her hand shook as she determinedly lifted her gun again. She was barely able to see the man as he loomed over her.

The clouds finally shifted, and in the pale moonlight shining down on the alley, Rafe was finally able to see. She stared up into the face of a monster. His vile features were cast in shadows, but his face appeared oddly misshapen and grotesque. Protruding from his temples were lethal-tipped horns. His eyes burned with fire. Rafe aimed the gun at his head, but he snatched it easily from her hand and held it to his temple, taunting her. He laughed down at her as he crouched to straddle her body. His bulk pushed Rafe further into the broken glass and other debris that littered the alley floor. His knee pressed into her ribs, causing her to stifle a scream as the pain lanced through her knife wound. Looking up at the man who held her gun, Rafe prayed like she had never prayed before. She closed her eyes as he brought the gun down to crack it against her skull. She swore she saw stars.

He bent down to whisper in her ear. "Now we're even." He held the gun to her forehead. "Now I put an end to your misery on earth."

Rafe remembered seeing a brilliant light, the purest white that seared her eyes and blinded her. She heard the sound of a gun going off but never saw the man take the bullet right between his eyes. She did feel him slide off her. His weight pinned her down, but all she could see was the light. It didn't call to her; it didn't draw her closer. It just surrounded her until she succumbed to it. She closed her eyes and slid mercifully into unconsciousness.

She woke up in the hospital, surrounded by doctors all prodding and poking her. Rafe knew how lucky she had been. The colorful bruises that covered her face would take their time fading, a vivid testament to the battering she had sustained. The hairline fractures to her skull were slowly mending. Dean's comments concerning the thickness of her skull had been echoed by the medical staff. Her hair being shaved off was the least of her worries.

It was only when she was finally lucid that Rafe found out that Dean had fired the shot that finally brought the man, Marcus Armitage, down. He was an ex-quarterback from a local team who'd kicked him off the squad for spending more time throwing the game to support his habit than he had spent throwing the ball in play. He'd been a six foot nine behemoth who, high on a mixture of cocaine and steroids, had nearly added cop killer to his hall of fame.

Rafe had made damn sure she never mentioned it to anyone, ever, the fires of Hades she'd seen burning in his eyes.

From the tone in Dean's voice, he'd been calling her name for a while. Rafe snapped back with a blink. "You okay there?" He slowly held the bottle of water out to her, taking care not to startle her with any sudden movement.

Rafe drank greedily from the bottle as soon as she twisted the cap off. The cold water eased her dryness but did nothing to wash away the acrid taste of brimstone she could feel clawing at her throat. "Stand down, Detective, I'm fine."

"Does that happen often?" Dean asked.

"No," Rafe said bluntly. She shook her pills from their blister pack, tossed them into her mouth, then swilled them down with more water. She then turned her attention to Alona, effectively ending the conversation. "So tell me about these data streams we have running."

Without a pause, Alona did as she was asked. "The data we have put in so far from these cases hasn't brought up any definitive matches, but we're still searching. With the countrywide DDUs just in their infancy, it might be some time before we get a match from another state."

"Time is something we can't afford to wait on. He's not going to stop. He has a specific and very definite MO. You don't start something that particular to just give it up after three attempts." Rafe tapped at her computer and brought up the crime scene photos from the first scene. As if she'd always used the software before her, she flicked the photos up onto the large screen, then stood to study them. The graphic stills hid none of the horror that had greeted the police who had responded to a caller's terrified find. Rafe's eyes lingered long on the pose of the woman's body. "Can we put the second scene up too?"

Alona swiftly brought them up, and the killer's pattern was easy to see. Two different locations, but the body placement was identical.

"Have we gotten the photos from last night's killing yet?"

Dean checked his computer and all three scenes were displayed on the big screen.

Rafe hoped to find something hidden among all the stills that would lead her to find the killer's identity. "So what do we see?"

"The bodies are left in the exact same pose. Arm outstretched, head tilted up unnaturally as if looking toward something, and clothes rearranged to cover the fact that their backs have been ripped open," Dean said.

"Last night's butchery of the woman's back was less than perfect, not his usual standard of clean cuts through the skin, yet everything was still arranged back in place. I'd say he felt rushed." Rafe leaned in to one particular still and Alona reached in and enlarged the photo. "I'll have to remember we can do that now instead of straining my eyes." Rafe thanked her. "However stuck for time he was, he still made time to leave his signature pose."

"There was quite a bit of foot traffic past that alley when I was called in last night. The local bar had a late-night party going on. That could have hindered him if he was aware people were nearby who could stumble by while he was doing his thing." Dean pointed at the photos. "He doesn't tend to go very far into an alley with them or even hide them once he's done. He seems to drag them toward the biggest shadow and start in on them there."

Rafe rubbed at the permanent frown line etched deep in her forehead. "I wish we could have pinned this on Marcus Armitage. He was damned handy with that knife, and he was certainly big enough to render a woman helpless." She shook her head ruefully. "Even one armed with a gun." Chewing at her lip, she searched the photos for anything to point her in the right direction. "It's just a shame the bastard was dead when this killer struck again. My being used as his punching bag would have been worth it if these killings would have stopped when Dean took him out."

"So we take out one scumbag and keep searching for another." Dean patted the computer behind him. "Maybe the killer resides somewhere in here and we just enter the magic word and he will appear."

Alona snorted. "You haven't had much to do with computers, have you, Detective?"

Dean smiled disarmingly at her. "I'm a beat cop at heart. All my data gathering is garnered on the street."

Rafe spared him a quick glance. "Well, *old* man, the rules have changed since you walked the streets. High-tech is the new law." She couldn't take her eyes from the one photo. The body of Andrea Mason, the previous night's victim, had been turned over and her back was flayed wide open. The skin had been pushed aside as if it were silk from a blouse. The woman's insides were all on view; the muscles were crudely chopped at and the revealed spinal column had been laid bare to the elements. The whiteness of the bone contrasted with the surrounding bloody mess of violated flesh.

Rafe deliberately looked away. She tried to find something else to focus on other than the last hellish moments of the three women posted on the screen. "I'm not seeing a sexual motive here. Usually they'd go for the breasts, or cut open the chest to get at the heart, but exposing the backbone doesn't ring any spurned lover kinds of bells for me." She looked at Alona. "Has there been any word from the profiler I contacted?"

"The agent you were in touch with was away on a case last week, but she contacted me this morning and said she was ready to present her profile to you as soon as you want it." Alona chuckled. "She mentioned something about you owing her big-time seeing as you'd issued an *unofficial* request."

"Have you got video linkups on one of these screens?" At Alona's nod, Rafe got out her cell phone and pressed a button. She waited to hear a familiar voice. "Detective Rafe Douglas here, I believe you have a profile waiting for me?" She couldn't help but smile at the excited tone that assailed her ear. "Have you got time for a conference call? We're all set on our end for a video link if you're up for it." She checked her watch and made a mental note of the time she was given. "We'll speak to you then." She closed her phone and gave Alona a thumbs-up. "Three thirty we have a conference call with Special Agent Kent. Can you have everything ready for that for me, please?"

"Absolutely. Wait until you see what this tech can do in that respect."

Rafe nodded distractedly, her mind already racing ahead. "Okay, now we need to gather this latest victim's last known whereabouts. Let's see if we can match anything from hers to our other victims. Let's check her friends, coworkers, Facebook buddies, places of employment from the start of their employment history. The answer has to be in there somewhere."

CHAPTER THREE

Hours later, after sorting through what seemed to be endless reams of paperwork, Rafe was relieved when Alona announced she had the video link ready. Nothing matched in any of the victims' private lives. They didn't work in the same jobs, didn't frequent the same clubs, and had never had cause to meet in one another's social circles. All were respectable women who had apparently been in the wrong place at the wrong time. Rafe shoved the files to one side, glad to rest her eyes from all the print. Alona directed their attention to a large monitor placed to her right. The screen's department logo disappeared and a small woman, arms covered in tattoos, appeared on the screen.

"Not what I was expecting from a profiler," Dean said, taken aback.

"Detective Douglas, Special Agent Kent will be with you shortly," the woman said then looked over her shoulder at the sound of someone entering the room behind her. The camera switched positions as another woman sat at the desk.

"Thanks, Trace." The profiler's husky voice held a hint of laughter in it as she settled down and faced the screen.

"Special Agent Blythe Kent, you look fantastic." Rafe grinned as she let her eyes drink in the features of her oldest and dearest friend. "You've had your hair cut." Blythe fussed with the now shoulder-length dark hair that brushed at her jacket collar with its unruly curls.

"And you look like hell itself," Blythe returned, her sharp brown eyes never leaving Rafe's face. "What did I warn you about city police work?"

"That it would be the death of me." Rafe shrugged. "Not this time, though, contrary to how I look and feel."

"You should have stayed with us."

"Maybe, but I have to say the pizza is to die for here."

Blythe tried not to smile. "You and your stomach. It's hard to forget you follow that more than you do safety."

"Blythe, I could have just as easily been beaten up by a perp in New York."

"True, but I could have been there to make sure you weren't a dumbass about leaving the hospital too early, or going back to work before your side had healed. And don't get me started on your poor hair, Rafe." The look Blythe gave her was too familiar. Rafe fought not to roll her eyes.

"She knows you well enough," Dean said quietly.

"Special Agent Kent and I go way back, but she took the high road to be an agent while I decided I wanted to trade my cop's badge for a detective's shield. And yet look at us now, both members of the fledgling Deviant Data Units."

"We can only hope the DDU does what it's set up to do, bring the forces together to catch the criminals."

"Which brings me to why I contacted you. You being the best profiler I know in a sister DD Unit."

Laughing, Blythe replied, "I'm the only profiler you knew that you could call up from your hospital bed while dosed high on whatever they had you on and still ask for me to profile your case and know I'd do it, no questions asked."

"You're a credit to the agency," Rafe said solemnly, trying not to grin and spoil the effect.

"You should have let me come down to Chicago to look after you. If only to try and keep you in check."

"There was no need. I'm fine. I'm back at work with minimal discomfort." She shot a dirty look at Dean's choking noise beside her. Changing the subject entirely before Blythe really started ripping into her, Rafe gestured to her team. "By the way, let me introduce my colleagues." She did so by drawing them before the camera and skillfully placing herself back a few steps from Blythe's pointed stare.

Rafe knew she'd be receiving a phone call soon full of solicitous words and threats that she'd better take it easy.

"Good to put faces to names," Blythe said, then looked to her side and nodded. "Trace is sending you a copy of my profile as we speak."

Alona checked her computer at the sound of an incoming message. "Got it."

"Now that I have seen you and am reasonably assured you're alive and kicking, though sporting more colors than are found in an M&M bag, let me get to the profile. Oh, and next time"—Blythe leaned forward, staring directly at Rafe—"consider calling me in before you go risking your life chasing down a thug who could have been better apprehended by officers more suited to tackling football players."

Rafe opened her mouth to argue but then thought better of it. She hoped she looked suitably contrite.

Seemingly appeased, Blythe sat back and straightened her shoulders, switching to her profiler manner. "The man you're after has a purpose; a mission. The kind of killer who takes his time to cut right through to the bone and lay out the body in pose is meticulous and driven. This man has a higher calling."

"I hate the ones who use God's will as an excuse to do their own dirty work," Dean said.

"But who's to say its God he hears?" Blythe replied. "Just promise me that the press won't be calling this killer something asinine like the Spine Tingler. You just know how they love to stick a headline grabbing name out there to label a killer."

"Detective Powell is seeing to all the press. She's trying to keep a tight lid on how much is reported. This is the third one in six weeks. We have a serial killer running wild and loose in Chicago. Tagging him by any name isn't going to stop the fear and terror from spreading," Rafe said.

Blythe shifted in her seat. "Then let's hope what I've come up with helps. The person you're looking for is a male, between the ages of twenty and thirty. He's in excellent physical shape because he can overpower these women with ease and he's able to cut open the bodies. He probably works in the meat trade or has knowledge of hunting because his opening up of the flesh isn't surgically precise but more the kind of cuts a butcher would make. Which would also explain why no one questions this man, who has to be covered in blood if seen afterward. If he's recognizable as a butcher, then no one is going to pay him a second glance. He's not someone who is going to stand out in a crowd. He doesn't go out of his way to make himself noticeable."

Blythe took a breath before continuing. "All his killings have so far been outside, in the open, swift and sure. But it's the time he spends after the kill that is important. He poses the body in a certain way, the same pose for each girl killed. That takes time, because he covers them back up, he moves their hair, he covers the slash marks in their necks. He tries to make them normal again and pleasing to the eye." Blythe unconsciously brushed at her own hair, momentarily causing Rafe to marvel at how attractive she was and how she was way-off-the-charts smart as well.

"He obviously has some kind of restriction that stops him from taking these women home. Something there stops him from spending more time with them. A girlfriend maybe, a wife, even a parent. He's cutting open their backs to reach the spine. This is his purpose, but the pose is obviously something he has to finish with. It's his signature. It has a meaning to him and we need to find it. His kills are not sexually motivated; you're not looking for a sexual sadist here. He redresses them after. That shows a degree of remorse. He poses them, but it's not a pose to degrade the bodies. I believe it's something of significance to him."

"Why cut open the body to expose the spine?" Rafe asked.

Blythe shrugged. "It's a curious area to go for, and he's not removing any organs or anything from the body itself. He cuts their throats quickly, so he obviously doesn't want them to suffer." Blythe made a wry face. "For all the horror he inflicts on them after. Do you want my opinion, Rafe?"

Rafe nodded, trusting Blythe's instincts and insights more than anyone else she knew.

"I think he's looking for something we can't see."

"What could he possibly be after?" Dean asked incredulously.

"Whatever the spinal area means specifically to him." Blythe moved forward to the camera. "You've got a seeker who won't give up killing until he's found what he's looking for. He's on roughly a two-week cycle, most probably because of his shifts at work. He's already killed this week. You need to check out the local meat factories, restaurants, anywhere that proficiency with a knife is required." She rested her chin on her hand. "Will you keep me informed, Rafe? Just in case I can build on the profile for you?"

Rafe nodded. "I'll keep you informed every step of the way, through the data stream and out of it."

"Then I'll look forward to speaking to you soon and wish you a speedy conclusion to this case." Blythe sat back in her chair. "And I'll call you sometime, just to check up on you health-wise."

"I'll appreciate that," Rafe said and had to smile at Blythe's laughter.

"Of course you will." She grinned wickedly back. Blythe made her farewells and their connection was cut.

Rafe brought up the photos from the crime scene again. She concentrated on the pose of the bodies and wondered what the killer was trying to say to her and the city in general. She had the feeling his conversation with Chicago wasn't over yet.

Chapter Four

The next morning, Ashley strode into the police precinct, well aware no one would give her a second glance. Having taken on the form of a young officer, Ashley easily blended in among the other uniforms. Unobtrusively, she searched out a floor map and found where the offices of the DDU were situated. She checked around the lines of desks for the name Officer Duncan Cook, which matched the one she wore on her breast. She'd been watching him all morning and finally, as he went off shift, she felt confident to take his identity.

Come on, Duncan, where do you sit? She caught sight of a framed photo of a doting husband and his wife holding up a young child. "Bingo," Ashley whispered, sliding into the seat and turning on the computer. She plugged in a small device to buzz past any firewalls and protocol and was only just able to flick the screen to a screen saver as someone's face peeked over the partition divider.

"Cook? I thought I just waved you off from your shift?"

Ashley smiled at the young woman. "You did, but I forgot to double-check something I entered, and you know what it's like. I'll be trying to pay attention to the wife when all I'll be worrying about is whether I spelled 'circumstantial evidence' right."

The woman laughed. "Conscientious to the last, eh, Cook?"

"Anything for a quiet life," Ashley looked at the officer's name tag, "Edwards. My wife, for some reason, wants my undivided attention when I'm home."

Edwards looked Ashley over with an appraising eye. "I can

understand why." She smiled. "I'll leave you in peace to check your statement, then for God's sake, go home."

"I hear you," Ashley replied, hurrying to log into the computer as it spat out Duncan's password and gave her entry into the system. With knowledge gained from too many illegal entries into police computer systems, Ashley began searching for any information concerning the DDU.

❖

After riding the elevator to the third floor, Ashley stepped off and headed toward the newly appointed DDU offices. She took a deep breath before she strode through the door and watched the occupants look up at her entrance, then jump to attention.

All but one.

"Detective Powell, what a surprise to see you here," the young female officer said. "Can we help you with anything?"

"I'm looking for the latest report on last night's killing."

"I can print you a copy right this minute." The officer turned to her computer.

Ashley recognized Detective Jackson from the crime scene, but she couldn't help but notice the other woman in the room staring at her, her eyes blinking as if looking directly into sunlight.

Oh crap.

"Who are you?" she asked Ashley bluntly.

"Rafe, you know who Detective Powell is." Detective Jackson nudged at her, giving her a concerned look. "That blow to your head didn't scramble all your brain cells, did it?" He whispered for Rafe's ears alone, but Ashley easily overheard his worried tone. Rafe threw her another suspicious look. Ashley decided she would be wise to beat a hasty retreat. Her glamour was fooling the others in the room, but something was definitely off when it came to this detective.

"I'll just take these papers," she said and hastily exited the office, clutching the reports to her chest and trying not to make it obvious that she was about to break into a run. She had barely made it to the elevator when a body slammed into her, spun her around, and pinned her to the wall. Rafe Douglas loomed over her, and from her closeness Ashley could easily see the tiny golden flecks of gold amid the chocolate brown of Rafe's eyes. Struck silent by Rafe's starkly handsome features, Ashley just stared up at her, even though as Detective Powell she would have towered over Rafe.

"I don't know who you are, but you sure as hell aren't Powell." Rafe pressed in harder, all but holding Ashley up against the wall by her chest. "And what's with all the lights around you?" She blinked furiously as if bothered by it. When she did look down at Ashley, she looked directly into her eyes.

Ashley's mouth gaped. *Oh my God, she can see through my glamour. She can see me.* Unable to stop staring at the angry face before her, Ashley inspected the cruel damage that had been wrought on Rafe. Without thinking, she reached up to touch the bruises. "What happened to you?" Ashley stroked Rafe's cheek gently, and for a moment the body holding her so tightly against the wall stiffened, then softened fractionally. Eyes closing, Rafe seemed to lean into her for comfort. Ashley murmured softly to her, touching each and every mark that marred Rafe's skin. She ran her fingertips over the vivid bruises that left their purpling trail across Rafe's forehead. A scratch mark, still rough and jagged, stood out on her temple. The raw edges all but burned Ashley's flesh, and she jerked her hand away, gasping at the pain. Rafe's head lifted as if she were awakening, her eyes dazed.

"You've been marked by a demon," Ashley said.

"A what?" Rafe sounded confused, if not a little drugged. She blinked at Ashley. "What are all these lights?"

Unnerved, Ashley slipped from Rafe's hold and made a dash for the stairwell. She knew full well that Rafe wouldn't be able to follow her. Mindful of the cameras positioned in every corner, she kept her disguise in place until she found a bathroom to rush into. Finally emerging as a female civilian, Ashley slipped free from the precinct armed with her report and a USB full of "Eyes Only" material she'd garnered from the police officer's computer. She'd slip back in later to see what she could gather from the DDU's own logs, but not while she knew Rafe Douglas was in the building. She opened her cell phone and pressed a button.

"Eli, we have a big problem."

❖

Rafe was struggling to stay awake. She slid down the wall until she ended up on her knees, lethargy seeping through every pore. All she could hear in her head were the soft comforting words from the blonde who had touched her so tenderly. Rafe blinked, her eyesight finally clear of the golden shimmers she'd witnessed surrounding the woman. Unsteadily, she ran her hands over her face and touched the jagged edges where Armitage's horn had cut her open. Rafe hadn't corrected the doctors when they had concluded it came from her being pistol-whipped. She hadn't said a lot about that night.

She tried to get to her feet, feeling unsteady and a little woozy. *I chase an intruder out of the office and she does what? Drugs me somehow? Mesmerizes me?* Leaning against the wall for support, Rafe was at a loss to explain her feelings. She felt bereft, adrift, and more than a little confused. When the blonde had touched her, she'd felt curiously safe. *Who the hell is she? Because she sure as hell wasn't Detective Powell.* She drew a finger along the scratch that broke her skin, tracing the path the woman had touched. It felt a little less raw. Rafe managed to push herself away from the wall and slowly made her way back to the office. Her mind spun. *What the fuck just happened here?*

❖

Never stopping in her mad dash across the city to her apartment, Ashley didn't feel safe until she slammed home the bolt on her front door.

"Productive trip?" Eli asked from his usual perch before the picture board.

"One of the detectives can see me."

"Really?"

Ashley balled her fists on her hips at his tone. "Yes, really. As in see me, *see me*. She can see right through the glamour to the real me inside." She was surprised to see Eli's eyes widen, since he rarely changed expressions. "And that's not all; she reacted to my healing."

"You were *touching* her?" His voice rose an octave.

"She's been hurt. I couldn't help myself. Her injuries called to me." Ashley threw herself into a chair and pulled her knees up to her chest. "You could have told me one of the detectives on this case was so damn gorgeous, for a start."

"Is she, now?"

"Wickedly handsome, all dark and brooding, with a face just this side of austere...until I touched her and she melted in my hands. But she's been hurt so badly. What happened to her, Eli? You have to know."

Eli remained quiet.

"She also sports a scratch from a demon horn. It scalded me when I touched it. How did a member of the newly assigned DDU get into an altercation with a demon, Eli? Can you tell me that at least?"

"She's a detective, so I'd wager one of her cases led her to a perpetrator whose blood wasn't entirely human."

Ashley scrubbed at her face with her hands. "You drive me insane sometimes, do you know that? I can never get a straight answer out of you."

"I'm not here for answers, Ashley."

"Yeah, yeah, I know. The old 'free will' speech. I've heard it all my life, Eli. I know the drill." She rested her head back against the chair and narrowed her eyes at him. "Did you have knowledge of her and the demon scratch *and* her role in the DDU before you sent me in?" She frowned as Eli looked at her with calm serenity. "You mention one word about destiny and I am throwing you out of the window."

"We're two stories up."

"Then you'd better hope that the rumors you can fly are true." Ashley dragged herself to her feet and handed him the file. "Here. See if there's anything in there that adds to what we already know." She grumbled as she slapped the USB stick down by her laptop. "Why I can't go in as the private investigator I am is beyond me."

"Because you're not searching for the same thing they are," Eli said.

Ashley stormed out of the room and locked herself in the bathroom. She caught sight of her image in the mirror, and for a long moment just looked. "She could see me. How long has it been since someone has really taken the time to see *me*?" She sat on the edge of the bathtub and hung her head. "And now she's never going to want to see me again."

Staring at her fingertips, she recalled how soft Rafe's face felt. "Trust me to find the only detective in the city touched by a demon. How's that for damned fortune favoring the foolish?"

CHAPTER FIVE

You've been off all afternoon, Rafe. Do you need to wait in the car at this place?" Dean pulled up at the fifth meat storage facility and wrinkled his nose at the unmistakable smell of animal flesh wafting through the window.

Rafe waved him off. "I'm fine. I'll probably never be able to order a burger again, but I'm okay, honestly. Second day properly back and all that. I'll get into my stride again soon."

Dean didn't sound convinced. "If you're sure. You've been awfully pale these past two hours, a little green even."

"I'm sure, and if you dare try to hold my door open for me again, I swear I'll pistol-whip you."

Dean struggled to hold back a laugh. "Now, there's the detective I know and love!" He pulled himself out of the car and watched as Rafe struggled to get out from her side. "How about we make this our last call today? I'm getting sick of seeing dead bodies hanging from hooks when they should be sizzling on my plate."

Rafe unobtrusively leaned against the car for support. "Sure. If you can't stomach any more. This one is the nearest to our first killing. Maybe we'll strike lucky."

"Keep dreaming, Detective." Dean snorted and led the way. "The previous factories were all the same—full to the rafters with illegal immigrants who scatter like cockroaches the second the light hits our badges, and suddenly no one speaks English when we question them. You'd think they'd want him caught."

"Maybe we can get some uniforms to canvass the area, some who have more than one language to their credit."

"Do you really think he's going to be a butcher?"

Rafe shrugged. "I trust Blythe's profile. She has an excellent success rate. Her team is very much sought after even without the profiling. She works with an amazing team of detectives."

"Is she single?" Dean asked, pretending to be looking at the building before them, but Rafe wasn't fooled in the least.

"Don't you ever give up?"

"You can't blame a guy for trying to find the love of his life, and you have to admit, Rafe, she's a stunner. All that black hair, and her eyes. A guy could get seriously lost in those eyes."

Smiling smugly, Rafe let him continue to rhapsodize. He finally caught her look.

"Oh come on, don't tell me she bats for your team."

"I'm not saying anything about Special Agent Blythe Kent other than she is an exemplary agent."

"Oh God, she is. She's a lesbian," he wailed. "But she's such a beauty."

"Yes, she is, and don't worry. Many of the women who fall at her feet appreciate what a marvel she is too."

Dean shook his head. "Another dream bites the dust."

"You saw her briefly on the conference call, Dean, and you were already building the little house with the picket fence?"

"Sometimes you just feel an instant connection, that recognition as soul meets soul, the instant rush of lust...er, attraction," he hastily amended.

Rafe's good humor died at his words. She'd all but climbed into the arms of the blonde who'd breezed into their office, then disappeared. *I can't believe I let her go.* Rafe had double-checked with Alona what reports had been given out. None of it was too sensitive that it couldn't be handled properly should it wind up in the hands of the press. On subtly questioning her, Rafe was still disturbed that Alona had only seen Detective Powell in the office with them.

I can't believe how out of character I acted and that I just let her slip from my grasp, she berated herself again. She couldn't help but wonder if it was the question of the woman's identity or the way she made Rafe feel that bothered her the most.

❖

Pretending to be part of the police headquarters night staff provided Ashley with her easy entry back into the department. She rode the elevator back up to the third floor and wheeled the cleaning cart she'd appropriated down the hallway. The DDU office was mercifully dark, and Ashley breathed a sigh of relief as she opened the door and eased inside.

"I wondered if you'd be back."

Ashley clamped a hand over her mouth to stifle her scream. She looked around the room until a small desk lamp clicked on, illuminating Detective Rafe Douglas.

"What are you still doing here?" Ashley went on the defensive.

"It's my office; I work here."

"It's also very late. You should be home resting." Ashley couldn't curb the sound of censure from her tone.

"I appreciate your concern. It's very kind of you, seeing as this is the second time today you've entered this office without permission."

Ashley held up the file she'd taken. "I was returning this."

Rafe stood and slowly walked toward her. "I'm sorry your earlier trip turned out to be a wasted journey. What were you hoping for? Something to curry favor with your boss at some newspaper or another? A *National Enquirer* exposé?"

Ashley shook her head. "I don't work for a newspaper. I'm in the same line of business you are, Detective."

Rafe propped herself against the table edge and folded her arms, her face stormy. "I *detect*. You seem to excel at breaking and entering. How are we remotely the same?"

"I'm a private investigator." Ashley frowned at Rafe's derisive laughter.

"Like I've never heard that one before." Rafe rubbed at her eyes. "You're always surrounded by light. Is that how you manipulate people? You migraine them into submission?"

"Are there cameras in this room?" Ashley asked, furtively looking around.

"The whole building is watched." Rafe gave Ashley a pointed look. "Though obviously not well enough."

"Then I can't talk to you here. Is there somewhere we can go to talk?"

"I was preparing to go home."

"Then take me home with you."

"Sure, why not? You've already gotten access into my place of work; what's giving you knowledge of my private address too? You want to case that place too?"

"I'm not a thief," Ashley said and had the grace to concede to Rafe's incredulous look. "It's really not how it looks." She was grateful Rafe had no idea that she was back in the building armed with another USB stick ready to raid their computer files.

"It never is," Rafe muttered.

Ashley edged closer to Rafe. In the pale light cast from the low light, she could see how pale and drawn she looked. Her eyes were bloodshot and she seemed unsteady.

"Were you really waiting for me to return, Detective, or were you too tired to make the move to get home under your own steam?"

Rafe instantly bristled and stood tall. "I'm perfectly capable of leaving here."

"Then let's go so you and I can start again on a more equal footing."

"You're an information thief," Rafe grumbled, wandering back to gather up her jacket and to turn off the lamp. "God, who needs a light when they can just follow the light you give off?"

Ashley resisted the urge to rest a hand on Rafe's arm to guide her out the door. The uneven gait to Rafe's walk belied her insistence she was fine.

"How long has it been since you were discharged from the hospital, Detective?"

"Long enough, and I don't need another mother." Rafe stared down at Ashley as she jammed her woolen hat over her shorn hair. "Who are you? What the hell do I call you when I arrest you for tampering with police property?"

Ashley guided Rafe to the elevator and they waited in silence.

Rafe was trying not to take her eyes off her, but she was starting to squint.

"I could just call you Sparky, what with all the bright lights you've got flashing around you like a million fireflies."

"You could just be imagining things, Detective. Your face tells the story of how pretty banged up you've been."

"No, I'm seeing everything perfectly, but you somehow managed to make my fellow officers think you were someone else when you sure as hell are not her."

Ashley pulled Rafe inside the empty elevator and pressed for the ground floor. "What *do* you see, Detective?" She tried not to flinch under Rafe's scrutiny.

"I see more flashing lights than there are fireworks at a Fourth of July party covering you from head to toe. I can see short blond hair and a pretty face that just doesn't lend itself to a life of crime, but I could be wrong."

She thinks I'm pretty. Ashley's body warmed under Rafe's constant gaze.

"I see street clothes, black leather, black jeans—a burglar's standard uniform."

Ashley laughed. "You just don't quit, do you? I'm not a bad guy, Detective."

"Sure, Sparky," Rafe said as she followed Ashley out of the building. Once outside, Ashley flagged down a taxi. With a sideways glance, Rafe gave the driver her address, then sat back against the seat, her eyes closing and her breath becoming labored.

Putting her hand to Rafe's forehead, Ashley was surprised by how chilled her skin felt, except for the burning area that was the length of the scratch. Ashley spoke to the driver. "There's an extra ten dollars in it for you if you can get us there quicker." She fell back in her seat as the man put his foot down and they sped ahead. "Rafe, try to stay awake, please. I can't carry you."

"You know my name."

"Yes, I do, and I know you're very sick."

"I'm fine, just tired. First days back at work and all that."

No, you're actually being poisoned slowly but surely by the demon scratch that no modern medicine can cleanse.

Ashley thrust a handful of cash at the driver when he pulled up in front of Rafe's two-story home. She pulled Rafe out of the back of the taxi and half carried, half dragged her to the front door. "Where are your keys?"

Rafe drunkenly patted at her jacket, and Ashley fumbled through her clothing to find them.

"Don't let the cat out," Rafe mumbled, leaving Ashley wondering what the hell she meant until she got inside the house and the sound of a plaintive meow rang out. Ashley kicked the door closed behind her, then followed the hallway through to a small living area where she was able to get Rafe to lie down on a couch. She eased her down to stretch out full-length and then knelt beside her.

"I've got nothing worth taking."

Ashley smiled at Rafe's one-track mind but deliberately ignored her comment. "Are you watching, Detective? You're not going to want to miss this." She removed the glamour surrounding herself and saw Rafe's mouth ease into a relieved smile.

"No more lights," she said. "How'd you do that?"

"Magic." Ashley took off her jacket and rolled up her shirt sleeves. "I'm going to need you to trust me."

"So much prettier without all the sparkly bits." Rafe's voice trailed off as she started to ramble. "Such beautiful blue eyes for a thief too."

"You're very sick, but I can help you." Ashley gently removed the woolly hat and placed her hands on Rafe's face.

"Your hands are soft," Rafe said. "What's your name, Sparky?"

"Ashley Scott."

Rafe repeated it. "Ashley." She opened her eyes to look at her. "Am I dying, Ashley Scott?"

Surprised by how easily and without fear Rafe asked the question, Ashley stumbled over her reply. "No, no, Rafe, you're not dying. You're very sick, though."

"I should have died that night in the alley, but Dean shot the guy. Big bastard he was too. He had horns that grew out of his temples as I watched, and these flaming red eyes." Rafe shivered under Ashley's touch. "Glowing red eyes. You don't have those. You have golden sparkles instead." She closed her eyes once more. "Am I going crazy, Ashley? Because it feels like I am."

"No, you're not. You're just seeing things no one is meant to see." Ashley felt something bang her elbow. A black head butted her again. "Hi, kitty." The big cat climbed into her lap and pressed in close, rubbing its head on her arm.

"That's Trinity."

"She's beautiful."

Rafe opened one eye directly at Ashley. "Yes, she is."

Feeling her face flame, Ashley was unaccustomedly flustered. "No flirting while I'm trying to heal you," she grumbled, gently nudging the cat out of her way and settling in nearer to Rafe's body.

"My ex said I didn't know how to flirt." Rafe's voice sounded slurred.

"Shows how much she knew." Ashley pressed her fingers harder on the jagged line across Rafe's forehead. Rafe's whole body jerked like she'd been jolted with a blast of electricity.

"I'm sorry," Ashley spoke softly, channeling as much of her energy as possible through her fingertips. "I think you meeting me today made you sicker."

"I was fine until I cornered you," Rafe said, her voice faint.

Ashley pressed a little harder. "I touched your wound, and it accelerated the seeping of its poison into your body, probably because it sensed my healing capabilities. I unintentionally stirred it up."

"Are you going to be trouble for me, Sparky?"

Ashley smiled at the wistful tone. She watched Rafe's face relax as she began to fade out. "I promise I'll try only to ever be good for you," Ashley said, sensing when Rafe slipped into unconsciousness. She turned her full attention to the matter at hand, removing the poisonous residue left by the demon's horn that was spilling into Rafe's veins. Ashley knew Rafe would have only gotten increasingly sick as the poison leaked into her body. Why she had felt the need to touch the angry woman who had pinned her against the wall hadn't escaped Ashley. It wasn't just the call of the poison to her healing capabilities; it was something more basic. Rafe had been injured, and it hurt Ashley to see Rafe trying so hard to mask her obvious pain. She'd wanted to take Rafe's pain away, make her whole again.

Ashley wiped away a trickle of sweat off her face and pressed ahead with the healing. "I wish I could heal your other injuries," she whispered, knowing that her skills were limited to the supernatural and could not accelerate the mending of Rafe's fractures and other wounds. Trinity curled up at Ashley's side, leaning heavily against her, the contented purr rumbling through Ashley's leg. "Guess you trust me with your mom." Ashley looked down at the cat and was met by large golden eyes looking back at her. "I promise I'm helping her. I need to get rid of the demon dross in her body. It would eventually kill her if left untreated."

Trinity let out a plaintive mewl.

"Yeah, I know, demons in Chicago. Who'd believe it, eh? Like the city isn't crazy enough."

The steady thrum of the cat's steady purring pulsed in rhythm to the energy coursing through Ashley's body. She was heartened to finally see the skin around the cut start to turn pink as the poison left Rafe.

"Just a little longer, Detective, and you'll be as good as new." Ashley could feel the poison entering her own skin, but her body was capable of fighting it off, rendering it useless, nullifying its vile disease. "See, now, wasn't it a good thing we crossed each other's paths? You were in need of a healer, and I just happen to have the healing you required." She frowned at her own comment. "*Eli.* I bet Eli planned this whole damn thing." She spoke aloud as if Rafe could hear her and be able to contribute. "Not the demon part. Eli wouldn't have set you up to meet with the demon. But our meeting has his stamp of interference masquerading as free will written all over it." She saw with some satisfaction the jagged skin marring Rafe's temple start to heal.

She made a face at Trinity, who was looking up at her intently, obviously fascinated by every word she was uttering. "He's Eli; he has *connections*; he knows everything." She shook her head. "Except for who this killer is in these crimes. Not even he has had that revealed yet." She felt the powerful push of a head against her arm. "Which is a shame, Trinity, because it would save me the bother of touring around the streets at night having to look at dead women who don't deserve to die. I could be putting that time to better use."

She lifted her fingers off Rafe's skin and examined her work. "There, that looks much better. I guess I was meant to help your owner live, because something tells me she's one of the good guys." Ashley sat on the floor with her back to the couch, shaking her hands out as if flicking off the remnants of the demon poison. She cracked her knuckles sharply as she waggled her fingers free of the cramp they had experienced from the intense pressure she'd placed on them.

Trinity climbed into her lap, demanding attention. Absently Ashley petted the cat, enjoying the simple task of running her fingers over the animal's soft fur. One-handed, she reached for her phone and called for takeout. "Can't let my blood sugar drop, can we?" she asked the cat, who just nudged her hand in a hint for less talking, more stroking. "Hope your mom likes Hawaiian pizza. I've got a strange craving for pineapple after that healing." She listened to the soft breathing behind her as Rafe slept in a healing-induced slumber. "I ordered enough for four people, so when she wakes up she should have a slice left at least."

The cat blinked at her.

"What? I'm starving. I've been reading dry old police files all day. It didn't give me much time to grab a snack." She picked the cat up and cuddled her. "Let's go see if we can find some plates and glasses. I ordered a bottle of cola, and if I can't find something suitable I'm drinking straight from the bottle and you can choose to be grossed out or not."

She wandered into the kitchen and began opening Rafe's cupboards to find what she needed. The domesticity of her actions made her pause for a moment. It had been a long time since she'd been in a home. A real home, as opposed to a hotel room hastily acquired for business reasons. Ashley couldn't remember the last time she'd sat down for a meal with someone, to share conversation and maybe move to something more intimate. She snorted softly, startling the cat in her arms.

"Sorry, Trinity. It's just sad when I realize you're the first thing I've held in my arms for a very long time." She nuzzled the cat's fur. "All work and no play makes Ashley a very dull date."

She looked over her shoulder to where Rafe was stretched out on the settee. "Your mommy is very lucky. She has someplace warm and cozy to come back to after a lousy day at work." The cat meowed as if adding her own comment. "Yes, and there's you to come home to as well. I have an Eli." Ashley made a face. "Oddly enough, it's not the same."

Ashley had never felt so keenly her being alone in the world. She clung to the cat a little longer. "How about we find you something you're not supposed to eat just so I can add to the list of things Rafe has against me?" She opened a cupboard door. "Though it would help if she had more choice in her pantry. Guess it's just plain ol' kibble for you, Trinity."

She busied herself looking after the cat. Anything to keep her mind off how lonely she felt and how unreal her life had become that simply feeding a cat was a delight.

"Maybe I should get a cat." Trinity's big golden eyes stared up at her unblinking. "Yeah, Eli would just love that." Ashley sniggered at the thought. "His immaculate suits and cat hair. God, it would be worth it just for that alone."

She kept herself entertained with that idea while preparing Trinity's supper, pushing aside all thoughts of demons and murders for a moment and just relaxing in doing something *normal* for a change.

CHAPTER SIX

The tantalizing smell of food drew Rafe from her deep sleep, and for a moment, eyes still closed, she just breathed in deeply to savor it. It had to be an olfactory hallucination; her fridge was empty.

"I've left you plenty to pick at if you feel up to eating."

Rafe's eyes shot open at the sound of a voice very close to her head. She shifted slightly and met the smiling face of Ashley seated on the floor beside her. Ashley held up a big slice of pizza and took a bite from it. She spoke with her mouth full.

"It's still hot, it hasn't been delivered long."

Rafe eased herself upright to swing her legs around and sit up properly. She reached for a piece of pizza and only after the first mouthful was she surprised to discover just how hungry she was.

"Did you eat at all today?" Ashley asked, handing Rafe another piece once she'd devoured the first.

"I can't remember," Rafe replied, her voice husky. Ashley poured out some cola into a glass and passed it back to her.

"Is there some reason why you're still in my home waiting on me? I thought you'd be long gone by now with my TV tucked under your arm." Rafe cocked her head at the sound of a familiar feline snore. "Ahh, I see you weren't going anywhere. You've been converted into a human cushion for my cat." Trinity slept contentedly in Ashley's lap.

"She's no problem. I fed her while I was waiting for the pizza to arrive."

"You're a regular angel of mercy," Rafe said around a mouthful of pizza. Ashley snorted but not with any humor. The look on her face gave Rafe cause to wonder what exactly had she said that had touched a raw nerve.

"Aren't I just." Ashley reached for more food.

"I can remember you bringing me home. I also seem to recall you 'turning off the lights.'" Rafe gestured at Ashley. "And I know you did something to this mark on my forehead because suddenly there's no pain when I touch it." Rafe ran a finger over the less pronounced scar. "So I need to ask. Just what in the hell are you?"

"I told you, I'm Ashley Scott and I'm a private investigator."

Rafe let out a sigh. "Yes, I'm sure that's all on your business card. What's not on there is the glitter show you apparently can produce on a whim." She waited, but Ashley merely continued with her meal and ignored her. "You know I can't share any information I have on a case with an outside source. But then I don't need to, do I? You've been in our office apparently gathering information by some means that I can't quite begin to explain."

"I'm working on the same set of killings you are."

"Who hired you?"

"A very interested party who wants the killer stopped just as much as you do."

"Is this interested party a member of one of the victim's families? Because I've spoken with all of them, except for this last one. Dean did their interview while I was being scolded by the doctors for being snuck out of the hospital in the middle of the night to visit a crime scene before I was *officially* released. To my knowledge, none of the families has ever indicated they were bringing in an outside investigator."

"I've been asked to investigate by someone else, Rafe. It's no reflection on your investigation or the work your people are doing."

"What were you doing in my office?"

Ashley looked chagrined. "You weren't supposed to know I was in there."

"Well, I could see you as plain as day, so I'm asking again, what were you doing?"

"How could you see me?"

Rafe blinked. "Excuse me?"

"Let me put it another way—what did you see when you first looked at me?"

Rafe cast a long, measured look at her but decided to humor her. "Like I told you, I saw a small blonde dressed as a cat burglar surrounded by a golden, shimmering light that burned into my retinas." Rafe picked up another piece of pizza. "I'm more intrigued as to why two of my most trusted people saw only Detective Powell in the room when I plainly saw you."

Ashley smiled sweetly. "I'm intrigued by that fact too. What makes you so special, Detective?"

Rafe let out a small laugh. "I'm nothing special at all, Sparky. But you obviously are. So what are we talking here? Special ops? Mind control? Hallucinatory drugs in the water cooler?"

Ashley's unfettered laughter made Rafe's heart trip in her chest. Ashley looked so beautiful when amused. Her eyes shone and her face lit up in a way Rafe's whole body responded to. Whoever this woman was, she was gorgeous. Rafe could appreciate that even though she tried to tell herself not to.

"It's nothing quite so conspiratorial, Rafe. For goodness sake, you cops are a suspicious lot."

"Comes with the territory." Rafe saw her hesitation. "What?"

"What would you say if I said maybe I was just magic?"

"I'd say you'd been sampling Trinity's catnip."

Ashley's eyes twinkled as she graced Rafe with a dazzling smile. "I'm going to like working with you."

Exasperated, Rafe laid her head back against the couch. "I am not working with you, and I'm going to make damn sure you can't step foot inside the Chicago Police Department again." The pout of Ashley's full bottom lip made Rafe want to lean forward and capture it between her teeth. She swallowed hard at the unexpected arousal that burned through her chest. It shook her and made her voice escape more angrily than she intended. "You took confidential files, Ashley. There's a law against that."

"Like you always follow the law?"

Rafe nodded, knowing full well she was blatantly lying. "Of course."

Disbelief was written all over Ashley's face. "And were you following the strict letter of the law the night you chased after a demon behind Castello's Bar and Grill?"

Rafe's body jerked with surprise. "How did you find out about that?"

Ashley pointed to Rafe's forehead. "I told you; you had the mark of a demon." She let her hand fall. "At least now it will fade with time and the poison he shared with you won't kill you."

Rafe was stunned. "It was going to kill me?"

"What he couldn't finish in the alley would have happened eventually from the cut. You don't usually get to escape a demon's death wish twice, Rafe. You might want to rethink that whole you being special thing again. Someone is looking out for you."

Rafe's mind swirled with the information she'd been given. She brushed a hand tentatively across her forehead, wondering just how much she owed Ashley for something she had done that Rafe could not explain. It confused and boggled her. It was also terrifying.

"What do you know of demons?" Rafe shifted uncomfortably on the couch, unsure whether she really wanted an answer to her question.

"I know more than you realize," Ashley said. "Not everything in your world is black and white. There are big areas of gray, and that is where the demons hide."

Rafe just stared at her, digesting her words. Then she was back in the alley, witnessing the birth of a demon right before her eyes, and she'd seen the endless fire burning through to his very soul. She blinked hard to dispel the image that haunted her. "You're insane," she spat out, fearing Ashley's truth.

"I'm not the one who chased down a demon in an unlit alley at night and nearly got her head caved in for the pleasure."

"How do you know that? None of those details were ever released." Agitated, Rafe needed to know who or what Ashley's sources were. If there was a leak in the department, Rafe wanted it plugged and fast. But no one knew the full details, only Rafe herself.

"I read your statement this afternoon on one of your officers' computers." Ashley reached for yet another piece of pizza and began chewing it slowly. "You left out a few little details in your report, if you don't mind me saying."

"You looked me up?"

"You're the lead of the newly formed DDU. I needed to know who you are so I could come to you. But nowhere in that report do you mention that the guy who tried to kill you that night was a demon. Why is that?"

Rafe clenched her teeth so hard her jaw ached. "Because I'd probably be in the psych ward wearing a fashionable straitjacket instead of back at my desk at the DDU. There was no demon."

"You told me yourself, he had horns and glowing red eyes."

"When?" Rafe racked her brain trying to recall when she had let slip the things she tried so hard to keep hidden.

"When I was healing you."

"The ravings of a delirious mind while you did whatever it is you say you did to me," Rafe blustered.

"Do you believe I healed you? Feel the scar for yourself, Rafe. Does it still feel like it's burning through to your skull?"

Rafe closed her eyes and groaned out loud. "No, it doesn't."

"Then stop being so frightened I'm going to tell people what you saw."

"I'm not frightened of anything."

"Obviously, hence chasing after a man twice your size and with demon strength to match. It's a wonder a scratch is all you got from him. I'm surprised he didn't tear your damn fool head off."

Rafe let out a shaky breath. "He tried hard enough." Her hand shook as she raised it to her forehead, and she fought against a wave of dizziness that threatened to engulf her.

"Now look at what you're doing. You're getting yourself all worked up, and it's not doing you a bit of good. You need to rest. You've just had poison drained from your system; you're bound to feel strange for a while." Ashley got to her knees, dislodging the disgruntled cat, who stalked off toward the kitchen in a huff.

"What have you done to me?" Rafe asked, finally afraid for herself.

"Healed you; nothing more. But I couldn't take the other pains away, so you still need to watch your side. And I can't make your hair grow back any quicker. I could only help with the one thing."

"Just the magic," Rafe said. "I think I'm going crazy, and you're helping me right along that path."

"You're not crazy, but you're damn lucky to be alive. Not many face down a demon and live to tell."

"I'm not telling. He was just a man," Rafe said.

Ashley smiled at Rafe as if placating a child. "When you looked into his eyes, did it feel like you were falling down an endless ravine of red fire? And that on your way down your skin was burned off piece by piece?"

Rafe tried not to react, but she knew her face gave her away.

"Two horns, either side of his temples, thick and banded. His face distorted until he no longer resembled a mortal man, and when he spoke it was with a voice so deep it rattled through your bones until you thought they would shatter into splinters."

Rafe's whole body twitched at the memory of how his words had vibrated through to her very core. *"Now I put an end to your misery on earth."* She felt bile rise to her throat. A numbing dread at what Ashley was revealing to her made Rafe search desperately for another answer, terrified that what Ashley was suggesting was truly real and hadn't just been her mind conjuring up terrifying images as she prepared to die. "Please just tell me you're from Internal Affairs."

Ashley laughed once, a short, sharp sound. "No. I'm not here to trick you into saying what you really saw that night. Your badge is safe, Detective. I'm here in the hope that what you saw will leave your mind open for what I need you to consider."

"What's that?"

"That the killer you're seeking may not be entirely human himself."

CHAPTER SEVEN

A shley couldn't stifle her groan at the inconvenient timing of her cell phone ringing just as she'd delivered her bombshell. She checked the screen and saw it was Eli. "Damn it," she grumbled and answered it. The conversation was short and sweet. Ashley hung up and looked over her shoulder at Rafe, who had barely moved since Ashley's revelation.

"I have to go. Will you be okay?"

Rafe just nodded.

"I know I've kind of given you a lot to process, but we seriously need to work together on this. It's not going to stop any time soon."

"What could you possibly bring to this investigation that we don't already know?"

Ashley slipped into her jacket. "The fact that I have been at the last two crime scenes while the body was still warm." She was satisfied by Rafe's gasp. "I believe that's quicker than you managed to get to them." She saw the intended barb bring some spark back into Rafe's eyes. "You want to talk, call me. I took the liberty of programming my number into your cell." She headed toward the front door. "You might want to shield your eyes, Detective. I'm about to get my glamour on." She shifted and Rafe immediately began to squint.

"Why are you doing that?"

"Because I came into your house as one person, I can't really leave as another. What kind of reputation do you want in this neighborhood, Rafe?" Rafe's face was so nonplussed Ashley flashed her a cheeky grin. "Call me before we get another body, Detective. You and I have a lot to talk about." She closed the door behind her, then hurried to the street to hail a taxi. She stood on the street corner, watching the moon begin its steady climb into the night sky. Ashley prepared herself for yet another night out in the cold.

"Like I don't have enough to deal with one killer on the loose, and now there are murmurs of another demon rampant in the city. Since when did Chicago become Demon Central Station?" She flagged down a taxi and got in, giving him directions to where Eli had reported a sighting.

"Cool night," the taxi driver said as he pulled away from the curb. "You going into work?" He obviously knew the office buildings Ashley had given him the address for.

"Yes, another late night, trying to keep the company afloat," she said.

"No rest for the wicked, eh?" he said, turning onto the main street and heading into town.

With one last look at Rafe's building, Ashley finally turned around. "You got that right," she said humorlessly, watching the lights from the street lamps streak across the night.

❖

Rafe got to work early the next morning. She sat before her computer searching for Ashley Scott through every database she could enter her name into.

Alona walked in, stopped dead in her tracks, and blinked at her. "Geez, you're in early, Detective. I'm used to having this office to myself for at least a few hours." She moved to her own desk and started up her computer. "Can I get you anything?"

Rafe distractedly tapped her pen against a Starbucks cup. "I'm fine, thanks." For the umpteenth time that morning she frowned as she brought up yet another screen and began typing Ashley's name in the required box.

"Anything I can help you with?" Alona asked, sidling over to see what Rafe was doing.

"I want to run this person through every system we have, but all I have is her name. I'm getting too many hits."

Alona pulled her chair over and straddled it. "You've got no other data at all? Date of birth? Address?"

Rafe shook her head, thought for a moment, then fumbled for her phone. "I do have her cell phone number, though. For Christ's sake, why didn't I think of that half a fucking hour ago?" She thumbed through her list of contacts but couldn't find Ashley in the A's so continued through the S's. "There's no Scott," she said, then found a new listing. "Damn woman." She shook her head at finding a new entry for "Sparky" displayed on her phone. She read the number out to Alona, who began her own search.

"Please don't let it be a disposable." Rafe peered over Alona's shoulder as she worked.

"This some woman you just met, ma'am?" Alona asked carefully.

"She's someone who says she might have information about our killer, but I'd like to know a little more about her before I accept what she says is true."

"If she can help." Alona brought up a screen full of Ashley Scott's details. "Wow, she's one pretty lady if this is the one you're after," she said on seeing Ashley's driver's license photo. "Looks like trouble is her middle name, too, by the twinkle in those eyes."

She's trouble all right. Rafe read what details Alona had found. Twenty-nine years old. Rafe was surprised she was only six years younger than her. *She looks so much younger. I wonder if that's got anything to do with all that golden glitter that surrounds her.*

"Says here she's a private investigator," Alona said. "Hell, she even got a commendation from the mayor of Kansas City for cracking a child porn ring. Says she helped save the kids from a group of predators."

Rafe wondered which variety, human or otherwise.

"Pedophiles are the worst scum," Alona said as she continued scrolling down the page. "I've got an address for you." She printed it off unasked.

"Do me a favor? Print it all out, license, newspaper mentions, commendation report, all of it. I think I'll keep a file handy on Ms. Scott, just in case."

"Are you going to call her?"

"I might just pay her a friendly visit." Rafe gathered up the information from the printer and tucked it into a file. "What do you think, Alona? Does Ms. Scott strike you as a doughnut for breakfast kind of person?"

Alona chuckled. "I'm sure she'd be more than grateful for your company at this ungodly hour of the morning, ma'am."

"I've told you before to call me Rafe, Alona. Ma'am makes me think my mother has entered the room, and God forbid that should ever happen."

"Thank you. While we're dispensing with formalities, if your lady here doesn't like doughnuts, I'll take one. Heavy on the chocolate and light on the sprinkles."

Rafe patted her on the shoulder as she walked past. "I'll see what I can come up with for you. When Detective Jackson finally drags his ass in, please tell him I'll be back shortly."

Alona called after her, "Can I say you look great today? Your eyes are less clouded and that gash on your forehead looks so much better. You must have had a healing sleep."

Rafe paused with her hand on the door. "Thank you, I feel... lighter." She cringed inwardly at her own words, but in truth she felt... cleansed. "Amazing what a good night's sleep in your own bed can do."

"Just watch yourself in that neighborhood, Rafe. It's not the safest part of the city. It's even got a reputation among the gangs as unsafe."

"Where is safe here?" she said as she left.

Her mind on the case, Rafe recalled Blythe's name for the killer: the Spine Tingler. She grimaced. Wouldn't the newspapers have a field day with that nickname splashed across the front of their tabloids to help spread fear across the city? People's views of being safe on the streets would plummet lower than they already were.

Rafe easily found a cab, seeing as it was barely six a.m. She hadn't been able to sleep for long after Ashley had left her. She'd felt strangely wired, energized like she hadn't felt since before the incident. Rafe was determined to find out just who Ashley Scott was, if she really was an investigator or something more sinister. Rafe was aware that for all her questioning the night before, Ashley had never explained what the glittery lights were. Magic didn't cut it in Rafe's world. She dealt in facts and things that were proven. She directed the driver to wait for her and got out in front of one of the biggest derelict-looking buildings she had seen in years. She would never have thought Ashley would have chosen to live there. It seemed too dilapidated for the woman whose leather coat had to be a name brand. Rafe pulled her own leather coat collar tighter around her neck at the bitter air that chilled her skin. The air seemed different here than it had in the city, and her chest ached as she breathed the cold in. Rafe shivered at the air's icy touch. She pushed through the building's main doors and startled a young man who seemed engrossed in whatever he was doing under his makeshift desk. Rafe wasn't sure she wanted to know, until he pulled out a PSP and put it aside hastily, flashing her a smile which only faltered fractionally when she showed him her badge.

"Can I help you?" he asked nervously, his fingers fumbling for the cell phone lying on top of the table.

"I'm just here to see my...girlfriend. I'd prefer not to be announced."

His hand drifting guiltily away from the phone that Rafe knew he used to give the building's occupants the heads up that police were on the premises. She had the feeling she had just walked into drug central, seeing as a building this run down had a watcher in the lobby. Someone was obviously paying him to keep an eye on their "business."

"Please, go right ahead. I'll just..." He sat back abruptly under Rafe's cool stare.

"Get back to your game," she said, already aiming for the elevator. "You never saw me here."

"Yes, ma'am, no, ma'am," he blustered.

Rafe was sure she heard him let out a sigh of relief when the doors closed on her. She pushed the button for the floor Ashley Scott supposedly resided on. "If this is a false address, Sparky, then you're the liar I believe you to be and maybe then I can stop thinking about you."

The landing was lit by a sad strip of weak light as Rafe stepped from the elevator. She instinctively drew her jacket back from her gun. She'd been in too many run-down apartment buildings not to be prepared for whatever came out from behind the doors. She hugged the wall, one hand on her gun, counting down the apartment numbers. Rafe raised her free hand to rap on the door. She heard footsteps and the door opened without any preamble. Ashley Scott stood there, dressed in the same clothing she'd worn the night before. She leaned against the door jamb, smiling at Rafe like she'd been expecting her.

"I figured you'd at least have given me the chance to change before you got here."

"You've been out all night?" Rafe found the idea of Ashley being with someone else until the early hours made her stomach clench painfully.

"I wish I could say it was for the pleasant company, but I'd done that earlier in the evening." She batted her eyelashes outrageously at Rafe. "I was working, Detective. Sadly, not painting the town red." She stepped back and ushered Rafe inside. "Now that you're here, without a phone call I might add, do you want to get straight to work or can I at least have a cup of coffee to start my day?" Without waiting for an answer, she moved back toward the kitchen. "Then you can tell me why you're to be found at my door before even God has gotten up."

Rafe followed Ashley into the apartment and looked around. "This isn't how I pictured you living," she said, finding the apartment impersonal and curiously empty. She caught sight of a large whiteboard, its back flipped toward her. It looked grossly out of place in the room.

"That's because it's not really mine. It's just a place to sleep while I deal with stuff before I move on to the next job." Ashley puttered about the tiny kitchen fixing two cups.

"Where's your home?"

"I don't have one. I go where the need for me is, then I move on."

Rafe heard the resignation in Ashley's voice. "I'm a workaholic, but even I have somewhere to call home."

"And a cat," Ashley added. "A big black cat to come home to and cuddle up with."

Rafe wondered at the wistful quality to Ashley's words. "I've had her from a kitten. She was a present from a friend who said with the job I did, I should always come home to a friendly face." Rafe remembered Blythe handing over the small scrap of fur that had grown into the beautiful animal Trinity had become. "Admittedly, a face with whiskers and kibble breath."

Ashley pushed a cup of coffee toward Rafe, then placed the milk and sugar within her reach. She eyed the file under Rafe's arm. "Do you come bearing gifts?"

Rafe placed the file on the table between them and opened it, spreading out the photocopied screen prints of Ashley's life, at least, all that she could find documented.

Ashley flipped through a few of the sheets, made a face at the driver's license photo, then looked up. "What? You don't have my latest Pap smear results? Your team must be slipping."

Rafe could tell Ashley wasn't very pleased but was holding back her anger. Sipping from the hot coffee, Rafe made her wait for her answer. "I've found out just the smallest slivers of information about you. You obviously manage to cover your tracks in all you do. But there's one detail missing that I really would like to know about that's not covered in any of these sparse details about you."

"What's that?"

"Why all that glitters is gold around you." She took another mouthful of coffee and watched Ashley's eyes sparkle a dangerous shade of blue. Dark clouds gathered; Rafe braced herself for the storm.

"It's not exactly public record," Ashley said, heaping sugar into her own coffee cup and stirring vigorously.

"So you have no real home. You have an investigative business that has no offices that I can find, yet you receive commendations from grateful folk for what you do in serving the public. So tell me, Ashley Scott, while I am not under whatever spell it was you wove over me last night, who the hell are you?"

"She's one of the good souls on earth."

The voice came from behind Rafe, causing her to spill her coffee as she spun around. She cried out in pain as a brilliant white seared her eyeballs and pierced through her skull. Even with her eyes screwed tightly shut, the light still pounded through her eyelids. Her knees buckled beneath her as the light overwhelmed her. The last time she'd seen light that bright she'd been waiting to mercifully die.

She could hear Ashley's voice calling, and the whiteness faded enough for Rafe to stop clutching at her head waiting for it to explode. Curled up on the floor in a protective ball, Rafe could feel hands on her back. She cracked open an eye to the room. A man stood before her, dressed in the most impeccable white suit she had ever seen. She opened her eyes a little wider and gasped as something behind him shifted in the light and just as quickly vanished from her blighted sight. She could smell Ashley's scent surrounding her and dimly registered that it was Ashley cradling her in her arms.

"You okay?" Ashley asked, running her hand across Rafe's forehead as if checking for a temperature.

"He's brighter than you, so much brighter," Rafe bit out.

"I do believe it's not just you she can see," Eli said. "This is more than a little unexpected."

Rafe looked at them both as best she could, desperately trying not to be frightened by what she could see or what she had gotten herself involved with.

"Rafe, this is Eli. He's kind of my boss, well, one of them anyway." Ashley grumbled at him. "For God's sake, Eli, turn it down if you can. I told you she was sensitive."

Rafe barely heard Ashley's harsh reprimand over the steady hum of white noise that accompanied the light. It sounded like a million voices suppressed into one endless tone. The brightness faded enough for Rafe to try to keep her eyes open a little longer, but she still ended up having to shut them. But there was no escape from the light. "What the fuck is going on?"

"Eli, *do* something."

Rafe flinched as unfamiliar hands grasped her face and held her head captive.

"What…" She gasped as white-hot pain lanced through her brain. She nearly blacked out as the agony threatened to overwhelm her. Then as suddenly as the pain had struck, it was mercifully gone. Rafe fell forward, saved only by Ashley's grasp. She opened her eyes to find Ashley's concerned face mere inches from her own.

"Are you okay?"

Rafe looked around her. She could still see the white light vibrating around Eli. It pulsated and flashed like a living, breathing entity. But looking didn't hurt her anymore and the sound was gone. Rafe turned to Ashley.

"Do *your* thing, Sparky," she said and watched as Ashley lit up in her familiar golden glow. "I can keep my eyes open when you do that now." She flicked a wary look in Eli's direction. "What is it with you two and the laying on of hands without consent?"

Eli cocked his head at Ashley. "You touched her *again*?"

"I healed her. That damn demon scratch was poisoning her. I'd triggered it, so of course I touched her to stop it from killing her."

Rafe tried to get to her feet as best she could without pulling at her side or needing too much of Ashley's help. Muttering under her breath at having to accept the arm under her elbow to keep her upright, Rafe grumbled, "Lights out, Sparky," and Ashley dropped the glamour. Rafe directed her attention to the man in the room. "So, Eli? What did *you* do to me?"

Eli began reeling off a complicated description that defied understanding. Ashley cut into his long-winded recitation.

"Without getting too technical, Eli. Not all of us share your far superior intellect."

Eli pondered for a moment. "I rerouted your brain synapses, effectively rewiring your brain with a dimmer switch. You can see the lights emitted, but now they are muted and are not going to cause your pain receptors to react."

Rafe stared at him. "Thank you. But if you can do all that, why not just stop me from seeing them altogether?"

"It's part of your physiology now. I can't tamper with that, which is meant to be, but I can help with the alleviation of the pain."

Rafe rubbed at her forehead, trying to get a grasp on all that was happening to her. "When the guy in the alley marked me, did I somehow slip through to an alternative reality? Because this sure isn't the Kansas I remember anymore."

"We're in Chicago, Detective." Eli tossed a look toward Ashley. "Just how badly was she brain-damaged in the demon fight?"

Ashley shook her head at him. "There's no such thing as alternative realities, Detective," she said to Rafe.

"And until you, there was no such thing as demons in my reality either, and look where that's leading me." She stepped into Ashley's personal space. "Right back to *your* door."

"I'm curious, how did you manage to find me? I don't usually leave a paper trail that can be found so fast."

"You gave me your cell phone number."

Ashley looked resigned. "So I did. I gave it to you so you could call me and we could set up a meeting. Guess you skipped that part."

"Who are you exactly? Because no PI I know would be camped out in a place like this unless they were undercover or out of luck. I've got enough fashion sense to know that your jacket probably cost more than the rent does on this place. So what gives?"

"We're here for the same reason you are, to find the killer of these women."

"Because you think it's a demon?"

"Because whoever or whatever he is, he's not entirely human."

"And you're here to do what exactly? Help me solve the killings in your own special way?" Rafe flicked a look up and down Ashley's body. "Forgive me, but I fail to see how much assistance you can be by supposedly changing your appearance."

"Supposedly?" Eli asked, watching their verbal sparring with great interest.

"She doesn't see who I become. Rafe has only ever seen me," Ashley said.

"Unfortunate."

"And the very reason why we're here like this now," Ashley told him.

Frustrated at how they were talking over her head when she was standing right there with them, Rafe butted in. "Actually, I'm here because last night you mentioned something about visiting the crime scenes. I have to ascertain just how much you may have contaminated both the scene and the evidence with your unauthorized presence." She brushed back her jacket and tapped the handcuffs attached to her belt. "Give me one good reason why I shouldn't haul you in right now for disturbing a crime scene."

"Because the person you'd be seen dragging into the station wouldn't be me but possibly Detective Powell. I can glamour her exceptionally accurately. How long do you think you'd still be at your shiny new desk at the DDU after that stunt?"

"How can you do what you do?" she bit out, furious at what Ashley proposed and powerless to counter her threat.

"The same way you can see the glamour when I wear it. Because I'm different. Just like you are now."

"But I didn't see any fancy lights before I got taken down by Armitage. My life was fucking normal up until then." She gestured between Ashley and Eli. "No glamours, no white lights, no healing when I damn well didn't ask for it. No rerouting whatever is going on in my brain that's making me feel so fucking paranoid!"

Rafe brushed off Ashley's hand that reached out to her. "I warn you, both of you, stay the hell out of my investigation or I'll arrest you both so fast neither of you will have time to turn on the lights." Rafe stormed out of the apartment, slamming the door behind her and wincing at the pull in her side the sudden movement had caused. She headed toward the elevator, muttering under her breath. "Rerouting of synapses. If I need healing, let's start with the fucking knife wound in my side." She pressed the button for the elevator, and when it didn't come immediately she pounded on it numerous times to vent her frustration. "If she's compromised any of my scenes I'll *glamour* her ass all the way to jail."

CHAPTER EIGHT

S o," Eli said, "that's your detective."
Ashley's ears were still ringing from the slamming of the door. *I bet that's woken most of the neighbors.* "Yes, Eli, that's Rafe Douglas."

"Humans don't usually survive a demon attack."

"She's like no other human I've ever met." Ashley busied herself leafing through the file Rafe had left behind. She was curious what Rafe had managed to find out.

"And?"

"And nothing, nosy. She's dedicated, determined."

"And very handsome. You said so yourself, I recall, after your first encounter."

Ashley groaned. "I admit it. She's so damn hot I'm frightened of going up in flames every time I see her."

"Is this a problem?"

Only if I can't manage to keep my hands to myself. Ashley thought back to the previous night when she'd held Rafe's face in her hands and watched over her as she'd slept. *Instant attraction, and I'm not the only one who felt it. And it wasn't the draining of poison talking when she told me I was beautiful.* Could she get Rafe to be that unguarded again, to put down her shield so that Ashley could reach the woman behind it?

"You've gone very quiet," Eli said.

"I have to go back and face her. I'm trying to think of the best strategy to do that without ending up behind bars."

"You can be very persuasive; I've seen you. You're good at getting what you want."

Ashley's breath caught a little at Eli's innocent words. *Want? It's just a job,* she told herself. *Solve the crimes and then move on to the next case.* "She's not going to make this easy."

"No, I don't think she will, but she'll be a worthy ally by your side. You complement each other."

"You got all that from her barging in here and yelling at me to stay away?"

"No. I got it from her eyes and heart and all that she didn't say out loud when she looked at you."

"Eli, you're just an old romantic at heart."

"I have no time for romance; it's too human an emotion."

"Thank God for that."

"My thoughts exactly."

Rafe was glad to see Dean and Alona hard at work when she returned to the DDU. She slipped a large box of doughnuts, along with fresh coffee, beside Alona as she headed back to her own desk.

"Where have you been, boss?" Dean looked up over his computer at her entrance and gratefully accepted his own coffee from her.

"I was following up on a lead I got last night, but it went nowhere." Rafe busied herself at her desk, picking up her telephone messages and discarding most of them. She was not willing to talk even to Dean about Ashley Scott or the bizarre happenings that kept occurring around her. She flicked on her computer and decided to just forget Ashley and all the crazy baggage that came with her.

"Alona, have we got the medical reports for the first two murders somewhere at your fingertips?" She waited while Alona brought them up on the big screen. Rafe read through them again, a frown gathering on her face. "I'm going to see if Dr. Alan can spare me a few minutes while he still has victim number three in his care." As quickly as she had entered the office, Rafe turned back around and left. She headed down to the basement, where the precinct morgue resided. The pale gray walls were in stark contrast to the rest of the CPD, but Rafe relished the coolness and the muted lights that ran the length of the corridor. She pushed open the door to the morgue and was directed further down the halls by a woman pushing a gurney. The body underneath the drape seemed shapeless and nondescript, but Rafe couldn't ignore the fact the white cloth covered yet another dead person to join the statistics that the city logged every month. She popped her head around a door and found Dr. Alan working away on a corpse.

"Dr. Alan, have you got a moment, please?"

The old man's face lit up when Rafe entered his room. "I knew it wouldn't be long before you were down here, Detective, chasing up the details." Dr. Alan grinned at her and waved her in. He gestured for her to put on a coverall so as not to get anything untoward on her suit. Stretched over the body between them, he fixed her with an intense stare, his eyes taking in her injuries with professional interest. "You took a mighty beating, and I know what you're sporting is only half of what lies beneath. I saw his body, and I have to admit to you, Rafe, I'm surprised you didn't end up on my table."

Rafe ran a hand over her face in a gesture that was becoming second nature to her, checking that she was still intact, assuring herself she was still alive. "To be honest, Doc, I thought I'd be toe tag material too."

He reached over the body and slapped Rafe gently on the shoulder. "I'm glad to have you back and in one piece. The place just isn't the same without you. And now that the DDU is fully functional, you're back where you belong. Which is why you're down here? I presume to ask about the latest victim your backstabber left the city to mourn?"

Rafe furtively glanced around the room before speaking in a hushed tone. "Actually, Doc, I want to ask about Marcus Armitage."

"The behemoth that nearly killed you? What do you want to hear? I'm sure you read my report."

Rafe's indecision crippled her. How could she seriously ask the coroner the burning question that was lodged in her head? She grimaced and gathered up her courage. "Was there anything *unusual* about Marcus Armitage when you performed his autopsy?"

"Other than the fact he was higher than three kites tied to a satellite orbiting Mars?" Dr. Alan shuffled over to his computer and, one key at a time, hen-pecked his way across the keyboard. "You know his tox screen. If it could be injected, swallowed, or snorted, it was in his system. He was grossly overweight, but I put that down to his being a quarterback who would rather snort a line than run down one." He glanced up from his screen. "Anything you looking for in particular?"

"Did he have any deformities?"

Dr. Alan blinked owlishly at her. "Deformities? He had several healed-up broken bones from old football injuries."

Shaking her head, Rafe took the plunge. "Did he have any…" Her words failed her and she patted at her head.

"Head injuries?"

"Horns," Rafe blurted out. "Did he have any horns?"

The silence in the room was absolute. Dr. Alan stared at her, looked at his computer screen, then out of the corner of his eye he looked back at Rafe again. "What medication have they got you on, Rafe?"

"Humor me, Doc, please. Did you find anything unusual on his X-rays?"

"On his head?"

Rafe shrugged. "On his head in this general area." She patted to just above her temples.

Dr. Alan gave her a measured look that made her almost regret bringing this conversation up. But he beckoned Rafe over to his screen and brought up the X-rays from Armitage's autopsy. "When he came in, his head was pretty much blown away, so he wasn't going to win any prizes for being handsome."

"Did he look odd?"

"His face was distorted, but no one's face stays normal after a bullet through the forehead. Once I'd peeled his face off and found what was left of his skull, there wasn't a whole lot I could piece back together." He looked over his X-rays again. "Can't remember seeing anything that resembled horns, though."

"I was just checking." Rafe studied the X-rays herself, desperately searching for proof of what she'd seen.

"He wasn't red either," Dr. Alan added.

"I beg your pardon?"

"He didn't in any way resemble Hellboy."

Narrowing her eyes at his sly drawl, Rafe had to smile. "This conversation stays strictly between you and me, right, Doc?"

"Of course. I'd hate for you to be back at work only two days and being chased by demons. Still, it would go a long way to explaining so many of the bodies I've had come past my tables." He stepped back from his desk. "Must have been really dark in that alley, Rafe. Your eyes were playing tricks, no doubt."

"No doubt," Rafe said, knowing he was giving her an out. "What can you tell me about our latest victim, then?"

"She didn't have horns either."

Rafe bit back a grin. "Let it go, Doc, or I'm telling your wife about your late-night poker games you host here when you're supposedly doing overtime."

He wagged his finger at her. "You play dirty, Detective."

"No, I play to win, which is why I clean you out every time. Now back to the victim, if you please."

"This latest woman was killed in exactly the same way as the previous two." He took off his latex gloves and slipped on a new pair. He handed Rafe a set as he guided her over to the fridges. "You have a serial killer on your hands, and a nasty one, judging by this killer's modus operandi."

Rafe followed him, standing aside as he pulled a tray out with a cloth-covered body on top. Rafe had seen Andrea Mason at her crime scene, but even now, seeing her face in rigor twisted in a mask of terror, it gave Rafe chills. She tried to hide her reaction from Dr. Alan. She didn't need to give him any more concerns.

"This is a bad one," he said as he finished rolling down the sheet. "I'm going to have to request that the family have a closed casket. They don't need to see their daughter looking like this at the funeral. It was hard enough when her father came to identify her."

"The stuff of nightmares," Rafe said, moving her gaze off the dead woman's face and down to the gaping neck wound.

"One clean cut, left to right, deep enough to cut open the jugular vein and have her bleed to death."

"A swift kill, executed with military precision perhaps?" Rafe examined the wound. "There are no hesitation marks at all."

"A hunter or butcher would be able to do the same."

Rafe thought back to the profile Blythe had given her. This was the second time the skills of a butcher had been brought up. "So this is

someone who knows how to incapacitate their prey swiftly and surely."
She studied lower down the torso. It had been left unmarked. The
woman's naked breasts looked pale and white in the stark light of the
morgue. "No signs of sexual trauma?"

Dr. Alan shook his head. "Not a thing, no fluids of any kind left on
or near the body. No vaginal tearing or bruising. There's no sign of any
sexual penetration taking place at all, before or *after* her death."

"So he's on his third victim and it's still not sexual. So what is it
that feeds his need to kill?"

Dr. Alan turned the body over carefully and Rafe got to see the full
extent of the butchery wrought on the woman's flesh. She couldn't hide
her wince this time.

"Fuck me. Without all the blood, it looks even more brutal."
She checked out the grotesque wounds. "And still there's nothing
missing?"

"Not a thing. All the organs are in place, the spinal cord is all
intact, and there are no teeth marks to indicate he sampled the flesh."
He folded back a wedge of muscle. "She was at her physical peak, and
from what I've learned from her family, she was a beautiful girl inside
and out." He laid her back down gently. "She didn't deserve to end up
like this."

Rafe couldn't bring herself to look away from the woman's face.
"What the fuck did she see just before she died that it seared on her face
like that?"

"Maybe she saw the devil himself."

Rafe flinched inwardly. She knew exactly what that looked like.

CHAPTER NINE

A shley sat on a bench opposite the Chicago PD and watched the endless parade of people milling in and out of the building. Legs outstretched, hands stuffed in her jacket pockets, she looked like someone merely enjoying the pleasantly mild late afternoon. Her eyes, however, were fixed on a certain window three floors up. She'd seen someone pass by it a few times but hadn't been able to tell if it was Rafe. She wished Rafe would just look out and see her to save her the wait of catching her when she left.

"Come on, Detective. See me down here. I'm playing by your rules. I'm not stepping foot inside your department. Come to me instead." Ashley wondered if somewhere in the strange and magical mix of genes her father had passed on to her there could be a smidgen of a siren's call. "Come on, Rafe, before I'm arrested for loitering." Still staring up at the window, Ashley concentrated all her energy toward the glass. She blinked with a start as a figure stopped at the window, looked down, then did a very visible double take. Ashley couldn't stop the grin from breaking across her face. "Oh yeah! Come get me, Detective. I'm out here waiting." She pictured Rafe storming out of the DDU and heading for the elevator. She knew Rafe would be fuming as the floors counted down. Ashley kept her gaze fixed on the front doors. Sure enough, Rafe came stalking out of the building, and with barely a glance at the traffic, walked right across the road toward her.

"For fuck's sake, Rafe, you should really brush up on your traffic code," Ashley said, wincing at the long, drawn-out horn blast from a taxi directed at Rafe's reckless crossing.

"What in God's name are you doing here? I thought I made myself perfectly clear this morning."

"You did. Crystal clear. But I can't let you not wanting me near these killings stop me from telling you yet again that you need me by your side."

"What part of no do you not understand?"

"The part that starts with an *n* and ends in an *o*," Ashley replied flippantly. "I'm sorry, Detective, but I don't do no very well. It's a bad trait and I try to be penitent about it, but it's something that's a work in progress for me." Ashley shifted on the bench, tucking a leg underneath her. "We don't have time for you to get all territorial over these cases. You can piss-mark all you want on your next case, but here and now you need me. This killer isn't done yet, and you need me working with you."

"I have the whole police force behind me. What makes you so damn important?" Rafe loomed over her, her dark eyes intense as she stared down at Ashley.

"Because of who I am, *what* I am, and who I know. You need someone who can recognize a demon soul." Ashley shrugged. "Who better than me?"

Rafe looked skyward and seemed to be offering up a prayer. Ashley was sure she heard "give me strength" escape from under Rafe's breath.

"There're no such things as demons," Rafe said finally.

Ashley couldn't help herself. She laughed. "Sure. Keep telling yourself that every time you wake up screaming when your dreams take you back into Armitage's eyes and you feel yourself burning in the sulfur." She felt a little remorse when Rafe's face registered the obvious shock of dreams remembered. "You've witnessed hell, Detective, seen it and been marked by it. Tell me the fires don't still scorch your skin when you recall looking into his eyes."

Rafe's face took on a haunted look and Ashley desperately wanted to reach out and pull her into her arms to hold her tight. Rafe sat on the bench beside her but wouldn't look her way.

"Your assault has left you open to these things, Rafe. That's why I could touch you and heal you. That's how Eli could help you not be so blinded by what you can now see. You're marked now."

Rafe's head lifted, her eyes filled with pleading. "Then take it all away, please. If you can do it, or Eli. Remove this from me, because I don't want to see things other people can't."

Ashley reached for Rafe's hand. She noticed how much smaller her own hands were as she held Rafe's hand tightly between them. "I'm sorry, *Neo*, but you inadvertently took the red pill, and once you start falling down that rabbit hole there's no turning back."

Rafe's eyes drifted to the people walking past her. "I just want my real life back again."

"I'm sorry, truly I am. I believe, however, you were marked for a purpose."

"That's not very comforting. I'm beginning to lose my mind. I found myself asking the medical examiner today if Armitage had any signs of horns."

"And?"

"He said it was too hard for him to tell seeing as Dean's bullet ripped off his face and took out most of his skull in the process. Part of which I'm grateful for—he saved my life—but it does rather destroy the evidence I needed to prove I'm not certifiable."

"It's for the best," Ashley said, then explained herself to Rafe's sharp look. "I mean, face it. What would people do if you'd gotten proof the guy who tried to kill you was demon bred? What panic would ensue? I say it's a good thing the majority doesn't realize it. Then the ones who are aware can deal with it and protect the city from harm and hysteria."

"It's not in my job description to be a demon hunter."

"It's a tiny clause, written in the fine print. It hardly ever gets invoked until a certain detective bearing the right shield gets initiated."

"You mean nearly gets herself killed by a demon football player."

"Semantics. You lived to tell the tale. Admittedly, you can't tell it to anyone or you'd be forced into retirement faster than a cokehead snorts a line of cocaine." Ashley smiled sweetly at her. "You're still one of the lucky ones."

"Tell me one good reason why I shouldn't just walk away from you again."

"You said I was beautiful."

Rafe shrugged, but her cheeks began to redden. "Being under the influence of demon poison running through my veins no doubt clouded what little judgment I had left."

"It still counts; you can't take it back. I heard it and Trinity heard it."

"Cats aren't known to be great witnesses."

"You'd be surprised what she'd say under oath if I promised her tuna."

Rafe grinned. "You're crazy."

"Then that makes two of us, doesn't it? We crazies have to stick together against an insane world." She looked deep into Rafe's eyes when Rafe turned to stare right back at her.

"And what are you exactly?" Rafe asked. "With the glamour and the golden light show. What does that make you in this world of two halves?"

"You don't think maybe I'm demon spawn too?" Ashley was intrigued how Rafe would answer. Intrigued and a little scared. Rafe never broke eye contact with her. Ashley felt like she could see into Rafe's very soul and, in that very moment, Rafe could see right back into hers.

"I don't see an endless hell when I look into your eyes."

"What *do* you see?"

"Too many things that I can't even begin to think about," Rafe said, looking away.

"We'll get back to those things," Ashley said, her heart lightening at Rafe's obvious interest. "Now, are you going to stop banning me from your office, or are we going to start up clandestine meetings where we share information and devise a plan of action to catch this killer?" Ashley stretched her arms along the back of the bench, her fingertips in reach of Rafe's shoulder. She ached to brush her hand over the stark white of the formal shirt. "I'm all for the cloak-and-dagger stuff, meeting in dark corners, sneaking around like erstwhile lovers." She quirked an eyebrow at Rafe's face. "Or I could just come into your office as myself or glamoured as someone else and we could go down that route."

"I don't want you employing your shape-shifting," Rafe said. "If I do decide to introduce you to the team, what do I tell them?"

"Tell them exactly what I am. A private investigator placed on the case."

"Placed by whom?"

Ashley hesitated. "A higher authority."

"The chief of police?"

Ashley laughed loudly, drawing the attention of the passersby. "I am going to love working with you. You're such a riot."

"I'm not trying to be funny. Who is your boss?"

"Someone who wants the demons put back in their rightful place. Can't I just leave it at that?" She recognized the suspicious glint in Rafe's eye, as well as the look that spoke of questions she wanted to press further on, so she was surprised when Rafe remained silent.

"Eli's your boss, though, right?" Rafe finally asked.

"Kind of. He's the one I get the heads up from to go find these ladies left in the dark."

"That might work. Still doesn't explain how you get a call to the sites before the police do."

"The demon telegraph has its own nine-one-one."

Rafe looked up at her building then back again. "Don't make me regret bringing you in on this with my people."

"You won't. And for the record, strictly between you and me, I'm not a demon. Not entirely, anyway."

"There are degrees of demon?"

"You'd be surprised what there are."

Rafe stood and reached down a hand to help Ashley to her feet. "I really don't need to hear any more. I already know way too much for what's left of my sanity."

"I can try to filter information to you on a need-to-know basis, if you like."

"I'd appreciate that."

"Do I get a desk right next to yours?" Ashley asked, smiling innocently up at Rafe.

"I've got enough trouble trying to work out some kind of plausible cover story for you as it is without you distracting me." Rafe led them both across the street with more care this time, then courteously held the door open to her HQ for Ashley.

Ashley smiled inwardly, enjoying the sweet kindness Rafe just couldn't hide from her even when she knew she drove her to distraction. It seemed only fair, as being in the presence of Rafe Douglas did curious things to her too. "I have a degree in religious and occult ideology and symbolism, which might be a way in for me here."

"You can get degrees in the occult?"

"I believe I mentioned religion first in that statement."

"Yeah, but no one studies religion unless they want to be a priest or something. You studied the occult in class? How does that work? Does everyone bring in their own Ouija board for 'Spook and Tell'?"

"Aren't you a wit?" Ashley made a show of looking around the police station. "This is a novelty. It's the first time I've stepped foot in here as myself," she said for Rafe's hearing alone and got a sharp glare in return. "Don't worry. I promise I'll always tell you who I'm glamouring as so you don't look like a total ass when everyone sees one thing and you're stuck seeing just little old me."

"Thank you, I think."

"I'd hate to make your life difficult." Ashley chuckled at the incredulous face Rafe made at her. Ashley followed her into the elevator, trying not to be obvious about checking out Rafe's butt in her suit pants.

"Difficult seems to be par for the course these days," said Rafe as she pressed the necessary button.

"Then let me try to make it a little less fraught for you. We'll catch this guy, Rafe. I know we will."

"From your lips to God's ears."

"Amen to that."

CHAPTER TEN

Rafe wasn't entirely surprised by how quickly Ashley won over Dean and Alona. There was something about Ashley that drew people to her and put them instantly at ease. Rafe was at a loss to explain it; she was afflicted with the same pull, no matter how hard she tried to fight it. She tried to pretend to be interested in something on her desk and not watch Ashley totally wrap her team around her little finger. She was brought out of her musings when Ashley brushed against her shoulder and handed her a USB stick. Rafe lifted an eyebrow at it suspiciously.

"You're about to let me in to share your work. Turnabout is fair play. I have my own photos of the scenes," Ashley whispered in her ear. Rafe's body instantly reacted as the erotic heat slammed straight down to her gut, causing her muscles to twitch. She barely heard Ashley continue. "I thought it would be prudent to share these, now that we're a team."

Rafe willed her body to stop reacting and coughed to draw everyone's attention. She shot up from her seat, careful not to touch Ashley and slipped away from her. She reached out a hand for the USB.

"I need to ask you both a very big favor," Rafe said, looking first at Dean and then Alona.

Dean seated himself on the edge of Rafe's desk. Folding his arms over his chest, he nodded. "Yes."

"I haven't told you what it is yet."

"I'd follow you anywhere, into anything, Rafe, and pretty much do anything you asked. I'm in, whatever the favor is."

"I second that," Alona said.

"Even if it might cost you both your badges?" Rafe watched them closely. Neither changed their expressions.

"If it comes to that, then we'll deal with it." Dean shrugged. "Now I'm just really intrigued." His grin ignited a matching one in Alona, and Rafe had to smile at their excitement.

She flashed a look over her shoulder at Ashley. Could she put her trust in a woman she barely knew? She took another look into Ashley's clear blue eyes and, choice made, held up the USB stick. "Ashley has certain information on this case that we don't have access to. I'm asking for you not to question it or her and definitely not to speak of it outside this room. We just need to use it in conjunction with what we gather ourselves. She's here to help us." Rafe paused before she continued, hoping she was doing the right thing. "There might be an occult angle to these killings. Ms. Scott is going to work that angle for us. She has a degree in religious and occult ideology and symbolism and is going to use her expertise to see if we need to look further in that direction." She hoped that was an explanation her team would accept and leave it at that. She caught Ashley's look of surprise. *Well, I can hardly tell them you hunt demons, can I? This way I'm touching close enough to the truth so I'm not lying to my team.*

"The occult?" Dean's eyebrows rose and he gave Ashley a steely glare. "You've got to be kidding me."

"Stranger things have happened," Alona said. "You can't honestly say this killer is normal. He's got something weird fueling his need."

"The bosses don't know about this. Detective Powell is not to hear a word about this. It stays in this room. We continue our side of the investigation, and Ms. Scott will follow her own leads. But we'll work both angles together." Rafe stared Dean down until he calmed.

"I don't give a fuck about jurisdiction or who's in the lead. I want to just get this bastard and take him off the street." Dean looked over at Alona. "What say you, Officer?"

"I deal in information that comes from many sources. I don't care what its origin is as long as it's accurate and can be used in a court of law." She held out her hand for the USB stick. "What do we have here?" she asked as she began pulling information from the device as soon as it was in her computer.

Ashley moved before the big screen as the photos were uploaded. She pressed into Rafe to whisper, "Why does no one pay attention to the religious bit?" before stepping away. Rafe barely heard her as her full attention was on the screen, her mouth dropping open as the first photo was one taken from a height above the alley. The vantage point clearly showed the victim's blood had been spread around the body as if fanning it.

"Why did none of our crime scene photographers go above the area?" Dean hastened to enlarge the photo. "Look how small she looks, yet check out all the blood. That isn't a natural pooling; it's spread too high." He looked at Ashley. "Did you take these?"

Rafe grimaced. So much for no questions asked.

Ashley merely nodded. "I was on a fire escape in the apartment overlooking the alley. I only had a few moments with the body on the ground." Copying what she'd seen Dean do, Ashley pulled another photo to the forefront, and the tide of blood was more visible around the body. "It looked like the blood had been *disturbed*."

"He's playing in it?" Alona asked, joining them.

"It looked spread out, messed with, as if its pouring out underneath her just wasn't enough for him," Ashley said.

"He needs a broader canvas for his art," Rafe said.

"He needs time for this," said Dean. "And he needs to be clean enough from spreading it that he doesn't draw attention to himself after. Christ, what does he look like when he's finished with this? He's got to be covered in blood."

"Which brings us back to the butcher in our profile." Rafe brought up a picture from the most recent killing, again, taken from above. The blood was once again spread out. She tilted her head a little to get another view. "He only managed to spread it on one side this time."

"We still think he picked a poor area to do all he wanted to for this one," Dean pointed out. "Too many chances of being caught by the people at the bar nearby."

Ashley pointed to a photo. "Can you get anything evidence-wise from him running his hands through the blood?"

"Not if he's wearing gloves, and we needed to have checked the previous scenes closely in the blood itself." Rafe groaned as a thought struck her. "Oh God, how many walked around her blood and never considered it was an actual clue here?"

"We'll consider ourselves warned for the next time." Dean made a face at his own comment. "Unfortunately."

Rafe continued going through the photos. The rest were like their own scene of crime pictures. She gave Ashley a sideways glance. "You should have been a CSI."

"Been there, done that," Ashley said. She then spoke under her breath for Rafe alone, "How do you think I get in so close once the police start arriving?"

Rafe asked Alona to make copies of the photographs. "Please send a copy to Blythe and tell her we think he's playing with the blood for some reason. Maybe she can add it to her profile for us."

"You have a profiler?" Ashley asked.

"She's a friend helping me out." Rafe felt Ashley's stare burning through her before she looked up.

"A *friend*?"

"We were at the academy together. She joined the FBI and I chose a detective's shield. We've been friends for years. I decided to ask her advice; she's not officially assigned to the case. It's strictly off-the-record."

"Oh, a sneaky friend. I like the sound of her already. I'd be very interested in what she has to say about this killer, if I can read her profile?"

Rafe reached over for the printout she kept on her desk. Ashley read through it quietly, then nodded. "When do I get to meet this marvel?"

"I might have to keep you two apart for my own sanity's sake."

"Oh, now I'm really interested in meeting her. I'm sure she could tell me plenty of stories about you."

"I'm sure she could, which is exactly why I'd make sure you two never meet." She caught Dean watching them with a thoughtful look in his eye. "Detective?"

"I'm just mulling over how Ms. Scott gets to the crime scenes before we get a call." He shrugged. "I know we're not supposed to ask questions, but you can't blame a guy for being curious."

"I have a great many informants on the street. I've cultivated them for years, both in this city and in others. Not everyone turns a blind eye to what happens in a city. They are the ones who call me."

"But you're just a PI. Don't you usually get the errant husbands to follow or the cheating wives to chase?"

Ashley laughed. "They are the bread and butter of my existence. It's a dirty job and someone has to do it. Some of my earlier cases had heavy religious undertones, so I took it upon myself to learn everything I could about the good and bad side of all beliefs, recognized and otherwise. It pays to know what you're dealing with. But, as in this case, sometimes I get a call that's a little more than I can deal with on my own, so here I am. Not everyone wants to talk to the police, Detective Jackson. Call me the go-to girl for those who'd rather not be seen talking to cops." Ashley ran a finger along the lapel of his jacket coyly. "Does that answer your questions?"

"Glad to have you on board." He nodded and gave her a small smile, seemingly disarmed. "Where do you hide your crucifix and holy water?"

Rafe's bark of "Who wants coffee?" was met by a unanimous agreement and effectively stopped Ashley from answering Dean's question.

"Ms. Scott, you're with me." She purposely steered Ashley out of the office, waiting until they were past the doors before asking, "What did you do to him?"

Laughing, Ashley shook her head at Rafe's bold accusation. "I did nothing, Detective. My glamour doesn't give me powers of persuasion. I merely wowed him with my charm and beauty." She looked up at Rafe. "Then I got a little too close for comfort to knock him off-kilter a little. Men are so easy. Their minds are easily distracted."

"Between your feminine wiles and your glamour, no one stands a chance."

"Except you. You've always seen just me."

"I'd rather see the real you," Rafe said. "I don't want there to be any pretense between us."

"I can't seem to pretend where you're concerned anyway."

Rafe steered her toward the elevator, recognizing the attraction between them was obviously mutual, no matter how hard she fought against it. "We're in such an awkward position here. We're working on a case; we shouldn't be fraternizing."

"Fraternizing?" Ashley snorted. "That's not the word I would have used."

Resisting the urge to take her by the arm, just to touch her, Rafe stuffed her hands into her pockets. "There's a Starbucks on the corner. We'll get the team coffee from there."

"You sure know how to show a girl a good time." Ashley bumped Rafe's hip. "And here I was thinking you just wanted to get me out of the office before I told Dean everything."

"Where I come from, getting coffee together is almost considered a date."

"Well, where I come from, a woman expects a meal on a plate and a candle on the table."

Rafe considered this. "So takeout pizza and one attentive cat doesn't constitute a first date in your book?"

"Not when one member of the party is out of her skull on demon poison, no."

"I may need to work on my act, then," Rafe said.

"I'll look forward to it."

"If we happen across any demons in human form will you point them out to me?"

"I won't have to, Rafe. You're going to have no trouble picking them out from the crowd yourself now."

Afraid that was going to be her answer, Rafe let out a disgruntled grumble. "Shit."

"Welcome to my world."

CHAPTER ELEVEN

Ashley read the coroner's reports on all three victims until she felt she had the details all but seared into her memory. She'd been quiet for a long time, poring over the paperwork and paying minute attention to the office dynamics playing out around her. She could see why Rafe was so well respected. She never talked down to her colleagues, was always eager to hear their thoughts, and never took credit for anything other than her own work. Ashley was surreptitiously listening to Rafe's side of a conversation she was having on her cell phone with an owner of a meat-packing factory.

"I merely asked what kind of protective clothing you issued your workers. For the second time, I'm not from the Health and Safety Board. I've already told you I'm Detective Rafe Douglas with the Chicago Police Department, and I need this information for an investigation I'm working on." Rafe was silent, then scribbled on a notebook. "Thank you. No, I'm sure you're up to code. Yes, I'm sure you follow every regulation to the letter too." Rolling her eyes, Rafe made Ashley chuckle quietly as she watched her rein in her impatience. "Yes, you're to be commended. Would you be agreeable to my coming to your factory to gather a sample of the clothes your staff wears?" Rafe paused a moment while the man obviously ran off at the mouth. "That's very kind of you. I'll be sure to ask for you myself. Thank you, no, thank *you*." She snapped her phone shut. "Geez! Forget the fact there's a murderer out there. As long as Mr. Canton's factory is up to spec, he couldn't care less. I bet he's running round the place now with a duster making sure I don't go in wearing white gloves to check how hygienic it is." She rubbed at her face. "Dean, I'm going to finish up here then head over to Canton's Meat and Poultry. His guys dress head to toe in protective clothing. If our guy has access to that kind of clothing, then he's only got to take it off and dispose of it in a Dumpster and he's clean as a whistle and no one would be any the wiser."

"Want a tagalong?" Ashley asked as she sat back in her chair and stretched. Not for one moment did she miss the flare of appreciation in Rafe's eyes before she turned away.

"Sure. You can distract Canton with your charm while I try to get a look at his crew. Maybe I'll get lucky and the killer will just stand out from the rest." Only Ashley caught the true meaning behind Rafe's statement. "But if I can get a sample of the clothing, I can send it to our CSI team and have them check for any fibers that could come loose and hide in the blood our killer seems to like playing in." She locked down her PC and told Dean and Alona not to work too late. "I've got a horrible feeling we're going to get another body every few weeks until we can stop him. And we're going to need to be prepared in case he evolves and starts killing more. We need more staff up here."

"It's being looked into," Dean said. "For now, I'll check further into staff lists for all the meat places around here to try and see if there is something or someone we've missed."

Alona waved a hand toward her computer. "All the data has been entered and the numbers are being crunched, but we're kind of screwed when we can't take into account layoffs, illness, and general shift-swapping between workers. No one has really stood out as always working when the killer has struck. There are too many people on too many shifts to narrow it down."

"I'll leave you to it." Rafe jingled her car keys in her pocket. "Ms. Scott and I are going to check out the clothing at Canton's."

Slipping on her leather jacket, Ashley shot back, "Cool. I wonder what their summer line is." She tossed a wave to Dean and a wink in Alona's direction, then preceded Rafe out of the office. She waited until they were out of earshot. "When I said I expected a meal out, Rafe, I kind of hoped it would be cooked and served before me. Not still frozen and hung in a freezer."

Rafe just grinned at her. "Who says the art of romance is dead?

How about after I've made this stop we go for a meal, a proper meal where we don't have to see where it comes from?"

"With lots of green leafy things. Something tells me this place isn't going to make me proud I eat meat."

"I know a great Italian place near here. Their vegetarian lasagna is wonderful."

"Sounds perfect."

"I know the owner. I'll ask for at least one candle," Rafe added shyly.

Ashley was warmed by the gentleness that every so often slipped from behind Rafe's barricades. She moved so that their arms brushed as they got into the elevator. "Why, Detective, you really know how to turn on the charm after all."

Rafe studied the floors counting down, studiously not looking at Ashley. "I hope so. It's been a long time since I've used it. I might be rusty. Besides, you deserve more in your life than just death and demons."

To her surprise, Ashley felt tears sting her eyes. She swallowed against the tide of emotion that rose through her chest. "That's the sweetest thing anyone has said to me in a very long time."

"I didn't mean to upset you."

"You didn't upset me. You made me very happy. There's a huge difference." She tucked her arm through Rafe's and held on tight for a moment before the elevator reached its last floor. "Let's get the factory over and done with so we can concentrate on the candle part of this deal." She let go of Rafe's arm, immediately missing the warmth from her body. She surreptitiously watched Rafe lead the way, enjoying the view from behind and noticing how people reacted to Rafe's presence.

"Your department is glad to have you back," she said as they stepped outside and felt the chill in the air.

"They're just surprised I'm still functioning after being taken down by Armitage. He was well known around here because of his football career." Rafe jammed her beanie hat on.

"And to think, they don't know the half of it. You'd be elevated even higher in their eyes."

"I'm happy to stay right where I am, thank you. The sooner that incident is ancient history, the better."

"They might forget it, but you never will."

"No, I don't suppose I will. He left his mark on me in more ways than one." She took her car keys out of her pocket and fidgeted with them nervously. "Now that I'm privy to my own private lightshows, and my world resembles something out of Dante's *Inferno*." At her car she opened the passenger side for Ashley. "Still, it brought you into my life, so I guess it can't all be bad. *Yet*."

"There you go again with that charming attitude. Who'd have thought that you kept that hidden behind your badge?"

Rafe closed the door for her and walked round to her own side of the car. Ashley was amused by the look flickering across Rafe's face as she settled into the driver's seat.

"You don't get told you're sweet often, do you?" Ashley surmised.

"Not in my line of work, no."

"Or out of it?"

"Hardly ever."

Ashley wondered at the kind of women Rafe had been involved with that hadn't seen just how gentle Rafe could be. *Their loss*, she thought, as she settled back to let Rafe drive them to their destination. A stray thought struck her.

"Could you really come up with nothing more than saying I deal in the occult?"

"Hey, I gave them your full degree title like you told me. It's not my fault everyone zooms in on the occult bit. It just seems a safer bet than saying what you really do."

Ashley couldn't argue with that line of reasoning.

After pushing aside her plate, Rafe reached for her beer and took a deep drink to wash down her food.

"You look like you needed that." Ashley finished up the remains of her own meal.

"I don't think I ate anything today," Rafe said, settling back in her seat and only groaning slightly when her side protested. She was less than happy that she'd had to take pain pills before her meal arrived, but the pain had gotten too much for her to handle with bravado alone.

"How are you feeling?"

Rafe made a face at Ashley's polite question. "Sore, achy, annoyed that the healing isn't instantaneous. Being stabbed is a major inconvenience. I don't recommend it."

"I'll bear that in mind. You don't do patience very well." Ashley's smile was without rancor.

"No, I don't. I've got better things to do than wait around for this wound to heal."

"And what about your head?"

Rafe ran a finger along the healing scar. "Alona told me I looked much better today, so I'm taking that as a good sign. But I'll be glad when my hair grows back and these stitches are out." She scratched at her bristly hair. "It's too damn cold to have a G.I. Jane cut." She leaned forward across the table and lowered her voice. "Can I mention I could have done with the demon knowledge *before* going after that guy on my own."

Ashley leaned forward too. "Something tells me you'd still have done it anyway, forewarned or not."

"Probably." Rafe took another drink from her glass and relaxed in the familiar sights and sounds of the restaurant.

"How often do you come here?" Ashley asked, picking up her glass of wine and savoring it slowly.

"Not often enough. The owner's son was a cop I used to work with."

"Used to?"

"He was killed in the line of duty, shot by a gangbanger. I come by here as much as I can to make sure his old man's okay, just to touch base with him."

"That's nice of you."

Rafe brushed her words aside. "Yeah, well, he also makes the best food in the neighborhood, so it's no hardship." Rafe looked across the table at her. "So tell me, why are you living in a building that should be condemned as unfit for human habitation?" Rafe's eyes widened as a thought struck her. "Unless you're the token human in an otherwise demonic high-rise?"

Ashley stared at her a moment in silence. Rafe wondered what was going through Ashley's head and if she'd even answer.

"It was the quickest place Eli could find for me on such short notice."

"Short notice?"

"I was called here the minute the second woman was killed. The pattern had been established, so I was brought in."

"That explains why you have no pictures from the first scene. You hadn't been to that one." Rafe considered this. "What was it about these killings that set off Eli's alarm bells?" Ashley's hesitation made Rafe smile. "Oh, come on. You've let me in on your strange world of demons and people who shape-shift. You're really going to tread warily around what you can and can't tell me now?" She took another mouthful of her beer and waited for Ashley to speak. "Unless there's something even more mind-blowing to impart that you don't think I could handle."

Ashley seemed to be considering her words. "Do you believe in God, Rafe?"

Rafe shrugged. "As much as anyone does, I suppose." She wondered at the turn in the conversation. "Though, when I was lying in the alley with Armitage crushing my head, I saw the most amazing white light." She caught the startled look on Ashley's face. "What?"

"You saw a white light?"

"Not *the* white light. There was no tunnel and endless reams of dead relatives beckoning me home. Just the most intensive white light I have ever seen and—" Rafe stopped suddenly as her mind raced on. "Actually, that was the first time I saw it. I've seen it again since." Rafe's brain scrambled for the clue. "Eli. Eli and his damn bright light show. That was the same kind of light."

"You were kind of out of it the first time," Ashley said.

"Yes, I was, but not the second time. I was in your shabby apartment being blinded by his rays of light. He's not just a glamour man like you, is he?"

"No."

"Then what is he that I could see him too? And then there's the fact he's a healer like you, only different. Retooling the brain different."

"You know we asked your team not to ask questions?" Ashley said, squirming in her seat.

"Questions about you. I'm asking about Eli. Mr. All Dressed in White, the man who is as straight-backed as an English butler." Rafe thought for a moment, her head filled with memories and flashes she vaguely recalled. She tried to remember the light without bringing to mind all the pain that was associated with that moment in time. "Could Eli have been in the alley that night I was demon bait?"

"Rafe, please…"

"It was the same light. You forget, Ashley, he's been in my head; he re-jigged my brain to turn down the brightness. And yet I never felt threatened, just like I didn't with you. I just lay there and let you do whatever you wanted."

"I wish," Ashley muttered.

"I felt safe and protected and at peace with you. The same with Eli." She stared at her empty plate, trying desperately to piece the clues together. Her head shot up. "Fuck me! He's a goddamned *angel*!"

Ashley grimaced at her choice of words. "Not so much of the damned, Rafe."

Rafe's jaw dropped open. "Seriously? He's an angel?"

"One kind, yes."

"One kind? Like different degrees of demons?" Rafe couldn't believe what she was hearing. "So angels really do walk among us?"

"Some do, some just pop in and out at specific occasions."

"Like when a detective is getting her head caved in by a demon? Could that be a specific enough occasion?"

"Maybe," Ashley hedged. "You'd have to ask Eli."

Rafe didn't know whether to be angry or elated. "Oh, you bet I will." Her mind was spinning trying to control all the new evidence swarming inside it. "Angels and demons, eh?" She waved over the waitress. "I think that calls for another beer." She added under her breath as the realization of her discovery hit her, "Or five."

CHAPTER TWELVE

A shley had to admit she was impressed by how calm Rafe was, considering how her safe world had been turned upside down and inside out over the course of dinner. They'd walked back to Rafe's house in a strangely companionable silence. "You're taking this incredibly well."

"I'm figuring it can't get any bigger than this, right? There's nothing that can top it for the most fantastical state of how this planet runs." Rafe opened her front door and ushered Ashley inside. "I've had too many beers to drive you home, so I am either calling you a taxi or I can gallantly offer to sleep on the couch while you take my bed."

"Why can't we sleep together?" Ashley enjoyed seeing Rafe's forehead pucker as she thought this over.

"Because I have had too many beers and I don't put out on the first date. I need to get to know someone first."

Ashley chuckled at Rafe's reasoning. "What else is left for you to know about me? You've already uncovered the biggest secret I carry around."

"What's your favorite film?" Rafe asked out of the blue, and Ashley answered without hesitation.

"Titanic."

Rafe frowned. "What a heartbreaking story. Where were the angels in that situation, Ashley?"

"Probably getting the survivors into what few lifeboats they did have," she replied.

"Was Eli there, or should I save that question for him too?"

"Geez, you're remarkably goofy on just three beers."

"I don't usually drink a lot, but tonight seemed to call for it." Rafe tried to step over the cat twisting around her legs and threatening to topple her to the ground. "Trinity!"

Ashley picked the cat up and cuddled her. "I'll see to the cat. Why don't you go and sit down?" She carried the cat into the kitchen and began preparing her food as if she'd always done so. She called through the doorway to Rafe. "What's your favorite film?"

"The Matrix Reloaded."

"You like the second one over the first?" Ashley scooped out some dry food for the cat and refilled her water bowl, then left her to it. Ashley found Rafe sprawled on the couch, still in her coat.

"The second one had more action and it had a love scene."

"Forgive me for sounding so surprised, but you really are a closet romantic, aren't you?"

"I can cheer for the straight couple to get it on. Especially when one is as amazing-looking as Carrie Anne Moss is in that." Rafe shifted a little on the couch as Ashley joined her. "Can God really see everything?"

Ashley tried not to be surprised by Rafe's question. "So I'm told. I've never actually met him myself."

"I don't think I can ever take you to bed knowing that."

Rafe sounded so mournful that Ashley couldn't help her reaction. She burst out laughing and got a dirty look for her amusement. "Contrary to what most fanatical God-fearing folk would have you believe, God rarely could give a damn about what anyone does in their bedroom, gay or straight. He's got a small matter of the universe to run. We're really just a small fraction of what he can devote his time to."

"Does he speak to Eli?"

"Eli gets his messages from all sorts of carriers. He then sends me out to investigate."

"But one of the carriers might know who the killer is, right? I mean, we may only be a fraction of God's attention, but he could focus in on the killer and tell us who it is, right?"

"Did you ever read your Bible, Rafe?"

"I got lost somewhere in the endless *begats* early on."

"God gave humans free will. Free will to follow a righteous path or free will to kill and cause havoc. He won't step in, not yet."

"But why send you to investigate? Why are you necessary?"

"I'm a demon hunter, a human one, even given my glamour gene. Demons aren't supposed to have free rein on earth, Rafe. I'm one of those who have to stop them from being here."

"Someone obviously forgot to send the demons the memo," Rafe said a touch too seriously.

Ashley smiled as Rafe closed her eyes. "You're a cheap drunk, Detective. Three beers and you're out of it."

"Probably shouldn't have taken the pain pills either. I think I took them, not so sure now. Not too sure how many I took either. My side hurt like a mother earlier."

"Oh great," Ashley grumbled. She pulled Rafe upright and steadied her with her arms about her waist. "Let me get you to bed before you fall down."

"I can sleep on the couch," Rafe said, heel-toeing her shoes off as she reached the bottom of the stairs. Ashley helped her out of her jacket then carefully guided her upstairs.

"Booze and pills don't mix, Rafe."

"I forgot to take them earlier and then the day got so busy and I was in so much pain I just took them first chance I got. I never thought to consider that a beer would react with them."

"You needed to take the recommended dosage, not pop them like candy, either. God, you need someone watching over you twenty-four seven." Ashley huffed as she waited for Rafe to point out which was her room.

"I'm sorry," Rafe said quietly.

"Why are you sorry?"

"That you're having to take care of me again. You shouldn't have to keep doing that." Rafe laid her head on top of Ashley's and hugged her. "Call a cab and take the money from my wallet. I won't be a bother. I think I'll just flake out."

Ashley was worried for a whole other set of reasons if Rafe did indeed pass out. She guided her toward the bed. She began to undo Rafe's shirt and their fingers clashed over the buttons.

"I can take my own shirt off, thank you. I'm not that far gone." With a slow, methodical seriousness, Rafe fumbled with each button until she could tug the shirt free from her pants. With Rafe clad in just her bra, Ashley got to see her scar from the knife injury for the first time. Her gasp caused Rafe's head to jerk up and she wobbled a little as her balance shifted. "Whoa, head rush," she moaned and sat on the side of the bed.

Ashley couldn't help herself. She touched the vicious looking wound that was healing but still stood out painfully vivid against Rafe's pale skin. "Shouldn't this still be bandaged?"

"It itched, so I pulled it off."

Ashley tried not to shake her head at Rafe's obstinate reply. She ran her finger over the length of the scar.

"You can't heal that. He used his knife for it." Rafe looked down at her side dispassionately. "No demon poison in there, just a fucking huge knife wound." She began pulling at her socks. "I hope he rots in hell."

Ashley knelt to assist Rafe. "He will."

"Did you know he was here?"

"No, he wasn't showing up on our radar yet. It looks like you found him first."

"Lucky me." Rafe fell back on the bed, then scrambled up the sheets while Ashley tugged off her pants. "I can't have beer again for a while," she said as she burrowed under the covers.

"You might want to take your bra off," Ashley said. Rafe fumbled under the covers, then threw the offending item over onto a chair. Ashley was charmed by Rafe's obvious modesty. "I'm going to sit with you for a while to make sure you're okay."

"Okay," Rafe mumbled, already sinking. "Thank you." She turned her head to gaze at Ashley. "Don't let Trinity smother you on the couch. If she sees you lying down, she believes you're fair game to be laid on."

"I'll consider myself warned."

"Blythe gave her to me."

"Did she now?" Ashley wondered if she should be jealous over the brilliant profiler who obviously had a personal connection with Rafe.

"She said she didn't want me coming home to an empty house every night."

"That was very sweet of her."

"She's a good girl. She needs a good woman to look after her. Take her mind off all the bad things she sees."

"And what about you, Rafe?"

"I've seen worse things. Things that I don't think will ever be erased from my mind. I've seen demons, Sparky, out in the world, living among us."

Ashley ran her hand over the stubble of Rafe's hair; it was soft under her palm. "Get some sleep now. I'll be right here if you need me."

"What if Eli needs you?"

"He knows where I am if he does. Don't worry about anything. Just sleep." Rafe turned over and was pretty much asleep within seconds. Ashley held up the bottle of painkillers she'd slipped from Rafe's jacket. She grimaced as she realized how lucky Rafe was that she hadn't been out on a job alone carelessly taking medication of that strength. *You really are the most stubborn woman I have ever met*, she thought, laying the pills down on the small bedside table and watching Rafe sleep. *You need someone to look after you too, whether you think you need it or not.* She bent forward to check that Rafe was still breathing. She slipped her shoes off and placed her jacket over a chair. Slowly, so as not to disturb her, Ashley snuggled down on the bed to listen to the steady breathing coming from Rafe under the sheets. She felt the bed shift as Trinity jumped up and strode purposely up Ashley's body to settle in between them. Ashley rubbed at the cat's ears affectionately, enjoying the contented purr that rumbled through her furry chest.

"You're easy to please," Ashley whispered, settling back against a pillow and basking in the luxury of being on a comfortable bed with two warm bodies keeping her company. "Ahh, Rafe. You don't know what you're missing out on tonight." She pulled up the sheet over a shoulder that had escaped from under the covers. Ashley moved a little closer, breathing in Rafe's unique scent from her naked skin and relishing the intimacy of snuggling on her sheets. She peered at the cat asleep between them, half of her furry body draped over Ashley's stomach. "Guess I'm not using that couch any time soon." She wasn't exactly disappointed as she settled in to watch over Rafe.

CHAPTER THIRTEEN

R afe opened an eye cautiously when she realized there was someone other than the usual feline sharing her bed. She squinted at the clock beside her bed. It read 6:05 a.m. She cautiously ran her tongue over her teeth, tasting the remnants of the previous night's beer. She turned her head on the pillow and came face-to-face with Ashley, who was leaning up on an elbow watching her.

"You do realize how creepy that is, right?" Rafe's voice was scratchy. Ashley just smiled at her.

"I've been keeping watch over you to make sure you didn't suffer any ill effects from mixing medication with alcohol."

Rafe groaned softly as her stupidity came back to her. "I still can't believe I did that. I'm sorry you got stuck baby-sitting someone who should know better."

"That's okay. It's had its perks." She lowered her gaze and Rafe looked down too. The sheets had slipped sometime during the morning and her naked breasts were now exposed. Rafe figured it was way too late to cover up and instead tried to brazen it out.

"You can't begin to know how much I'd like to kiss you senseless right now, but you have beer breath, and at the moment, that ranks right up there with the tuna kibble breath your cat shared with me all night."

Rafe laughed and surreptitiously slid a hand under the sheets to make sure she still had her boxers on. Relieved they were in place, she eased herself out of bed. The floor held steady beneath her feet. With her back to Ashley, Rafe stared at the carpet, searching desperately for the right thing to say. She'd been surprised by the desire that lit up Ashley's eyes. She was even more astounded to realize it was directed at her.

"Then I am really sorry that I imbibed too much last night," was all she could honestly say. Rafe gathered up clean clothing out of her dresser, holding it to her modestly. "I need a shower, then maybe I can try to redeem myself in your eyes."

Ashley slid off the bed and walked toward her, her gait deliberately sensuous. Rafe was captivated by the sight. Ashley moved nearer, stilling Rafe's nervous hands.

"You have nothing to redeem. You do have to promise me you'll start taking better care of yourself."

"The doctors warned me to be careful with the meds, but I was only listening with one ear. I just wanted to leave the hospital so bad. I slipped up. I won't again." Rafe pulled a pair of socks from a drawer. "Am I right in remembering us talking about the presence of angels last night?"

"That's pretty much when you started knocking the beer back," Ashley said.

"Damn, I'd so hoped that was part of the alcohol talking."

"I'm sorry. I just keep piling on the unbelievable for you to carry, don't I?"

"Are there any more secrets left? If there are, I really don't think I can cope with them before a cup of coffee."

Ashley shook her head. "I think you've reached your allotted quota of 'angels and demons news flashes' for now." She plucked at her shirt. "I need a shower too. Do you think I can borrow something of yours to wear? I believe your cat drooled on me sometime during the night."

"I've got plenty if you don't mind tucking it in or rolling up the sleeves. I'll get you a clean towel and then I'll make you breakfast to hopefully make up for my appalling lack of manners last night."

"You have nothing to apologize for. You're incredibly sweet when under the influence, be it devil's poison, alcohol, or medication." Ashley appeared to think this over. "Actually, you're a lot easier to handle then too. I might have to remember that."

"I'll try to be nicer without the assistance of mind-altering substances, if that's all right with you. I need to keep all my wits about me around you as it is."

"Do I make you nervous, Rafe?" Ashley ran a finger along Rafe's naked forearm.

"You make me crazy to start off with, but then crazy in other ways too."

"What kind of other ways?"

"The kind that make me wish I had sweeter breath and that I wasn't the only one half-naked." She deliberately took a step back. "And that we aren't due in the DDU in just over an hour."

"I like that kind of crazy you speak of. I've felt it too since the moment I saw you and you saw right through to me." She shook her head. "Damn work," she grumbled. "Go shower and use plenty of mouthwash. I at least want my kiss when you're done if we can't call in late."

"You do realize that fraternization is frowned upon at the department?"

"I'm not on your payroll, Detective, so you can fraternize with me any way you want to."

Rafe groaned at the heat that stirred at Ashley's seductive tone. "Damn it, now I need a cold shower." She pushed past Ashley in haste, feeling their bodies touch as Ashley refused to budge.

"Tell me about it," Ashley said loud enough for Rafe to hear before she shut the door behind her.

❖

Rafe shook the cereal box experimentally and was relieved to hear a remarkable quantity of flakes rattle around inside. She looked down at Trinity, who was winding herself around her legs in a bid for attention. "I've fed you already. Quit fussing." Rafe checked on the state of the last carton of milk in her fridge. It was still fresh, so she placed it on the table too. She stared for a moment at the two bowls, two spoons, milk, and cereal laid out on the kitchen table. She couldn't remember the last time she'd had someone who'd stayed long enough for breakfast after.

Usually she was steering them out the door once they were clothed. She moved the cereal box a little to the right, wondering if it would be enough.

"You're muttering to yourself." Ashley entered the kitchen with her hair still damp and curling at the edges. She ran a hand down her front, smoothing the borrowed shirt. "Thank you for this."

Rafe couldn't take her eyes off Ashley's cleanly scrubbed face. Though she was aware Ashley wore the minimum of makeup, seeing her without it made her look even younger. Rafe gestured to the table. "I prepared breakfast."

Ashley snorted. "You laid out cereal. That's not the same as preparing it, Detective."

Undeterred, Rafe pulled back a chair for her. "Semantics, Sparky. Hope you like your flakes frosted." She was surprised when a small hand reached for her neck and pulled her head down.

"I want that morning kiss you promised," Ashley whispered against Rafe's lips.

Rafe complied without hesitation. Ashley's lips were soft beneath hers, full and moist. Rafe explored every inch before teasing her tongue inside to taste, then retreat, then push inside again. She pulled Ashley to her, startled by how well they fit together. Ashley's full breasts nestled against her own, hip fit to hip for all the difference in their heights. Ashley pulled Rafe's shirt out from her pants and Rafe jerked at the heat from her hands as she touched her. Reluctantly having to draw breath, Rafe pulled back and rested her forehead against Ashley's.

"About last night—" she began, but Ashley cut her off with a finger placed upon her lips.

"Enough already."

"No, I need to know what happened. I remember figuring out Eli's angelic status, and I think I ate dessert, but after that all I remember are snatches of stuff, and I really need you to fill in the blanks for me."

"We shared a large piece of chocolate gateau, but by then you'd started to get very sleepy. I noticed your speech going first and then your eyes just started to droop. So I paid the bill and helped you walk home."

Rafe groaned. "You paid? It was supposed to be my treat."

"I didn't know how to charge it to your card, otherwise I would have." Ashley grinned up at her.

"Fuck, I can't even do a date without messing it up." Rafe tried to pull back, but Ashley held on to her.

"Our next date won't have you scarfing down multiple painkillers with a Budweiser chaser. And the conversation won't be about work, angels, demons, or anything else inflammatory."

Rafe sighed and lowered her chin to rest it on top of Ashley's head. "Did I say or do anything stupid?"

"No more than usual," Ashley said. "You asked me my favorite film. That's a first date question, so you aced that."

Rafe racked her brain for the answer, then relaxed a little. "Kate Winslet."

"You remembered." Ashley hugged her in delight.

"I remember asking why Eli didn't save the passengers." Rafe grimaced as bits and pieces of the night filtered through her brain. "And you gave me the free will speech."

"It's what makes us human, Rafe. Free will, the choice to screw up should we wish to."

"I sure screwed up last night." Rafe was acutely embarrassed and disgusted with herself. Her behavior was not how she wanted Ashley to see her.

"You were exhausted. You're barely back behind your desk, and you're still getting used to your medication. Will you stop beating yourself up about it and get back to kissing me!"

Framing Ashley's face between her hands, Rafe pressed tender kisses all over her skin. She started at her forehead and traced every feature on Ashley's beautiful face reverently with her lips. When she reached Ashley's mouth, she was ravenous, seeking comfort, wanting more than just kisses. She pulled Ashley to her; her hands slipped under clothing to rest on Ashley's waist. Rafe began restlessly tugging up Ashley's shirt, seeking further.

"Stop." Ashley gasped the word against Rafe's lips, kissing her sweetly before reluctantly drawing back.

"Why?" Rafe's body was primed for more.

"We have to be at work soon, and besides, not in front of the children," Ashley murmured, cocking her head to one side.

Trinity sat up on a kitchen chair, looking like some serene Sphinx. Her eyes were half-closed as if their antics were boring her, but she couldn't be bothered to look away.

With shaking hands, Rafe reached for the cereal box. "Sorry I can't offer you more," she said, trying to calm her pulse and steel herself from reaching for Ashley to taste her lips again.

Deliberately letting her fingers brush over Rafe's, Ashley retrieved the box. "Oh, believe me, Detective, what you have to offer isn't anywhere on this table." She ran the tip of her tongue across her upper lip as she teased Rafe. "At least, not yet *you* aren't."

Rafe stifled the moan in her chest and grumbled. "You're going to drive me insane."

"Probably, but you said it yourself, with all you've seen you're already halfway there."

Trying to act normal and not give in to the urge to pull Ashley back into her arms, Rafe changed the conversation. "What's on your agenda today?"

"Other than finishing off your frosted flakes?" Ashley tipped out a generous bowl full and handed the box to Rafe. "I'm going to check in on Eli to see if he's heard anything more. What about you?"

"I should be getting results back from the crime lab from the second killing. I rushed them through to get it done in a week."

"It's always processed quicker on TV crime shows."

"They can piece everything together in forty-five minutes too. I could only wish for that kind of solve rate."

"Are you busy tonight? I thought maybe I could show you the bright lights."

Rafe answered around a mouthful of flakes. "You forget. I've already seen *your* bright lights."

Ashley laughed at her. "Aren't you witty in the morning? I'll have to remember that. I thought you might like to take a walk on my side of the city, Detective."

"You're taking me demon hunting?" Rafe blurted, rubbing at her forehead distractedly. "The last time I did that I failed abysmally."

"You'll be merely looking, not tracking. I promise I'll keep you safe."

"You're doing an excellent job so far," Rafe said. "It's like having a guardian angel or something." She looked suspiciously at Ashley but got a firm shake of a head in return.

"That would be Eli's role, not mine. I'll just stick to trying to keep you out of trouble."

"Some would say you've got your work cut out for you."

"I can handle both it and you, Detective, never fear."

CHAPTER FOURTEEN

D ean rose from his chair the second Rafe entered the office. "Boss, we might have a break." He waved her over to his desk and handed her a folder. "Cops last night brought in a guy for attacking a woman. He's being brought over here for us to interview."

Rafe perched on the table edge reading the report. "He was caught in the act?"

"He was seen strangling the woman in an alley, right under the nose of a guy in the apartment across the way."

Rafe flipped through the rest of the report. "Was he carrying a knife at all?"

"Yes. Looks like he was caught before he had a chance to use it. Forensics has it."

"But our guy's M.O. is a murder and mutilation, not manual strangulation."

Dean held up a hand, forestalling the rest of Rafe's arguments. "The kicker is this guy is one of the butchers at the Epican Meat Factory. Come on. That has to mean something."

"It means we have a suspect here who isn't sticking to the pattern we've gotten established for our serial killer. We'll investigate him, certainly. Maybe he's devolving, trying something new." She didn't believe that for a second. The man they were after had a specific undertaking in his kills. He was searching for something. He wasn't going to switch back to something as basic as strangling, not when he was able to rip open flesh to find what he was looking for.

"You don't think this is our spine killer, do you?"

Rafe shook her head. "No, but I'm open to the possibility he might be. All are guilty until proven innocent, right?"

Dean leaned back in his chair. "I was hoping this might bring an end to the case. I don't like the fact we're getting no evidence and all we can do is wait for him to kill again."

"I know, but I learned the hard way that suspecting someone because you think he might fit the mold isn't going to get you any closer to finding the true killer." She turned her attention to Alona, who was hard at work at her desk. "Anything new on the shift schedules from the local factories?"

"I've narrowed it down to a few names that came up on the nights in question. But one pinch-hits for anyone who wants him to do their shift and the other is a sixty-year-old woman."

"Can we really rule her out?" Dean asked.

Alona nodded. "I'm afraid so. She doesn't fit any of the profile except for her vocation, and then there's the little matter of her being only four foot six."

"I'd say we can safely rule her out." Rafe handed Dean his report back. "Keep looking. I've got another set of officers going around tonight to the meat factories. I figure if no one has anything to say on the day shift, maybe the cover of darkness might loosen a few tongues." She wandered over to the window and looked down at the bench Ashley had sat on. She was startled by the sigh that rose into her chest.

"Where's the PI today?" asked Dean.

"Running her own checks."

"I've never known you to bring in an outside source that dealt with..." Dean stopped and seemed to think his words over carefully. "...magic."

"The occult isn't magic tricks, Dean. It encompasses science, religion, spirituality."

"And Ashley believes our killer uses his twisted belief in the occult to go out and kill these women?"

"She's trying to rule it out for us so we can do our side of the investigation without the ritualistic side of it clouding our judgment." Rafe knew she should have just introduced Ashley as a PI and left it at that while warning Dean not to question it, but she couldn't do that. She hoped twisting the truth a little wouldn't come back to bite her in the ass. Rafe was already apprehensive about getting involved with someone she was working with. Added to that was the fact that Ashley wasn't entirely human. Rafe remembered their shared kisses that morning and her body made no pretense that, human or otherwise, Rafe wanted her. *It figures that the first woman I'm drawn to in ages has supernatural magical powers. I can never do anything by half.* She tried to refocus on what Dean was saying to her.

Dean cocked his head toward the photo on the screen where the body of the second victim, Erica Lane, was spread out and captured from above. "This isn't a natural killer leaving these women like this, boss. If Scott can find something out in what she does, then I'm all for it."

Rafe stared at the photo for a long time. "We can use all the help we can get. I really don't want to have to stand over the body of victim number four because we didn't explore every avenue open to us."

❖

"If I had known you wouldn't be using this apartment to sleep in, I wouldn't have paid the deposit," Eli said as soon as Ashley wandered in through the front door.

"Good morning to you too. If it's any of your business, I stayed over at Rafe's."

"Ah, the fine detective."

"The *oh so fine* detective," Ashley said with a grin. "But my plans of seducing her got lost somewhere between her painkillers and one too many beers."

"Oh dear."

"You got that right. She doesn't do convalescing well at all. She'd try the patience of a saint." Ashley cocked her head at him. "Know of any?"

Eli ignored her. "I'd say she never usually has to worry about recovering. She seems a very capable woman."

"Going up against a demon kind of threw her off her game," Ashley said. "We're getting nowhere, Eli. This killer is going to be back in business soon. Have you heard anything at all?"

"Nothing. This killer is remarkable for not drawing attention to himself." He rubbed at his chin. "Which is strange because demons are such showy fellows and usually end up drawing attention to themselves whether they desire it or not."

"Any new ideas on why he's cutting them open from the back? No demon would eat human flesh, so it's not like they're after a meatier part."

Eli made a disgusted face. "The taste is like chicken, or so I'm told. Most unpalatable for a demon's digestion."

"There's nothing mystical about the spine, and he's leaving the organs in place. What are we missing here?" Ashley tugged at her hair in frustration. "Why did you get re-mixed up in this world, Eli? It's nothing but endless death and cruelty. It wears on my soul."

"You can see both sides of this world; you alone have that unique perspective."

"I'm not the only child of mixed blood. I'm not the chosen one. I'm just the one you chose to recruit."

"And very good at your job you are too."

"I want to catch this guy. I want Rafe to be able to put him away."

"You know that can't happen. We can't let a demon be incarcerated. He has to be banished."

"Then I at least want her to have the satisfaction of knowing he's caught and is going to be punished." Ashley turned to Eli. "If I asked you something personal, would you answer me truthfully?"

"Have I ever lied to you?" Eli looked affronted.

"You're not averse to masking the truth, Eli. I want a straight answer to a simple question."

"Then I will do my best."

"Were you in the alley the night Rafe was nearly killed?" Ashley caught his immediate hesitation. "I need to know if it was you or someone like you."

"I was there."

"Why didn't you stop the demon from hurting her?"

"That wasn't my job. I just had to keep her from dying."

"Yet the scratch she sustained was poisoning her. She was going to die anyway."

"But you healed her."

"Was I sent to her just to heal her?" Eli hesitated again and Ashley fumed. "I'm going to keep asking until you tell me the truth. *All* of it. I know we're meant to investigate these killings together; I can see that much myself. But why her? Was it just because of the demon?"

Eli let out a sigh and looked heavenward, seemingly for an answer. "It's because there is a distinct possibility that she's your *One*."

Ashley flushed with a heady pleasure and then experienced a chill as the weight of those words descended on her shoulders. "Oh my God, I knew it! That explains the instant connection we felt. Well, that *I* felt anyway. She's probably going to take a little longer to acknowledge it." Ashley hugged herself and danced a little on the spot. "She's my soul mate. It's really true. Not just something from myth and legend. Two souls uniting." She reached for Eli. "You saved her for *me*."

"She's your One. I'm your guardian angel. You needed guidance to find her. You've found her, so now your path together is up to you both to figure out."

"My soul mate," Ashley said softly. "Why did it take so long for you to guide me to her?"

"You're not exactly ready for retirement, Ashley," Eli said dryly. "I have no concept of time. It's infinite and endless. You humans put too much reliance on it. You're together now, so don't waste any more of it."

"I thought you said time was infinite?"

"For me, yes. For you mortals, though, time is precious. Each moment is to be treasured." He paused. "I envy you that."

"You're envious we die?" Ashley was stunned.

"I regret that time holds no meaning for me. It just is and always will be."

Ashley looked at him with new eyes. Who knew being an angel came with its own set of baggage?

"Wait, you said there's a distinct possibility she's my One. Why only a possibility? Why aren't you certain?"

"You still have free will in this choice, Ashley. If you didn't consider her *hot*, as I remember you describing her, then you could reject her and your souls would not be joined."

"So I could continue on without her in my life?" Ashley didn't like the sound of that at all. She was already feeling the necessity to be near Rafe every moment she could spare.

"Yes, you could. That would be your choice as a child born of free will."

Ashley thought this over. Would Rafe be willing to be soul mates with one of her lineage? Racial differences, sexual preference, none of it really mattered when your girlfriend was blessed with strangely supernatural powers.

"Are you seeing your detective tonight?"

Ashley nodded. "I have work to do first, though." She opened her laptop and hoped her mind wouldn't keep drifting to thoughts of Rafe naked and the mantra of not wasting any more time. Rafe had already had two brushes with death. Ashley was determined nothing was going to hurt her again. Rafe was her soul mate, her One. Her guardian angel had told her so.

"Rafe told her colleagues I deal in the occult," she said, smothering a smile as Eli blustered loudly beside her.

"Sacrilege!" His voice rose uncharacteristically loudly.

"I thought you'd be impressed. But you can't smite her for it; she is my One, after all."

"I could make an exception," Eli said, making Ashley just laugh even more.

Rafe stared through the one-way mirrored glass of the interrogation room at the disheveled man handcuffed to the table. She scrutinized him, mentally processing his appearance, his demeanor, the way he kept tugging at the handcuffs as if one more pull could set him free. He looked incredibly irate for someone who had just been arrested for the attempted murder of his girlfriend. His features were nondescript. He had dark hair, was average height; nothing stood out about him. However, his face was getting redder by the second as he pulled against his restraints.

Dean appeared beside her and handed her a fresh cup of coffee along with a file with the man's details. "So, what do you think? Is this our man? He tried to take out three policemen when they arrested him."

Rafe didn't answer. She was trying to see if there was anything unusual about the suspect that blatantly stood out. She couldn't tell Dean she was looking for signs of horns or a glittering only she could detect. *That damn woman has me searching for demons everywhere.* She took a long drink from her coffee. *This stops here. Real police work doesn't involve the supernatural. The killer has to be human. What I saw had to be a one-of-a-kind occurrence. An aberration. One big demon-sized figment of my overactive imagination.*

"You are going to interrogate him, right?" Dean asked, looking at her cautiously.

Rafe squinted one last time to see if anything remotely sparkled in that room. *Sorry, Ashley Scott, but this one is all mine. A scumbag of the human variety.* She nodded at Dean and walked into the room, closing the door behind her.

"Mr. Epcot, or can I call you Ben?" Rafe settled herself in the chair opposite him. She set her coffee down and opened her file. "It says here you were apprehended trying to strangle your girlfriend tonight."

He wrenched on the cuffs. "I don't like being restrained."

Rafe took a sip from her cup. "I'm guessing Ms. Downs didn't like your hands wrapped around her throat either. The cuffs stay on."

"The bitch had it coming to her. She's a cheating whore."

"So you thought the best way to deal with that was to take her down an alley and strangle her?" Rafe took out a photograph taken at the scene of the bruises on the victim's throat. "These look pretty damaging, Ben."

"She's lucky I only got that far before the cops got me off her."

"Did you have other intentions tonight for her, Ben?"

"I'd have gutted her once I'd gotten my knife out. I'd sharpened it real smooth for just that purpose."

Rafe resisted the urge to look over her shoulder where she knew Dean was probably crowing over that admission. *Our killer doesn't gut,* Rafe thought. "What's your job, Ben?"

"I'm a butcher at the Epican factory, surely that's in your file there?" He tugged again at his bound wrists, making the handcuffs jangle. "This is a little over-the-top isn't it? After all, I was stopped from strangling the bitch." He looked at her slyly. "Or are you worried I'll go for you next?"

"You said she cheated on you?" Rafe saw his face darken and she couldn't help herself, she stared into his eyes to watch for the fires to start burning. There wasn't even a flicker of a flame. Rafe wasn't entirely sure if she was disappointed or not.

"She had it coming. Caught the bitch myself last night," he said.

"But you didn't attack her last night. You waited a whole day before going after her." Epcot looked uncomfortable with that fact, so Rafe dug a little harder. "Why? Was the man she was with bigger than you and would have put up a better fight than she did?"

His head dipped. He mumbled his answer into his chest. "I just wanted to deal with her; she was the cheat."

"What? Do you have no argument with the other guy? He a friend of yours or something?"

"It wasn't a guy," he muttered finally.

Rafe noted his discomfort at this admission. "So it was another woman? But you have no problem attacking women, Ben. What would another one be?" She waited for a long moment for his answer.

"She was fucking my sister," he finally answered. "I walked into my house and there they were in my bed. I could hear my baby sister egging her on to stick her tongue—" He stopped suddenly and began yanking on the handcuffs again with more ferocity. "Take these fucking things off me now. I don't like being tied down."

Rafe removed a pen from her pocket and made a note in the file. She got up, retrieved her coffee, and took a step back from the table. "You need to calm down, Mr. Epcot."

"Calm down?" His wrists began to bleed as he cut himself straining against the steel cuffs. "All women are the same. They deserve everything that is coming to them. I'd kill them all if I could. I'd take my knife and I'd cut them wide open and rip their insides out. They are no better than the animals I slaughter." He gave Rafe a calculating look. She could all but see his mind working. "I've done it before. Killed in alleys. It's been all over the news."

Rafe was surprised by this admission. "How many women have you killed so far, Mr. Epcot?"

"Just a few." His smile widened. "I'd say three...that you've found, anyway. Guess you'll have to check all the alleys just in case, won't you?"

Rafe made a subtle gesture behind her and the door opened to admit two officers.

"Please take Mr. Epcot back to his cell while we corroborate his statement," Rafe said.

Epcot immediately began to put up a fight as the officers unlocked him from the table. They manhandled him until one of them was able to subdue him enough to get him free from the restraints then the other cuffed him for transport. They dragged him from the room. By now he was screaming at the top of his lungs.

"I killed those bitches, all of them. They asked for it. They all ask for it!"

Rafe could hear his voice reverberating down the hallway as he was taken back to his cell. Dean popped his head around the door.

"Seemed like a nice enough guy," he said.

"Whether he's our man or not, he needs to be locked up. Obviously, in his current state of mind women aren't safe around him."

"That dude has some serious sibling issues." Dean chuckled to himself. "It's no wonder he's so pissed. I would be if my sister was a better fuck than I was." He was stopped from making any further comments by Rafe's censorious look. "I spoke to his girlfriend. She's picked a right family to get involved with. Seems Epcot's sister has a thing for bondage and restraints. I'm betting brother dearest has been trussed up like a turkey one too many times. Those kind of traumas leave scars." He handed Rafe the woman's statement. "So do you think he could be our guy for the murders? He's confessed to them."

"Our killer is leaving a carefully crafted message in the bodies he leaves for us to find. I doubt Epcot could draw a smiley face on a steamy window." Rafe handed Dean her file. "Check into his background; keep him locked down and away from anything sharp."

"It would have helped if he'd used his knife. The guys who collared him said it was meticulously clean," Dean said.

"Then our victim would have been yet another dead woman in an alley. Don't wish that on us for the sake of closing the case." Rafe checked her watch and brushed past him. "I have an appointment to keep. Let me know if you find anything out about this guy. He fits part of the profile but not all of it."

"Come on, Rafe. What are the odds of two crazies running loose in Chicago?" Dean called after her.

About the same as the odds of demons running rampant and my being able to see them as clear as day.

CHAPTER FIFTEEN

There was nothing more soul-destroying than interviewing the family of a murder victim. Rafe hated having to tell them that the police were doing everything in their power to catch the man who killed their daughter, while Rafe still had no clue as to who he was. She had sat holding the mother's hands while she sobbed. The father, eyes red-rimmed and face ashen, still bore the haunted look of someone who'd had to identify his daughter's body. Rafe wondered if the memory would ever fade of how his daughter's face had been twisted in terror.

Seated at her desk now, she stared unseeing at her computer screen.

"Rafe?" Alona spoke quietly as if unsure whether to break into Rafe's thoughts. "You okay?"

"I hate dealing with those left behind. Their daughter's dead, just like the two women before her who left similar families bereft. And we've got nothing to show for it. No clues left behind, no identity. Just his ghoulish signature spread out in three different alleys." She rubbed at her face. "I need him to slip up, but in order for him to do that he has to kill again."

"There's nothing on the data stream. If he's done this before, we've got no information on it."

Rafe peered over her shoulder at the photos left up on the screen. "It's a very evolved pattern for a first-time killer. He's already got a signature and everything."

"Maybe he's been planning it for a while."

Rafe nodded. "Maybe. Are you sure there's nothing like a knifing that even roughly foreshadows this?"

Alona shook her head. "Nothing like what he does. He's unique, Rafe. And if he did do something before these, then he never got caught and it was never reported. I've got bar stabbings, honor killings, and general knife fights, but nothing that matches this M.O."

"Is Dean still checking out the meat factories?"

"Yeah, he took four uniforms with him to canvass the area of the latest killing. Said he needed company."

Rafe didn't envy him his retread of scenes already canvassed.

"Can I ask a question?"

Rafe gave Alona her full attention. "Sure."

"This PI, is she safe on the streets? I mean, she's gathering her information from the areas even our guys go into in pairs."

"She tells me she's careful," Rafe replied. "You worried about her?"

"She seems like a really nice lady. I wouldn't have pegged her for a PI and definitely not one who deals with the occult. I guess if you don't see what you expect, she could blend in anywhere."

Rafe bit the inside of her cheek to hold back a bark of laughter that threatened to erupt at Alona's innocent but accurate remark. To her, Ashley had never blended in at all. Rafe hadn't been able to ignore her from first sight.

"Do you think she'll be able to help us with her connections?"

Rafe hoped so. She was desperate for any glimmer of a lead. "Here's hoping. I'll take all the help I'm given." *From this world or the other*.

"Did you see Detective Powell on the ten o'clock news last night?" Alona asked, changing the subject just enough to catch Rafe's curiosity.

"I swear I've never seen a cop so dedicated to getting her face on TV every night."

"Maybe the city sleeps soundly once she's told them the police will keep them safe."

Rafe laughed at Alona's piqued tone. "I wish she sent me to sleep that easily."

"The police force needs a friendly face to promote us. After all, the last spokesman we had didn't do us any favors."

Rafe grimaced as she recalled the last person designated the force's public liaison. "Chief Staenberg did make a mess out of his five minutes of fame," she conceded. "Nothing smells worse than a corrupt cop covering up for his own family."

"Especially when he knew there was an innocent man in jail for the crime his brother had committed."

Rafe remembered the case well, and the very public outing on TV. While the chief was trying to report on a successful case brought to a close, he was interrupted by the wronged man's wife. She had been armed with enough evidence to wreck Chief Staenberg's career, and did so, on live TV. Rafe hadn't liked him or held any respect for his position. He had been a blowhard with little thought for the officers under his care. "And now we have Miss America tucking us in every night." She knew Detective Powell was a good cop in her own right, but all that had been sacrificed for her to issue placating news bites to the general public to lull them into thinking the city was crime-free.

"She's a good cop," Alona said. "I like seeing her."

Rafe snuck a look at a disgruntled Alona. "I bet she doesn't send you to sleep…" she drawled and grinned as a red tide of embarrassment bloomed on Alona's face. *So that's why you defend her honor.* Rafe tried to put a stern look on her face. "Well, if you like her that much, you can liaise with her instead of me having to do it. The woman drives me up the wall."

Alona stammered. "But…but I can't…"

"Yes, you can and will, should we ever find anything worth reporting for her to impart to her awaiting public." Rafe settled back in her chair and sighed. "That's one less thing for me to worry about." She ignored Alona's muttering from behind her and checked her watch. She wanted to talk to Blythe but knew she'd be at work, and she didn't really want to compromise her a second time there. She'd wait until they were both home and then ask if Blythe had any more ideas about this killer. She hated the feeling she was going to get another body before she was going to get any nearer to finding the killer.

❖

Ashley wondered just how much longer she should stay with Eli before she could leave without him being unduly suspicious.

"Do you have somewhere else to be, Ashley?" he asked.

So much for being inconspicuous. She shook her head as she snapped her phone closed and wondered, not for the first time that afternoon, just how many people she could talk to who had no idea, other than what they saw on the news, that there was a serial killer loose in the city. Humans and demons alike were unaware of anything new stirring aboveground. "I'm getting nowhere. No one knows who this guy is or has any idea *what* he is." She gave Eli a pointed stare. "Do you have any news from a higher source?"

"You know we're on our own in this, Ashley," he said.

"What's the point of all-seeing, all-knowing if you don't use it to put a stop to evil?"

Eli turned his back on her and looked over the photos for the umpteenth time, studiously ignoring Ashley's comment. She muttered something under her breath about free will being a pain in the ass, and reached for her jacket.

"Where are you going?"

"I'm not getting anything from my contacts, so I'm going to head out to go see if the word on the street is any more informative. I'm not helping anyone sitting in here just staring at the photographs," she said.

"They tell a story."

"They tell the story of one sick individual." She flipped the board over, startling Eli. "I can't look at their faces anymore. I'm going out."

"Leave your phone on," he called after her.

"Like I can ever leave it switched off," she said over her shoulder irritably before leaving the apartment. She checked the time on her watch and wondered if Rafe was in her office or out canvassing the areas with Detective Jackson in search of this elusive shadow dancer. She paused before pressing the elevator button. Could they be looking for the type of demon who haunted the dark areas of the night and only stepped out to hunt? She hadn't come across one of those in years. Those types of demons were rare and extremely difficult to track down. She'd never seen one kill for sport, and couldn't remember the last time one actually killed a human. They preferred animal prey.

Ashley was more than a little frustrated. This killer wasn't exhibiting the usual traits that demons did. Maybe he was just human after all, but that didn't explain her being brought in. She was always placed on a case for a specific reason. She pressed the elevator button, wondering what the catch was this time around. Demon or not, she had been brought to Chicago for a reason. If it was just so she could meet Rafe, she would have preferred a more traditional introduction, something with a lower body count between them. She wondered at Eli's involvement. He always had his reasons; she was just never aware of them until after the fact, and she'd learned not to question. She was questioning it all this time. Something wasn't right, and she didn't think this series of events had been set in motion just so she could meet the woman of her dreams.

Chapter Sixteen

Rafe wasn't surprised to find Ashley waiting for her on the bench opposite the Chicago PD. She was more surprised by the feeling of peace that surrounded her heart. A grin formed unbidden and Rafe had no way of stopping that either. She watched as Ashley rose from her seat and negotiated the traffic to come meet her.

"I'm glad you took my call to spring you out of work and saved me the job of dragging you out of there. I wondered if you'd care to join me tonight on a stakeout?"

Rafe's hopes soared. "You have something?" Her excitement deflated at Ashley's apologetic expression.

"Sorry, I didn't mean to get your hopes up. I just wanted you to come see where I work."

"Sure. I'm not doing anything tonight. I had plans to work late, but Dean took over what I was aiming to do once he knew it was you on the phone. He all but ushered me to the door. I understand why everyone is still walking around on eggshells with me, but I'm *okay*."

"Take it easy while you can. Your partner won't always be willing to cover for you. Make the most of his generosity and spend the evening with me because of it."

Smiling, Rafe had to admit she liked the sound of that. "Even after last night? I'm surprised you are willing to risk it after my latest jackass performance."

Ashley linked her arm through Rafe's. "Which is exactly why I'm taking you to eat first. I will also be policing your intake of alcohol and painkillers and then will keep you beside me at all times during the evening while I show you the sights."

"Sounds good to me," Rafe said, then qualified, "The food and the company bit at least. I'm not so sure I like your side of the city after seeing where you're staying." She leaned in to Ashley and kept her voice low. "The air is weird there."

Ashley's eyes widened. "You really *are* sensitive." She tugged Rafe into motion and led her up the street. "The air is different because it's a demon hub."

"A demon what?"

"Hub. It's where the demons come out from hell to walk on the earth."

Rafe pulled them both to a stop, staring down at Ashley until people began to bump into her because they were blocking the sidewalk. She tugged Ashley over to a store window out of people's path. "You know where they get in and haven't plugged the fucking hole up?"

"We don't employ demon border patrol, Rafe. It's not like it's one big revolving door we have to watch. But the area is a weak spot, and the demons use it to their advantage and slip right in."

Lifting her head to the heavens, Rafe muttered, "I'm moving to Kansas. Big, endless fields of nothing there." She looked down at Ashley's snigger. "What?"

"You really don't want me to tell you what's in Kansas."

Rafe had the horrible feeling Ashley wasn't joking. They continued walking in silence. Finally, Rafe risked a sideways glance.

"You still don't want to know," Ashley said in a tone that Rafe had never heard from her before. Authoritative, the kind of tone that made Rafe realize maybe she shouldn't ask about things she didn't need to know about. She had already learned way too much about things not of this world to ever go back to a normal existence.

"So, do you like Mexican food?" Ashley asked with a cheery lilt to her voice that hadn't been there just seconds before.

"How do you remain so unaffected?" Rafe was amazed by how normal Ashley was once she got past the glamour and the fact she knew about demons and hung out with an angel.

"I've grown up in this world, Rafe. I've seen it colored by demons right from the start." She tugged at Rafe's sleeve gently. "Come eat and I'll tell you my entire family history."

Rafe followed her. She was a touch apprehensive at what she was going to learn about Ashley. She knew when Ashley employed her shape-shifting ability she could see the golden glamour. Yet nothing ugly ever surfaced to cover Ashley's true beauty. Rafe had always been able to see her, and what she saw was someone who called to the loneliest part inside her heart.

"You've gone awfully quiet," Ashley said.

"Just enjoying the night in your company," Rafe said. Ashley's answering smile was something beautiful. Rafe's heart clenched at the sight and she had to fight to stop herself from pulling Ashley into a doorway and kissing her senseless.

"You're quite the charmer under all that bluff," Ashley said.

"You mean you couldn't see through *my* glamour straight away?"

Ashley's laughter sent tingles down Rafe's spine. "I could always see right through you, Detective. I just didn't realize how deep you were going to let me look."

"As deep as you want to go."

"I've a good mind to skip the food." Ashley cuddled into Rafe's side.

Laughing, Rafe wondered why she was going to stupidly disagree when all she wanted was to take Ashley somewhere private and kiss her for hours on end. "We both need to eat, and I'm most intrigued about your lineage, so you're not getting out of telling me your life story. Then you promised me a night out with you. There's no reneging."

"Can I get a rain check on what I would rather be doing with you?"

The low, husky quality of Ashley's voice warmed places in Rafe that had lain dormant for too long. She groaned at the spark of fire that burned in her gut and spread lower. "Yes, please," she replied, surprised by the blatant yearning in those simple words. Suddenly food was the last thing on her mind, but she tagged along behind Ashley blindly, happy to just follow her lead.

❖

"So let me get this straight. Your father was an angel. He fell in love with your mother and fell to earth, losing his angelic status. He then became a demon who could take on human form, moved in with her, and they created you." Rafe's mind sifted through all the fantastical information Ashley had given her. "You displayed your particular talent early on and your mother couldn't cope, so she left you with your father. He, in turn, worked his way through a line of mortal females who couldn't resist his particular brand of angelic/demonic charm until he found a woman who kept him on a short leash and he fathered another kid with her."

Rafe sat back on the old deck chair that was placed on the roof of Ashley's apartment block. The location afforded her a grand view of the run-down area and beyond. In the distance, Willis Tower stood tall, its dual antennae looking eerily like horns reaching heavenward. Noticing this gave Rafe pause for thought. They sat eating take-out burritos, neither seeming to notice the cold air that surrounded them high up on the roof. "Ashley, to be honest, your folks sound like some weird and wacky country-and-western song. Something along the lines of, *My daddy was a demon and my mama was a woman who took the devil by the horns*."

Ashley nearly choked on her mouthful of food. "Thank you, now I'm going to be trying to fit those lyrics to music in my head." She wiped at her mouth with a grin. "He was a lover with an incredible wandering eye. He spotted my mother and, damnation or not, nothing was going to keep him from her." She edged forward in her seat as something on the street below caught her attention. "Oh, the drug runners are out again." She sat back and reached for more food.

Rafe shot upright and tried to pick out faces. "I'm too far away to get a proper ID." She reached for her phone. Ashley's hand stopped her movement.

"I promise I'll tip off the police the next time they're around here so they can come collect them." She pointed to each one of the five men below, picking them off. "He's the ringleader. I can get an address for you since he's a neighbor. Newbie, newbie, regular customer, and ringleader's bodyguard."

"You haven't called this in before?"

"I've got more important things to deal with than folk dealing in mind-altering substances."

Rafe sat back, but her eyes never wandered from the transaction taking place below. It chafed at her not to do anything about it. "I could just call it in. It wouldn't take me a minute."

"But the paperwork would, and the disturbance would be detrimental to the area tonight. I don't want your guys swooping down here. Not tonight, Rafe. Please?"

Rafe stared at the warm hand touching her own where she clutched her cell phone. Rafe slipped her phone back inside her pocket. "I just want scum like that off the streets."

"You can be Dudley Drug Buster another night, Detective. Tonight, I want you to see something else once these players have exited stage right."

Rafe took a deep breath and purposely turned her head away from the street activity to regard Ashley. "So your mother was human."

"They met, fell in love, and had me. Dad said I began to show signs very early on that I wasn't your typical baby. I did all the usual things, crawled, walked, cut teeth, but Mom was never sure whose baby she was going to find in my crib. If I spent a day at the nursery, I would come back and change into all my little friends. The first time it happened she swore my father had brought the wrong kid home by accident." Ashley shrugged. "That's when Dad had to tell her I wasn't just any kind of kid." She grimaced. "I'm told it didn't go down too well."

"It's a hard concept to swallow, I'd imagine," Rafe said.

"She stayed until I was school age, then she took off and left me behind."

Rafe heard the underlying sadness in Ashley's offhand comment. She wrapped her fingers around Ashley's clenched fist. "It was her loss. She missed out on seeing you become someone beautiful."

"With the power to shape-shift at will."

"Sure, you have a little something extra going on. Aren't all mothers desperate for their daughters to be exceptional? Mine sure as hell was."

"She's not impressed with your detective badge?"

"She'd rather it was my husband's while I stayed at home and raised the kids and played happy little homemaker."

Ashley laughed. "Forgive me, but that image just does not sit well in my head."

"The whole lesbian thing nearly pushed her over the edge." Rafe shrugged it off, not wanting to bring up her mother's disappointment at Rafe not being all she'd dreamed. "She's got my sister-in-law fulfilling her perfect daughter fantasies. I'm the gay black sheep of the family."

Ashley gave her a sly look. "Should we inform your mother you've kissed demon spawn too?"

"Not unless I want to induce a heart attack." She pretended to consider it. "Another time, maybe. And don't refer to yourself as that."

"But it's true. My daddy was an angel who fell to earth to copulate with a human woman."

"Gee, when you put it like that it just leeches all the romance out of the tale." Rafe shifted in her seat carefully as the chair creaked beneath her. "You're the product of love, albeit a little unconventional and religiously frowned upon, but they say the same about gays, so you're screwed either way."

"It doesn't bother you?"

Rafe shook her head. "I can't honestly say I'm not a little freaked by what you're telling me. But when I look at you, I don't see the same thing I saw in the alley. I never have." She searched Ashley's face and smiled. "You must have gotten the angel part of your father because I don't see any demon at all." She was horrified to see Ashley's eyes suddenly tear up. *What did I say?*

"That's the sweetest thing anyone has ever said to me."

Rafe relaxed a little, relieved she hadn't messed up. "It's true, besides which, you have a guardian angel. Surely you wouldn't have one if you were considered to be fighting for the other side."

"Eli's always been there. I used to see him when I was a child. No one else's imaginary friend had wings, though. But from the age of about twelve he came to me. He said that was when my calling began."

"Your calling?"

"To help contain demons."

"Tough call considering your father was one."

"Eli said my father was living on borrowed time, but he promised I'd never have to be the one to return him to his rightful place."

"Is your father still here?"

"No, Eli banished him some years back. I watched him *leave*, for want of a better word." She shook her head. "I was old enough to be parentless, but he'd left another child fatherless at a much younger age."

"So you have what? A sister? Brother?"

"A brother. Lucas Thorpe. I think he'd have been about twenty-one now. I remember seeing him as a baby, and I think the last time he was about ten years old. Last I heard he and his mother were in a car crash where no one survived. I hardly knew them, so it was hard to mourn their loss. I didn't get on with Marion. To be completely honest, for a human, she was more demonic than my father. She didn't like some other woman's brat taking my father's attention away from their child." Ashley picked at her food as she spoke. "I got used to my dad not always being at our home while he made nice with his other family. It made me very self-sufficient."

Rafe hated him for what he'd put Ashley through as a child. "He had two homes going? He's no different from many a mortal man."

"I never kept in touch with his other family. Marion knew I had powers. Dad told me he got drunk one night and spilled the whole demon lineage beans, so she was always afraid of me after that. I didn't do anything to provoke it, but I was always daddy's little angel in her eyes and she hated me for it."

"Did Lucas display any talents?"

Ashley shrugged. "I was never there to know. Not all demon born do, though. I hope for his sake he didn't. It would be nice if one of us had been normal."

"Families," Rafe said.

"I only saw my dad on occasion until his time to depart was set."

"Is he still *alive*?"

Ashley nodded. "Yes, and residing happily in hell."

"The hell of brimstone and endless torment?"

Ashley nodded again. "Some people like that kind of thing."

"Do all bad people go there?"

"No, just the demons. Don't believe all that you read. A lot of it is propaganda for the masses, to keep the people in line and living in fear."

Rafe only just managed not to let escape the sigh of relief pressing at her rib cage. She looked out into the darkness instead, wondering at what else the night had in store. She decided to share her day's news.

"There's been a development in the case today. We had someone confess to all three murders." Rafe watched closely for Ashley's reaction.

Ashley didn't even feign surprise. She just continued fixing her next burrito. "Really? Tell me about him."

Rafe described Epcot in detail and his crazy familial bonds.

"Well, he certainly ticks a lot of your profile's boxes." Ashley took a small bite from her burrito. "Did you see any sparkles?"

Rafe fought the urge to roll her eyes. "No, I didn't."

"Any smell of sulfur? A hint of Hades in his eyes?"

Rafe bit back a sigh. "No, he was decidedly human from what I could tell."

Ashley shrugged. "Then it's not your killer." She took a more generous mouthful from her food, then spoke with her mouth full. "You're wasting your time pursuing him."

"I still need to rule him out. After all, he confessed to the crimes I am investigating. You know, the ones currently terrorizing the city?"

Ashley waved a dismissive hand in her direction. "Hand it over to Dean to wild goose chase. You've got better things to look into."

Rafe bristled at Ashley's flippant attitude. "What if this is our killer?"

"I've told you he isn't."

"So I'm to just believe everything you tell me?"

"It would make my life so much easier. But then it wouldn't be as exciting as me arguing with you and getting to see your eyes ignite with such passion." Ashley's voice dropped a register. "It's very sexy."

Nonplussed, Rafe tried not to be drawn in by the wicked twinkle shining from Ashley's eyes. "Why do I feel you're going to be more trouble to me than a whole hoard of demons on the loose?"

Ashley's playful chuckle only added to Rafe's disquiet. *I'm certain to go down in flames and probably enjoy every singe and scorch mark she burns upon my heart.* She reached for her drink, suddenly wishing it was something stronger.

CHAPTER SEVENTEEN

Ashley contentedly chewed her burrito. She finished a mouthful, then asked idly, "So tell me about your family, Rafe. After all, it's got to be more normal than mine."

"Don't be so sure," Rafe replied. "I'm one of three children born to Carmine and Alisha Douglas. My mother is a trophy wife, my father a dealer in antiquities."

"You're kidding me. You're not from a long line of cops?"

"Nope, my father is still horrified by my less than academic choice of professions. But he's got my brother Mike, who's an art dealer in Toronto, working his way to the top in his own right until he can take over my father's reins. Then there's Leo, who is learning at the master's side so he can take over the paperwork while Mike does the creative stuff."

"Mike? Seems a bit pedestrian a name considering yours. And Leo?"

"Michelangelo, to give him his full name, and Leo is short for Leonardo." She watched as Ashley digested this. A glint lit up her eyes. *Damn, she is fast*, Rafe thought, cringing at what was going to come.

"Your full name isn't Rafe, is it?"

"I *prefer* Rafe."

"You've got to be Raphael, though, who, along with Michelangelo and Leonardo, were the great masters of the Renaissance." Ashley sounded immensely tickled by this.

"Like I said, I prefer Rafe." Ashley sported a wicked grin that

Rafe caught immediately. "Don't you dare mention the fucking Ninja Turtles or I will throw you off this roof!"

"I prefer Ray-fe," Ashley drawled out Rafe's name, "over Raphael. That's so not you. Does anyone call you Raphael?"

"My parents do, and Leo because he knows it pisses me off."

"No one whispers it in your ear at intimate moments of sheer pleasure?" Ashley's voice dropped a register that made Rafe swallow hard.

"No, I think I can honestly say no one has dared to use my given name in that setting." She wondered at Ashley's grin. "So now you know."

"Yeah, now I know. You're the turtle with the sais, the rebellious, sullen one."

"Don't make me regret telling you," Rafe said with a growl and leaned forward to reach for Ashley when something caught her attention out of the corner of her eye. She looked down and did a double take. "That body down there is *glowing*."

Ashley peered over the edge of the roof. "So he is. What color do you see?"

Rafe squinted. "He's red with a shot of yellow."

"Then he's a Class E demon," Ashley said.

"Class E?"

"Minor demon, kind of low on the food chain."

"So he's a lesser demon but a demon all the same?"

"Sure is."

"And shouldn't he be returned to hell before he does whatever demons do?" Rafe watched the guy amble his way along the sidewalk.

"He will be." Ashley pointed to two white lights that flashed brightly in the sky. The lights shone like stars, growing in size until Rafe could see a distinct humanoid shape and the recognizable shape of wings.

"Can't he see them?" Rafe whispered, watching as the white lights descended.

"No, he won't until the last minute. Demons don't see the light, Rafe. Their souls aren't pure enough."

Rafe saw the angels ready their weapons, long spears tipped with lethal points. One flew down and ran the man through with it, pinning him in place.

"He killed him!"

"No, he just trapped him with the Spear of Light. Now he can see them and he knows he has no way of escaping."

Rafe didn't blink for fear of missing anything that happened on the street. The first angel had the man held in place. The other descended at a slower rate and circled them, surrounding them in a ball of silver light. Then, like a soap bubble popping, they disappeared in a flash. Rafe blinked at the suddenness. "They're gone."

"Yep, on the fast track back to hell with that one." Ashley picked up a handful of nachos and ate as if nothing extraordinary had just transpired.

"Why him, though? Why catch him and not Armitage?"

"Your demon was a Class B, from what you described. They blend in better, find lesser-traveled portals to enter in by. They also hide better among humans, so they are harder to spot. Unless you know what you're looking for."

"The horns being a dead giveaway, eh?"

"You'd see right through their disguise now, but Armitage had quite the life here masquerading as a human. He fit in, so he didn't send off as much as a blip on our radar. Class B demons can sometimes mask their demon form even from angels. So we have to wait until they do something that exposes their soul. Then and only then can the angels come and take them back."

"So that night, Eli was taking the demon Armitage to hell? But we had a body. The angels who just took that guy away left nothing behind."

"Lesser demons can't form a proper human outer layer. They just pretty much glamour themselves to fool human eyes. That demon wasn't strong enough to pass fully. Armitage was."

"And we're left being unable to tell the difference between demon-shed skin or a real human cadaver."

"Eli removed the demon from its 'host,' if you like and left you the remains. After all, the body is just a shell for what lives inside."

"What about the Class A demons?"

"They run for government."

Rafe stared at her aghast. She barely dared to breathe, terrified by the implications, until Ashley finally cracked a smile and then began to laugh. "Shit, Ashley, don't even joke about that!" She glared at Ashley, who was doubled over with laughter at her expense. "Bitch," she grumbled, which only set Ashley off more. Rafe reluctantly had to smile when Ashley finally calmed down enough to wipe the tears from her eyes. "You're such a smart-ass. This zone, do you keep a watch on it in your PI status?"

"Not just me. I'm still new to this area, so I've just been taking my turn. We have watchers. They keep tabs on the goings-on and inform those who need to know."

Rafe nodded slowly, digesting this. "If I hadn't passed out, I'd have seen Eli capturing Armitage before my very eyes." A part of her was disappointed she hadn't witnessed that event.

"You weren't ready to see it then, Rafe. The light was still blinding and you were too injured to have appreciated it. If you think about it, you helped capture a demon, though."

"Inadvertently." Her hand strayed to touch her forehead in what was becoming an unconscious act of self-comfort. "Do you ever get tired of it all? The weirdness?"

"It's not weird to me. I grew up with it. This is my idea of normal."

Rafe looked out into the moonlight. "Mine too now, it would appear."

CHAPTER EIGHTEEN

The rest of the evening passed uneventfully. Rafe stood and stretched to remove the kinks from her spine left by the rickety chair, then she took a careful step nearer to the roof edge. "Guess I've had my show for tonight."

"You got the best seats in the house too. You saw something no one else would have seen had they looked out their windows. You and I alone witnessed that command performance." Ashley shivered as a chill air blew over them. "Though I think it's time we head back inside."

Rafe helped clear up their belongings and followed Ashley back down the stairs to her apartment. Once inside, Rafe looked around it with a critical eye.

"This place is just not right for you." After throwing away the trash, she wandered back to the tiny living room and cocked her head questioningly at Ashley. At her nod of agreement, Rafe flipped over the whiteboard. Her eyes fell on the familiar photos. "I've wondered at the significance of this board since the last time I was here."

"You mean when you came to yell at me?"

"I didn't come to yell, merely to chase you off my case." She eyed the photos. "For all the good it did me," she said. "How many other police investigations have you been in on?"

"None here. You're my first. But I've 'assisted' on a few cases here and there. You are, however, the first one I've walked up to and told you point-blank that I needed to be brought in."

"Why?"

"Because you need me and because you'd already been dragged into my world. I knew we could work together."

"Yet with the other investigations?"

"Strictly professional. I fed them information, they did all the ground work, and I took what I needed from them by glamouring up and walking right on in."

"And the child porn case?"

Ashley looked surprised. "I forgot you had your computer whiz dig up my files. That one I wasn't able to keep out of the limelight quite so well. I went in as myself because I had the lead they needed to follow. Huge case, very nasty."

"Were they demons? The guys you stopped?"

"No, they were the worse scum of humanity instead. The demon was the one using their sordid depravity to line his own pockets by distributing it over the Internet. He was who I was after."

"But you got him?"

Ashley nodded. "He's back where he belongs."

"Do you always get who you want?" Rafe asked, hoping her gulp wasn't audible as Ashley's eyes heated and she moved purposely to invade Rafe's personal space.

"If I'm lucky." Ashley pushed her way into Rafe's arms and cuddled into her.

Rafe couldn't draw Ashley close enough to her. She breathed in deeply of her scent and just held Ashley tight. Soft lips began working their way up her neck, and Rafe tilted her head so Ashley could reach everywhere she wanted. Teeth nipped at her pulse point and her knees threatened to buckle beneath her. Clinging to Ashley so she wouldn't fall, Rafe struggled to speak. "God, woman, what you do to me. How can someone so small rock me off my feet so fast?" She rubbed her cheek across Ashley's hair and trembled as Ashley's hands pushed under her heavy jacket to spread across her back. Rafe pressed fevered kisses along Ashley's hairline, then dropped her lips to capture Ashley's in a hot meshing of mouths. She thrilled to the sound of Ashley's moan as their mouths locked and tongues tangled.

She cradled Ashley's face between her palms to hold her still to deepen the kiss. Rafe ran her tongue along Ashley's full lower lip, caught it gently in her teeth, tugged slightly, then ran her tongue back over to soothe. She lowered her hands to tug up Ashley's shirt, kneading at the taut muscles in Ashley's stomach. Ashley's body tumbled into Rafe, almost knocking them over in her need to get closer. Rafe's back hit something solid. She looked over her shoulder and caught sight of the lifeless stare of one of the dead women posted on the board. Rafe pulled back. "We have to stop."

Dazed eyes met hers, disbelief clouding Ashley's face. "Why?"

"Because this is too fast, too soon, and we have a case to solve."

Ashley pulled out of Rafe's arms. "Too fast, too soon?" Ashley tugged her shirt back down to cover her bare midriff.

Rafe's mouth watered at the sight of the belly button shyly peeking over the waistband of Ashley's jeans before it was hidden. She all but reached for the shirt to expose it again and explore further. Common sense won out, to her own sense of dismay.

"Rafe Douglas, life is too short. Do I need to remind you that in the space of just a few weeks you have almost died twice? The first time I couldn't stop, but the second time I was right by your side pulling you back from the edge." She poked Rafe sharply in the chest. "I have it on good authority life is too short and too precious to waste."

Rafe hugged Ashley to her, trying desperately to wrap herself around her. "I'm no good at any of this. I'm sorry. You make me nervous and exhilarated all at the same time. I can't decide between getting hot and naked with you or running as far away as I can from you."

Ashley caressed Rafe's cheek. "Why run, sweetheart?"

"Because in the few days I've known you, I feel like I've known you forever. It scares me, and yet, I can't explain it away."

"Do you believe in soul mates?"

Rafe's eyebrow rose a little. "The idea that someone has only half a soul and when they meet their other half they're finally at peace?" She smiled crookedly at her. "It makes for a nice romantic tale."

"What if I told you it's all true?"

Rafe slipped out of Ashley's arms to stalk off a few steps only to turn around again. "Is there nothing you don't fucking know about!"

Ashley's quiet voice broke through Rafe's agitation. "I don't know how you feel about me."

One look at Ashley's face and Rafe's heart reached out for her. She took an involuntary step forward as if physically pulled by it. "How can I tell you when I don't even know myself?"

"But you care for me, right?"

"You've been in my house, slept with me and my cat, and I made breakfast. That's more intimacy than I have shared with most of the women I've been with." She stuffed her hands in her pockets and again caught sight of the board displaying the scenes of crime. "We have a duty to these women to find their killer. Until then, we have to stay focused."

"I am woman. I can multitask and focus on many things at once."

"I'm a detective, and I need to concentrate on one thing at a time."

"So how many dates are we talking, Detective, before you can speak of soul mates without freaking out?"

"I don't know. Our dates seem to be a little odd in and of themselves."

"And this is what, our third one already? I'd say things are looking bright for you with me."

"You deserve better," Rafe said.

"But, Detective Douglas, you forget, I can see you too. All the way through those strategically placed walls, past the badge, right through to your heart. Because I feel like I've known you forever too."

Rafe reached for Ashley's hand just as her phone rang loudly in her pocket. She snatched it up quickly, fearing another dead body found. "Douglas here." She let out a soft breath at the voice on the other end. "No, it's okay. I'm…" She gave Ashley a look. "I'm not home yet. I'll phone you when I get back." Rafe checked her watch. "Give me half an hour or so." She finished up the call. "I've got to go. I have to return a call to Blythe about this case."

"You could talk to her here. You don't have to leave."

Rafe was torn between duty and need. She threw caution to the wind and caught Ashley up in her arms. The kiss she gave her was almost bruising in its ferocity and in her desire. She only pulled back when she could no longer breathe. Ashley was left gasping in her wake.

"Soul mates, eh?" Rafe rubbed her nose against Ashley's. "Just when I think you can't surprise me any further."

"I've got to keep you on your toes to keep you interested," Ashley said before Rafe kissed her again, long and hard.

"Oh, I'm interested." Rafe dragged herself away from Ashley's tempting body. "Just for the record again, there was never anything at all between Blythe and me."

"I know. That's why I'm letting you go." Ashley touched her lips with shaking fingers. "For now."

Rafe pulled the door open, wondering if she was crazy to leave behind what Ashley was so obviously offering her. "I'll see you in the morning?"

"I'll pop into the office before I go do some of my own work."

As she stepped over the threshold, Rafe paused in the doorway, hesitating to shut the door behind her. "Why don't I want to leave?"

"Because your heart recognizes what your head doesn't yet," Ashley said.

"Which is?"

"That you belong with me."

Rafe's whole being filled with a soothing warmth that was unfamiliar. *Peace. Is that what this is?* "I've never belonged to anyone before. Other than Trinity, and I think she only stays for the food and the scratching post."

"You should go back to your cat. She'll be feeling lonesome." Ashley edged nearer. "Are you going to tell Blythe about any of this?"

"You mean tell her about the demons running rife in my life? Hell no! She's my friend and I love her, but she doesn't need to know. I want her to be blissful in her ignorance."

"Can you keep it from her?"

"I'm going to give it a damn good try. I don't tell her everything; what's one more secret?" Rafe made herself take another step away. "I'd better go. I need to ask her about reworking the profile."

Ashley grabbed Rafe by the lapel of her jacket and tugged her down for a long, lingering kiss. "Go. Be careful driving home."

Rafe ran her tongue over her lips, relishing the gentle throb the kiss had left behind. "Sure I will, because if the demons in Chicago aren't trying to kill you, the crazies on the road are." Rafe left before she found another excuse to stay.

CHAPTER NINETEEN

Alone in her apartment, Ashley took off her jacket and waited for Eli to appear. His sense of timing was always impeccable, so she knew it wouldn't be long after Rafe had left that he'd show up. Ashley felt cut adrift without Rafe beside her. She missed the warmth that naturally radiated off Rafe, missed her presence and her intelligence. Now that they were getting more intimate, Ashley was loath to let Rafe out of her sight. She touched her lips gently with her fingertips. They still tingled from the forceful kisses they had shared. She smiled and hugged the sensation to her.

"You look happy."

Ashley spun around to greet Eli. "I had my detective over to share some quality demon-watching time," she said.

"So I saw."

"Were you spying on us?"

"No. I was merely doing my job observing humanity."

"Do you watch *everything* I do?"

"No. I grant you your privacy when it's warranted. I'm not a pervert. I know when to draw the veil over my eyes."

"Are you ever afraid you'll be tempted?"

"I saw what it did to those I considered brothers. I don't envy their life and what they have become." Unexpectedly, he brushed his knuckles across Ashley's cheek. "But your father helped bring you into this world, and sometimes I envy him for that. You are a marvelous woman."

Ashley's eyes welled up. "May you always think so."

"I have no doubt you'll continue to surprise me, but you will always be favored."

"Because you're my guardian?"

"Because you are the daughter of my beloved brother angel and you are my friend." He smiled at her, a truly beautiful smile befitting such an angelic soul. He then turned his attention back to the board filled with photos. "Anything new?"

Ashley followed him so they stood side by side, just as they had every single night since the second killing, staring at the stark images pinned on the board. "There's nothing significant that points to one man or demon. I fear he's going to have to kill again and hopefully slip up. So far, he's invincible. He kills at will and no one can stop him." Ashley stared at a photo and something tugged at her memory. "You know, I'm sure I've seen something like this pose before." She studied it harder, racking her brain for an answer. "I just can't think where."

"A statue perhaps? Some kind of sculpture?"

Ashley chewed at her lip, pensive. "I'm not sure, but something about it is nagging at my brain."

"Maybe it will become clearer as the hours pass."

"Maybe. But not tonight. I'm going to bed. *Alone*, might I add."

"Your detective didn't want to stay?"

"I think she wanted to stay but wouldn't let herself."

"An honorable woman, a rarity these days."

"Honor is overrated, Eli. Sometimes you just want a warm body to cuddle up with on a night like tonight." Ashley wanted Rafe like no other woman she'd been with. Not just for the physical release their lovemaking could bring them both, but for the comfort, the tenderness, the sheer need to just be with her. This feeling was soul deep and almost desperate. *And I sent her home to talk with another woman instead of keeping her here with me. What's wrong with that picture, Ashley?* She continued to berate herself as she took herself off to bed.

❖

Settled in her living room, her lap taken up by her cat, Rafe called Blythe's number. She answered on the second ring.

"Tell me you weren't really still at work this late not long after being discharged from the hospital."

"No, Mom. I was out on a surveillance that saw me just sitting around on my ass. I got fed and everything, so you can quit worrying." She heard Blythe's exasperation with her loud and clear through the phone. "Honestly, I'm getting stronger every day."

"Your hair is too damn short."

"I had them just shave it all so it was the same length instead of me looking like a complete fashion disaster. It's growing already." She brushed her hand over the soft bristles on her scalp.

"You frightened me," Blythe finally admitted.

"Yeah, well, I frightened myself there for a while. But I'm on the mend, and the guy who did this is well and truly dealt with." *In every way.* "So how's the FBI treating you these days? Are you in charge of the DDU yet?"

"No, and I don't think I want that responsibility either. I like my job just fine as it is. I spend way too many hours working. I have no time for a social life. Sometimes I barely find a moment or two in the day to breathe."

"And you love every second." Rafe knew that feeling well.

"Yeah, I do. I just wish I could do something more about my woefully lacking love life. I really don't want to strike up a romance with someone in the office, though. If it ends badly, I don't want to be the one reassigned from a job I love so much."

"You'll just have to trust that your heart will lead you on the right path." She listened to the silence on the other end of the line. "Blythe?"

"Just how badly were you hurt in that fight, Rafe?"

"Enough to shake my perspective on life. I've come to realize it's too short. You need to grab happiness wherever you find it." Ever the cop, she couldn't resist adding, "As long as it doesn't compromise the evidence or interfere with your case."

"What happened to By the Book Douglas?"

"She's still here, but sometimes you have to step into the gray areas. I'm treading in some now."

"Are you okay, Rafe, seriously? Health-wise? And no fudging."

"I'm fine. I am healing and getting my strength back more every day. And I'm...seeing someone."

"A woman?"

"Yes, a woman! I do date, you know."

"Yes, but it's so rare and I never hear about it until well after the fact."

"This is still new. Early days if I'm honest." *Literally days. God, it seems like forever.*

"She must be special if you're mentioning her."

"She's special, all right."

"What's her name?"

"Ashley Scott. She's a PI assisting on the case."

"Ashley Scott? Where do I know that name from? A PI, you say?" Rafe could all but hear Blythe's brain ticking away. "Not the same Scott involved in the child porn ring we busted?"

"Small world, isn't it?"

"I remember meeting her briefly. She was more involved with the Internet side of the ring, but I saw her in the department a few times. Small and blond, right? Very pretty."

"That would be her."

"And she's helping you how?"

"She has contacts on the street, some of the great unwashed who don't want to talk to cops. She's also checking into the weirder aspect of these killings. She's investigating an occult angle."

"I don't recall any occult references in the profile I gave you."

Rafe knew her lame excuse for having Ashley involved in the investigation was going to cause more trouble than it was worth. She considered for a brief moment just telling Blythe the truth, to have someone else see how crazy the world had gotten since she'd had her head caved in. To have someone to confide in, worry with, be frightened with. She thought of Ashley and the trust she had placed in Rafe and decided against it. "It's just another angle. It's not in my team's investigation; it's something she is pursuing on her own." Rafe fingered the scar on her forehead. "She's not on my dime, so she can chase after shadows as much as she likes."

"And you're dating."

"Kind of," Rafe hedged, gasping as Trinity chose that moment to stick her claws through her pants almost in reprimand. "Yes." She glared down at the cat, who blinked at her, unrepentant. "We've seen each other a few times now."

"But?"

"No, no buts, well, not really. I'm just cautious, and it's all happening so suddenly. I'm still getting my head around the fact I nearly died in that alley, and now I have this woman in my life and she's wonderful and funny and makes my head spin worse than the medication does."

"Oh, Rafe, that's how it's supposed to be."

Rafe shifted in her seat, needing to get off this topic of feelings and romance before Blythe started asking about Ashley's background. *Oh yes, she's wonderful and funny and just happens to be the child of a fallen angel. We watched a demon being banished tonight. It's the latest craze in dating for lesbians.*

Rafe cleared her throat indicating the need for a subject change. "Did you get the information I sent you about the new guy, Epcot?"

Blythe had no problem changing tack with Rafe. "Yes, I did. He's a classic attention seeker. I predict a long line of sibling rivalry, starting with the vying for attention from their parents. He's trying to go one better than she did on him. She slept with his girl. His move was to remove that object from the playing field. He failed, though, in his intentions so he had to up the stakes. His admitting to the serial killer's crimes is his way of proving his superiority."

"It sounds desperate and a little crazy," Rafe said.

"Psychopaths don't think like the rest of us, Rafe. You might want to keep an eye on his sister. They sound like a pair who never grew out of their childhood competition for attention."

"It makes me mad we have to put manpower into investigating his false claims."

"Better to prove them false and know you're going in the right direction for the true killer. The trouble is, Epcot fits a great deal of the profile. But your killer is much more complex. I've added to the profile. Thank you for the new photos, by the way. Rather artistic ones too for the crime scene guys."

Rafe didn't comment. She didn't want to have to explain why Ashley was at the scenes well before the police were.

"Anyway, this killer's apparent fascination with the blood could be because he's turned on by it, but you can exsanguinate a person so much easier than ripping open their back to do it. It could be an expression of his desire to make the crime scene look even more horrific, but he carefully poses the body after the act and tries to make them appear beautiful again. It's contradictory. The rearrangement of the blood does not make sense in context to his killing."

"So what's your theory?"

"I think he's framing his work. After all, the blood is spread in a very specific area. Whatever he's painting we just can't see yet. He's chosen the wrong terrain to show us what he's depicting."

"Great, now we have fucking Rorschach images left in blood." Rafe stretched over to snag the end of a folder and managed to pull it toward her without disturbing the sleeping cat sprawled in her lap. Rafe looked at one of Ashley's photos again, this time with Blythe's insight. "It does look like he's tried to smear the blood out and above the body."

"Whatever it is, it's not a natural blood formation," Blythe said. "His signature is bigger than we thought. The blood is linked to the pose. It's all a part of how he wants them to be seen."

"What the hell is he trying to tell us?" Rafe stared at the photo, searching for that elusive something she hadn't seen previously. This time she tried to decipher the blood as it was spread above the body of the second victim, Erica Lane.

"When you can see his creation, maybe then you can find him," Blythe said. "He needs a better canvas. His killing them in alleys doesn't let him move the blood where it obviously needs to be positioned. On the last killing, the dirt is scuffed around the body. Maybe that isn't from him killing her but from him trying to push the blood up to frame her shoulders. I think he'll try to pick a better surface to display his meaning on. His message isn't being heard."

"I pray we catch him before he strikes again."

"You have no leads at all?"

"Not a thing, just a bunch of photos that leave us with more questions than answers and three dead women."

"Then look to the blood. I feel he's all but signing his name in it for you."

CHAPTER TWENTY

The amount of paperwork left piled on her desk made Rafe sit down more heavily in her chair. She turned on her computer, reached for her now cold Starbucks, and drank the dregs sparingly while sorting through her in-box tray. She flipped a few files over into Dean's in-box and continued perusing the rest. Though the spine killer was her top priority, Rafe still had other cases to deal with, and she read through the reports that had finally made it to her desk. She made notes on each one, where to follow up, what was a dead end, what could lead to more information. She picked up the file concerning the death of Andrea Mason, the third spine killer victim. All the results were in and the paperwork concluded. Something in the autopsy notes caught her eye.

"Morning, boss," Dean said as he entered the room armed with a cardboard tray full of fresh coffee.

Rafe eagerly took the proffered drink from him. The red-hot liquid scalded her tongue as she hastily drank it down. "I think the killer unwittingly gave us a clue with his last victim." She waved the file at Dean. "Natalie Gray, our first victim, was five foot four and blond. Erica Lane, victim number two, five foot five and blond. The last victim, Andrea Mason, five foot four again and brunette."

Dean folded his arms, waiting. Rafe continued. "When Andrea Mason was brought into the morgue, after she was processed and washed down, there was a chemical residue found in her hair. The results concluded she had coloring in her hair at the time of her death. One of those wash-in, wash-out jobs. She was a natural brunette."

"But when she was killed—"

"She was blond," Rafe declared. She slapped the file on the table. "In the dark, in the night, you're not going to tell a dye job from a natural color."

"He's not stalking these women beforehand. He'd have known she wasn't a natural blonde."

"He's specifically targeting small blond women." Rafe's thoughts immediately went to Ashley. *You'd better be safe out wherever you are today.*

"So not only has he got a definite signature with the ripping open of their backs, posing them and messing in their blood, he's also got a specific female type he sets his sights on." Dean reached for the file. "Nice to know they can rush evidence through when they need to."

"It's a serial case; they knew we needed it processed ASAP." Rafe reached for her coffee and took another long drink. "We can catch this guy. We just need to figure his motives out. Maybe find the blonde who triggered his killing streak."

Alona sauntered into the room and greeted them both. She made a point of staring at Dean. "You're in early, Detective. The woman who picked you up last night kick you out before her husband came home?"

Rafe laughed into her coffee container at Dean's reddening face. She'd missed her colleagues' teasing banter. Things were finally getting back to normal in the office.

"Actually, she said she had an early appointment." He handed her a coffee and hid himself behind his monitor.

Rafe watched Alona accessing her computer. "I need you to run some checks for me today."

"What do you need?"

"I'm looking for assaults on blond women, all short in stature, five foot five the tallest, in and around the areas of the killing zone we have for the spine killer. Go back a couple months to start us off."

"You've got some new information?" Alona began tapping away at her keyboard.

"We've finally got a chink of light to the darkness this guy is hiding in. Let's see if we can't widen it and find him."

❖

"So this is my good morning from you? I walk in and you promptly take me down to visit the morgue." Ashley tried to tame her windswept hair as she walked beside Rafe. "You could at least let me warm up first with coffee before taking me down to the icebox."

"Sorry, but we only have the body for today. It's been processed. Andrea Mason is being released to the funeral home tomorrow."

Ashley understood the urgency. She stopped fussing and just enjoyed being able to see Rafe again. "Still, you never even gave me a kiss hello."

Rafe never slowed her pace. "I hardly think the morgue is the right place for that, Ms. Scott."

"You owe me."

"I'm sure I'll enjoy it when you collect too," Rafe replied and ushered Ashley in to meet Dr. Alan.

Ashley recognized him. She'd spoken to him at the last two crime scenes, each time as someone other than herself. Rafe introduced them.

"You're here to examine Andrea Mason's body again?" he asked as he directed them into another room lined with steel doors.

"Yes, I want Ms. Scott to see the body. You're aware she's assisting us with the case?"

"I heard a rumor you had a PI in tow, yes." He gave Ashley a curious look. "Do you have a medical background, young lady?"

Ashley smiled at him. "No, but I've seen enough dead bodies to know when something isn't quite right. I think Rafe is hoping I'll hit on something she can use."

"I've examined the poor girl inside and out and found there was a lack of evidence left behind. No transference of bodily fluids, no DNA, nothing that hints at who was behind this." He pulled open a door and pulled out the pallet with a shrouded body on it. Gently, he lowered the sheet.

Ashley knew, as with the previous bodies, that this was a human body, not one shed by a demon. The subtleties were minor, but Ashley was well versed in recognizing them. She pulled on a pair of gloves and began gently palpating the skull. She overheard the words Dr. Alan whispered aside to Rafe.

"Tell me she's not looking for horns too."

Ashley looked up in time to catch Rafe hushing him. "Horns, Dr. Alan?" Ashley decided to tackle him head-on. "What do you usually autopsy in this room?" She felt along the line where the skull had been cut open and admired the work that had allowed for the woman's brain to be removed yet still let her look reasonably normal. The contorted look on her face ruined the neatness of the autopsy cuts. "Nice job, by the way. You can hardly see where you cracked her skull open."

Dr. Alan's smile was crooked. "I wanted her to look her best, but whatever she went through left its mark."

Ashley checked in the woman's mouth, felt along her throat, and then lowered the sheet and checked the places she knew demons scratched, bit, or invaded. She knew that some demons were exactly like humans in their violence, though they generally didn't seek out humans as prey. When they did, they were as predisposed to fighting and rape as much as any human degenerate. "Your report said there was no sign of sexual trauma, just like with the last two victims."

Dr. Alan nodded. "None of them were penetrated."

"Thank God for small mercies," Rafe muttered.

Ashley turned the body over carefully and made a face at the ruined flesh. She pressed her fingers into the wound. "No sign of teeth marks." She searched for the minute signs of a demon's hands but nothing lit up before her eyes. She bit back a growl of frustration.

"This was all done by knife," Dr. Alan said. "In my experience, the biters like to sink their teeth into the flesh, not cut it open and bite at the innards. I have to admit, with this ferocity, I was surprised there was no consumption of anything. Seems like a great deal of trouble to go through not to get something out of it."

Running her finger along the exposed spinal bone, Ashley wondered what this demon wanted. The spine wasn't usually high on their list of needs. She carefully laid the body back down and covered her again. She snapped the rubber gloves off her hands and threw them away. "I don't think I can add anything more to what Dr. Alan has already written up," she said with a shrug.

"Fuck," Rafe said.

"What did you hope to find?" Dr. Alan asked.

"Answers, just like you search for. He left no trace I could see."

"And you'd know this trace how? I thought you weren't a doctor, and I didn't see you use any equipment in your examination."

Ashley smiled at him. "We all have ways and means, Dr. Alan. You see answers in the body and Detective Douglas sees hers in the evidence. I have my own ways of seeing things."

"The rumor mill rolled down here that you'd gotten a religious scholar with occult leanings involved in this investigation," Dr. Alan said to Rafe. He turned his attention to Ashley. "I didn't believe it at first, but I'm just wondering how far you lean toward the occult, young lady. Or maybe you're a witch?"

Ashley laughed. "Sorry to disappoint you, Doc, but I am no practitioner of any faith. I'm just bringing an extensive knowledge of the occult and symbolism into the mix." She eyed the covered body. "This poor soul bore no marks I could point to and say that's what she fell prey to." She gave Rafe a look. "Sorry, Detective, the search continues. Whatever this killer is up to, he's not going to make it easy for you." She shook Dr. Alan's hand. "Thank you for letting me come down here and see her. I appreciate that."

"I wish you'd have found something, I wouldn't mind being shown I'd missed something if it led to this bastard's capture."

"You're not going to miss anything," Ashley assured him. "You're very likely going to be kept in the dark also."

"Are you a psychic?"

"No, sir, I'm not that either. If I was, I'd be the best-paid private investigator in the business!" She bid him farewell and tagged along after a clearly frustrated Rafe.

"We're going to have more deaths, and the city is already frightened by the three we can't explain."

Ashley remembered watching the late-night news as she'd lain in bed alone. "Your chief, Detective Powell, gives many of the news conferences, doesn't she? Shouldn't it be you up there seeing as you're the lead on the case?"

"She's young, attractive, and chosen to be the department's figurehead to tell the city we have everything under control. Better they see her than have my battered face and crew cut splashed all over the nightly news. How can I say I can protect the city when I couldn't even protect myself?"

Ashley grabbed her arm and pulled her to a halt. "I'd rather have you reassuring me that everything is being dealt with than hear it from Detective Barbie!"

"Don't let Alona hear you call her that. She has the biggest crush on her."

"Let me guess, the no-fraternization rule is holding her back?"

"No, I just don't think she can work up the nerve to confront her yet. Not everyone acts on their impulses like there's no tomorrow."

"Oh, there's always a tomorrow. It's just you never know what it might bring."

"In my experience, it's usually another body."

Ashley feared that in Rafe's line of work that was sadly true. She smoothed her fingers down Rafe's arm and captured her hand to squeeze gently before releasing it. "Want to go get some fresh coffee for the troops before we go sit and pore over more files and data? I'd like to clear my nostrils of the morgue smell."

Rafe led her out the back of the CPD and out into the cool morning air. A morgue van pulled up as they were leaving and they stepped aside to watch Dr. Alan and his team welcome another body into their care.

"Tomorrow never came for that unfortunate soul." Rafe sounded uncharacteristically morose.

"Their journey here has ended, but they start a new path that we can't begin to imagine."

"Are you religious, Ashley?"

She shrugged. "I *believe*. I don't think it's entirely the same thing."

Rafe's eyes drifted toward the sky. Ashley saw her shut them for a moment, then let out a soft exhale of breath. "I don't know what to believe anymore. I'd like to believe that after this life there's somewhere better to go, but I've seen the terror left on those girls' faces and wonder what hell we have to tread first in order to reach whatever peace there is."

"Not all people die like that, Rafe. We just have an exceptionally cruel killer on the loose."

"I want him caught." Rafe gave Ashley a sideways glance. "Dean is still looking into Epcot's claims."

"Is he sparkling today?"

Rafe huffed. "Of course he isn't."

"Then it's still not him," Ashley said bluntly, then added more softly, "Don't start pinning your hopes on the reality you used to know, Rafe. It doesn't exist anymore."

Rafe grumbled under her breath. "I still want him caught."

"He's going to slip up. Nobody, human or demon, is perfect."

"Promise?"

Ashley's heart softened at how wistful Rafe sounded. She sought only to comfort and caressed Rafe's cool cheek, ever mindful of their surroundings but needing to touch her. "You can count on it. You know your humans; I know my demons. Together, we'll put a stop to whatever this monster is."

CHAPTER TWENTY-ONE

"Rafe, will you please put your hat on? You're making me cold just looking at you."

Rafe rummaged in her jacket pocket and pulled out the woolen hat. She jammed it over her ears then cocked her head at Ashley. "Happy now, Mother?" She stuffed her hands into her pockets, only now noticing the cool evening air. "You know, I should be at work, not slinking off home."

Ashley linked her arm through Rafe's and crowded in. "You've been popping pills all day. Don't think I was the only one who noticed either. Dean is manning the office, but even he said there was nothing for you to stay for."

"Thanks for pointing out again that we have no leads to investigate."

"You can't make evidence appear out of thin air, Detective. Sitting for hours staring at the data streams isn't going to make the answers magically spring out either."

"It would help if your contacts were a little more forthcoming. You know, the whole *eye in the sky*? And I'm not talking Google Earth here."

"You know it doesn't work like that, sweetheart," Ashley said.

Rafe was annoyed that Ashley couldn't just get her angel *friends* to point a finger at the culprit, but the unexpected endearment took the ire right out of her. "You're trying to make me forget what I'm being grumpy about."

"I don't want you grumpy. I'm just taking you to your home to eat, seeing as you have decided my perfectly functional apartment is beneath you."

"Your apartment is in the middle of a demon-infested hellhole. It's not somewhere that helps me relax when there's so much activity going on." Rafe wrapped an arm around Ashley's shoulder, wishing she could just whisk both of them away from anywhere connected to demons.

"And you've got undercover narcotic cops watching the street corner for the guys we saw last night, haven't you?"

Rafe stiffened at the accusation. "Shit," she ground out. "Does *nothing* escape you?"

"I'm getting to know you too well, Detective Douglas, for whom duty comes first and foremost," Ashley said with a smile. "And I got a message from Eli saying we had lots of new faces in the area trying to blend in. Humans do tend to stick out there."

"So much for them being inconspicuous." Rafe tugged on a piece of hair at the nape of Ashley's neck. "Are you angry?"

Ashley shook her head. "No, it means I get to meet Trinity again, and I'm not so stupid that I don't appreciate a nice home over the place I sleep in."

As they walked down her street, Rafe looked at her house with fresh eyes. She'd taken it for granted for many years. It was a place to come back to after work to sleep in, feed her cat in, to just exist in before she went back out to work. Now, with Ashley beside her, it felt so much better to go back to.

"It feels like a home when you're in it," Rafe said, surprising herself when the words came tumbling out. Ashley looked up at her silently. "Well, it does. It's the darndest thing. I can't explain it."

"Life just keeps surprising you at every turn, doesn't it, Rafe?"

Rafe could hear the amusement in Ashley's voice but just handed her the house keys and had Ashley let them inside. "Here kitty kitty," she crooned down the hallway. Trinity came running, her answering meows loud and obviously joyous. Rafe picked her up, petting her fur and rubbing behind her ears.

"Now that's a welcome home." Ashley stroked the cat's head. "I wonder if I could get Eli to try it?"

"He's more winged than furred. Trinity would think he was

a bird to be chased." Rafe grinned at the thought. "Wouldn't that be something to find left as a gift for me?" She let the cat down and helped Ashley out of her leather jacket. She hung it up along with her own. Rafe scratched her head blissfully after removing her hat. "The sooner this starts growing out, the better."

"It's going to be interesting seeing what your hair really looks like." Ashley ran her palm over Rafe's head. "Not that you don't look gorgeous like this."

"I look like someone I'd arrest."

"Your bruises are fading." Ashley touched at Rafe's face gently. "You're going to totally break my heart with how handsome you are when you are all healed."

Rafe captured Ashley's wandering hand and pressed the palm to her cheek. "Don't say that. I don't ever want to hurt you."

"I just meant you're going to be even more beautiful."

"You're the beautiful one." Pressing her lips to Ashley's palm, Rafe fell into the fathomless blue of her eyes. She was only brought out of her spell by Trinity head-butting her leg. She looked down to where the cat was weaving her way through their legs, grumbling in a plaintive voice.

"Guess someone is feeling left out." Ashley chuckled. "Maybe we should get the food ready and leave this conversation for later." She stepped back from Rafe. "Besides, you need something other than the standard cop diet of doughnuts."

"You got me a sandwich for lunch," Rafe said, recalling the amusement of her colleagues when Ashley had taken their orders and told them, "If you eat, she'll eat."

"And now I'm fixing you pasta." Ashley held up the bag of groceries she'd refused to let Rafe carry from the little corner shop a block away from Rafe's home. "You sit," she ordered and pushed Rafe in the direction of the couch, then handed her the TV remote. "Channel surf and stay away from the news channel or else."

Instead, Rafe craned her neck to try to watch Ashley start puttering around the kitchen. "There'll come a time where you won't be waiting on me," Rafe said.

"Good, then you can show me how good you are at fixing stuff other than cereal."

"I hope you're partial to cat food." She warmed to the sound of Ashley's laughter. She slipped her shoes off and pushed them under the coffee table, then rested her sock-covered feet on top. Clicking between the channels, Rafe listened to the running commentary going on in the kitchen between Ashley and the cat.

"You know, I think you've fed that cat more than I have the past few days."

"I like it. She doesn't complain about the menu."

Rafe finally stayed on one channel. She settled in against the seat cushions and tried to relax.

"Dr. Alan was particularly cooperative today," she said.

"No shop talk," was shouted back.

"I'm just thinking. It was funny when he called you a witch." Rafe grinned. That comment had tickled her though she'd tried not to show it in the morgue.

"Good thing he doesn't know the half of it."

"I wonder how many demon bodies he's had on his slab and just never had a clue."

"Rafe, I'm going to feed your pasta to Trinity if you don't find something else to talk about."

Rafe stayed silent for a moment. She wasn't used to having someone she could talk to about work, or anything. Actually, now that she thought about it, she wasn't used to having someone to talk to period. She tried to watch the TV, but it was just a blur of motion before her eyes.

"Good grief, don't tell me you can't hold a civilized conversation?" Ashley said from the kitchen.

"I've already found out what your favorite film is. That's about as far as my repertoire goes." She could hear Ashley laughing at her but took it in good part. She was more aware than anyone of her own shortcomings.

"You're a hopeless case." Ashley walked into the room carrying a glass and handed it over to Rafe. "No booze for you. I still don't trust you with it."

"One mess-up," Rafe grumbled, accepting the soda and drinking from it thirstily. Had she drunk anything today other than coffee? She guzzled nearly half the glass away.

Ashley was watching what was playing on the TV. "You're watching *V*?"

Rafe had to look at the screen to check. "It would appear so."

"You can watch a show that portrays aliens living amongst us, but you quibble at there being demons actually walking the Earth?"

"I'm trying to be more open-minded, but there isn't exactly a support group for demonophobics."

Laughing, Ashley grabbed Rafe's head in her hands and kissed her soundly. "I love your sense of humor. You're so freaking funny!"

Rafe watched her disappear back into the kitchen. "But I wasn't joking," she said. She turned her attention back toward the show and watched as the alien leader furthered her plot against the human race. *Us against them*, she mused, but cheered up when a familiar blond character came onscreen brandishing her gun. *And the heroic female cop rides in to save us all.* She tipped her glass to the screen in a toast. *Here's to those who carry the badge and fight to protect and serve against all evildoers.* She only hoped she could be strong enough to face what lay ahead in her own future.

❖

Sprawled out on the couch, snuggled up against Rafe's side, Ashley savored how perfect the moment was. *For one so hell-bent on rushing headfirst into everything, she brings a calm to my life like I've never experienced before.* She slipped her fingers over Rafe's stomach and pushed past the soft cotton shirt to find warm skin beneath. She caressed it, thrilling to the strength of muscle twitching beneath her touch.

"You keep that up and I'll be purring almost as loud as Trinity," Rafe said lazily, running her fingers through Ashley's hair. They both looked over at the cat curled up in front of the fire, her purrs vibrating through the air.

"That's one happy cat," Ashley said. "Of course, it might have been the pasta sauce I added to her kibble."

"I hope she doesn't expect that every day now." Rafe tugged at Ashley's hair gently in reprimand.

Ashley reached up to nuzzle Rafe's neck. Rafe tilted her head to give her easier access, apparently more than willing to let Ashley do whatever she wished. Ashley took full advantage of that, spreading kisses from Rafe's chin up to the soft spot behind her ear. Rafe jumped a little as Ashley teased her by nipping at her earlobe and then sucking it between her lips.

"Ashley," Rafe rumbled as Ashley kissed a path across her cheek.

"Have we waited long enough for me to have my wicked way with you?" She breathed the words into Rafe's ear and felt a shudder vibrate through Rafe's body. She let out a squeal of surprise when Rafe suddenly moved from under her and was on her feet as swiftly as her body would allow. She reached for Ashley's hand and pulled her up from the couch. Rafe led her up the stairs, switching off lights as she went. The lamp beside the bed was switched on and Rafe turned to pin Ashley with serious eyes.

"Last chance to bail."

Ashley shook her head. "I'm not going anywhere without you right beside me."

Rafe pushed Ashley down on the bed and climbed over her. Ashley gasped as the weight of Rafe's body pinned her to the mattress. She barely had a chance to delight in it before Rafe's mouth covered hers and kissed any comment from her lips. She clung to Rafe's back and dug her nails in at the pleasure Rafe wrought from her. Ashley tugged at Rafe's shirt, trying to pull it free from her pants until Rafe stopped her kisses and reared up. Rafe straddled Ashley's hips and slowly, deliberately, began to unfasten each button. Ashley had to force herself not to reach up and rip the shirt off with her bare hands. Unable to help herself, she groaned as flesh was revealed inch by tantalizing inch.

"I knew you'd be passionate," Ashley said, hooking a finger through Rafe's belt and pulling it free.

"Thought about it much, have you?" Rafe tossed her shirt aside.

"All the time since that day you barged into my apartment and told me to stay out of your investigation. Seeing you so fired up like that made me incredibly wet."

Rafe halted in removing her bra. "You were pissing me off," she said before undoing the last catch and baring her chest. Ashley let out an appreciative moan at the sight.

"And you were turning me on," she replied, her hands instantly on the exposed flesh, gliding up from Rafe's stomach to rest between her breasts. Her fingers itched to capture the hard nipples that crowned Rafe's chest, to see how long it would take to break Rafe's composure.

Rafe pulled Ashley up and unfastened her shirt and bra with quick, efficient hands. She pushed her back down and Ashley let her, intrigued by the serious look of determination written on Rafe's handsome face. She found it decidedly sexy. Rafe divested herself of her pants and underwear. She then stripped Ashley naked and was back in her arms.

They both released moans at the first feel of nothing but naked skin between them. Ashley's hands were captured and put above her head, held in place by Rafe's left hand. With her free hand, Rafe brushed down Ashley's body and cupped her breast to bring the hard nipple up to her lips. Arching her back, Ashley tried to press more of herself into Rafe's hot mouth. Her hips bucked as Rafe sucked her in deep, then licked hard across the thickened tip. Rafe alternated between sucking and licking first one breast, then the other to afford it the same pleasure.

Sharp electricity jolts flooded from Ashley's nipples straight to her sex. Desperate for relief, she shifted her leg and Rafe's thigh pressed in between, adding pressure to her already swollen mound. Ashley's hips undulated as she began to smear her wetness on Rafe's thigh. Rafe pulled back, making Ashley moan in desperation.

"You are not getting yourself off, Sparky." Rafe nipped at a breast, tearing a gasp from Ashley's throat. She let go of Ashley's hands, levering herself upright to capture both of Ashley's breasts in her palms. Caressing them, chafing her thumbs over reddened tips, Rafe rubbed herself on Ashley's stomach. Ashley could feel her wetness coating her skin.

"Oh God, you've got to let me have you," Ashley moaned, grabbing onto Rafe's hips and urging her on as Rafe rode her in a lazy rhythm. Ashley couldn't take her eyes off Rafe's face as her desire was so blatant there, so unabashed and so beautiful. Ashley didn't know which was more distracting, Rafe's hands molding her breasts or the feel of Rafe's swollen sex smearing wetness all over her skin. She shifted her hand between Rafe's legs but was only afforded a brief stroke through hot silk before Rafe slipped from her grasp.

A bruising kiss silenced Ashley's complaint, then Rafe's tongue flicked its way down her body in a maddening trail. She teased over Ashley's breasts, down her stomach, and dipped into Ashley's belly button to tease before going lower. Mindful of Rafe's injuries, Ashley had to stop herself from grabbing Rafe's head and forcing her to where she needed her the most. She cursed the fact Rafe's hair wasn't even long enough for her to pull on to direct her to where she wanted that teasing tongue to rest. Without preamble, Rafe slid a finger deep inside Ashley's wetness. Ashley's back came off the bed as she bowed to Rafe's strength.

"Oh my God," she groaned, her breath catching as Rafe eased out again, then pressed in deeper. "Yes, like that, exactly like that." She knew she was soaked inside. Rafe had no problem sliding in. Two fingers pressed for entry and Ashley sensed Rafe's hesitation. "Do it," she said, grabbing Rafe's arm and urging her on. Her insides clenched around the intrusion, welcoming Rafe home as she built up a delicious friction that threatened to make Ashley scream. Firm lips closed around Ashley's clitoris and Ashley gasped. "Oh do it, suck me in," she begged, all but mindless as the sensations Rafe brought to her body threatened to overwhelm her.

Rafe speeded up her thrusts, timing them to each roll of Ashley's hips. Ashley's hand pressed on top of Rafe's head, pinning her in place, all the time scraping her palm over the short, stubbly hair for comfort. Rafe licked Ashley's sensitive bundle of nerves, then blew on it. Ashley's moans began to escape as keening wails.

"You're driving me insane. Fuck me," she pleaded, pulling roughly at her own nipple and blindly letting her body follow every move Rafe desired from it. The rough friction of Rafe's fingers buried deep inside her and the constant worrying of her clitoris by a talented tongue caused an explosion to cascade through Ashley's body like no other had ever brought her. She let out a scream and came in a series of violent waves that burst through her like a volcanic eruption. Her body shook and pulsed and she spilled her pleasure all over Rafe's hand. Ashley lay stunned and shaken, her body twitching with shock waves. "My God, Rafe, what did you just do to me?" she managed to whisper, tears stinging her eyes, then rolling unchecked down her cheek.

Rafe looked decidedly pleased with herself. She gently removed her fingers from within Ashley and studied the thick moisture on them. "I'd say I fucked you senseless," she said smugly.

"And how do you come to that conclusion, Detective?" Ashley watched Rafe lick at her fingers. A groan rumbled from her chest at the erotic sight and her insides clenched at how sexy Rafe looked, flushed and sweaty from her exertion and self-satisfied as only a good lover should be.

"I have examined the evidence. It never lies." Rafe gently kissed Ashley's clitoris. The soft pressure made Ashley twitch again as a series of tingles shot through her from Rafe's intimate kiss.

"Come up here and hold me." Ashley pulled weakly at Rafe's shoulder. Rafe gathered Ashley in her arms and cradled her while Ashley tried to recover her senses. "You are amazing." She snuggled into Rafe's breast and breathed in deeply of her unique scent. *I've found my home at last in her arms*, she thought, burrowing in and rubbing her face against Rafe's warm skin. *I've found my One.* Her face pressed against Rafe's skin, Ashley could feel the soft tremors that made Rafe's body quiver beneath her. Recognizing unreleased passion, Ashley smiled to herself and shifted her head just enough to be able to rub her cheek over Rafe's right nipple. The answering catch in Rafe's breath told Ashley all she needed to know. She lifted her head to meet the dark eyes staring right back at her. Her strong features, austere in desire, took Ashley's breath away.

"You are so damn beautiful." Ashley breathed her words across Rafe's breast, flicking her tongue out to taste and tease.

"That should be my line." Rafe's voice was strained as Ashley's tongue ran over her nipple roughly.

Ashley took Rafe's reddened tip into her mouth. She sucked at the hard nub, then flicked at it with her tongue, loving the sound that was forced from Rafe's throat. Rafe's hands ran agitatedly through Ashley's hair, then clenched at her shoulders, urging her on. "Lie back, sweetheart," Ashley whispered and followed Rafe down. Once settled onto her side, Ashley continued her play across Rafe's breasts. They were smaller than hers, firm yet soft, with nipples thickening at every touch of Ashley's lips. She ran her fingernails across Rafe's chest, down the flat stomach, watching fine tremors erupt in their wake.

She made sure to brush carefully around the wound that stood out starkly on Rafe's otherwise perfect body. Ashley laid a kiss beside it. She moved again and settled herself between Rafe's legs, and both of them groaned as their mounds met. Rafe bumped against her, seeking further pressure. Ashley held back enough to drive Rafe crazy. She saw the light dawn in Rafe's eyes when she realized Ashley's intent was to tantalize.

"Don't you fucking tease me now," Rafe pleaded desperately.

Ashley just grinned as Rafe bucked her hips, aching to be touched. "I'm going to have you slowly but surely. I've been waiting forever to be in this position. I am not rushing it."

"It's only been days," Rafe said, reaching for Ashley only to have her hands pressed down by her sides.

"Seems like forever to me." Ashley kissed Rafe into silence with a slow, measured teasing of lips and tongue that had Rafe's mouth clinging to hers for every last touch.

"You're killing me." Rafe's voice was husky. Ashley loved how it sounded.

"You've had previous brushes with death. Believe me, this will be all pleasure." With feather-light touches Ashley kissed Rafe's face. She was fully aware she was driving Rafe to distraction by not rushing to take her. She could feel the body beside her taut and trembling in her need to come. She savored her power over her. Ashley slipped to Rafe's side again, her hand skimming once more over Rafe's tight nipples. The darkened tips thickened as Ashley flicked at them, then tugged.

"Fuck," Rafe gasped. "If you don't do something soon, I'm going to come on my own."

"Hold on, baby, I promise to make it worth your while." She brushed her hand through the soft hair framing Rafe's sex.

"Please, just—"

Shushing her with a kiss, Ashley slid a finger between the soft folds. She caressed her gently, then teased along lips and ruffled edges until her fingers were saturated with Rafe's juices. Her heady scent tugged at Ashley's senses; it made her want to bury her face in Rafe's desire. Instead, she dragged her fingertip across the top of Rafe's clitoris, and the answering groan Rafe released sent shivers of pleasure down Ashley's spine. Rafe buried her face in Ashley's shoulder, panting erratically against her skin.

"Please," she whispered against Ashley's flesh, "make me yours."

Ashley dipped her head to take Rafe's lips with her own. "You've been mine since the moment I laid eyes on you." She gently squeezed the hard clitoris between finger and thumb and watched as Rafe's head fell back. Eyes closed, mouth open, Rafe surrendered herself to Ashley.

"You're mine, Raphael, do you know that?" Ashley's thumb brushed over the turgid flesh and Rafe hissed out a strangled sound of agreement. "All mine, every part of you, heart and soul." Ashley pushed a finger inside Rafe and began to set up a rhythm inside that she echoed with every brush across Rafe's clitoris. She watched as a flush of red began to blossom across Rafe's chest and thrilled to the pleasure etched on her face as Ashley brought Rafe ever closer to orgasm.

I've been in the company of angels, and even that never moved me as much as seeing her face right at this moment as I make her come. Ashley's name was shouted hoarsely as Rafe's body wrung out every ounce of pleasure from Ashley's hands when she climaxed, then she curled into Ashley, trembling and shaking. Ashley cuddled her, spreading soft kisses in Rafe's hair. She slid her finger out, hearing Rafe's breath catch as she did so. Ashley left her hand between Rafe's legs, cupping her and letting her fingers soak in the hot passion Rafe had spent.

"You need to stop that unless you aim on setting me off again," Rafe said in Ashley's ear when her fingers started to explore once more.

"I can't stop touching you," Ashley said, trailing her fingers through the sticky wetness that covered Rafe's legs. She felt a sharp intake of breath brush against her throat as her finger brushed over Rafe's exposed clitoris. Rafe's hand stilled hers.

"The rest of the body is willing, but the clit says touch me again and I'll spontaneously combust." She gave Ashley a weak grin. Ashley removed her hand reluctantly. "I've never been taken so slowly with such gentle hands and yet come so damn hard." Rafe shifted and shivered. "I swear I'm still coming inside." She pressed Ashley's hand low on her stomach.

Ashley took the time to take in Rafe's lean body, committing to memory every scar and freckle. She felt Rafe's hand tighten on her own.

"Don't think I missed you using that damned name of mine."

Ashley smiled unrepentant. "I wanted you to have it said just once while someone made love to you and was worshiping your body."

Rafe grumbled at her. They were silent for a moment until Rafe asked, "Is this what soul mates do?"

"What? Make love until neither can think straight?" Ashley pulled back a little to look into Rafe's quiet face. "What, sweetheart?"

"Is it the soul mate thing that makes you never want anyone else to ever touch you again but that one person?"

"I think so," Ashley said. "Is that how you feel?"

"That's how I've felt from the moment you laid your hands on me outside my office. I was high on demon poison and all I could wish for was that you never took your hands away from my face."

"I wasn't supposed to touch you then, but your soul called to me."

Rafe's smile was wry. "It's very forward like that." She took a deep breath. "You know, we hardly know each other, and technically, we've only just met. This isn't how I normally act."

"Has *anything* been normal the past few days?" Ashley asked softly. "You and I were meant to be, Raphael Douglas, get used to it."

"Again with the name calling."

Ashley chuckled and relented. "I'll stop, but only because you called me Ash so beautifully as you came."

"That might be because I couldn't get all your name out in what little breath you left me with."

"It was wonderful and sexy and I hope to hear it more from your lips as I bring you pleasure. Though I think next time I want to take you with my mouth." Rafe shuddered under her. Ashley's own heart started to pound a little harder.

"You can't just say things like that." Rafe groaned at her words, her body pressing into Ashley's. She swore under her breath. "Fuck."

With a seductive grin, Ashley pounced. "Why, Detective Douglas, I thought you'd never ask." Her kiss ended any further response, and soon only the sounds of soft moans filled the bedroom.

CHAPTER TWENTY-TWO

Sometime during the time they'd actually slept, Rafe had ended up spooned along Ashley's back, as close as she could be, savoring her warmth. She woke up slowly, and Rafe could just about make out the numbers on her clock. She was surprised it was barely after midnight. She stretched her body a little, enjoying the aches that came from their lovemaking. She listened for a moment to Ashley's soft breathing. *She's everything I would have wished for had I known I needed it. God, are we moving too fast? I'd hate to lose her because we have rushed into things.* She pressed her nose to Ashley's neck and breathed in her scent. *I don't think I could bear to lose her. But damn her and her talk of soul mates, because now I can't think straight.*

"Stop thinking," Ashley's voice murmured sleepily from beside her.

Rafe stilled. *Christ, can she read my mind now?* Ashley reached back to caress her leg, and instantly, Rafe wanted her again. Pushing all thought aside, she kissed at Ashley's nape, then began to nudge her over onto her front so she could explore further. She rained kisses down Ashley's back, and in the pale light of the bedside lamp she caught sight of curious markings under her hands. Rafe's eyes widened as she took in the two huge tattoos emblazoned on Ashley's back.

"Fuck me," she said.

Ashley shifted a little to look over her shoulder. "I was all set to, but it appears you have gotten distracted by my artwork." She lay back down on her front, letting Rafe have a proper view of the designs on her back. "Now, had you been up to date with your dating etiquette, you'd have known to ask if I had any piercings or body art."

Rafe couldn't take her eyes off the tattoo. "That's one huge tattoo, Ash." She ran her finger gently over the edge of one marking. "Two, to be correct, I guess."

"Do you hate it?" Ashley's voice was hushed.

As she examined the artwork on Ashley's back, Rafe reached out to touch again and explore it. She traced the detail from each shoulder down to the start of Ashley's hips. "This is *just* a tattoo, isn't it? This isn't another secret of yours only I can see, right?" She was heartened by Ashley's soft chuckle.

"You're safe, it's just a tattoo. I got an amazing artist who worked on it for me." She cast a glance over her shoulder again. "What are you thinking, Rafe? I can't quite read your expression."

Sitting cross-legged beside her on the bed, Rafe shook her head. "I'm overwhelmed by the sheer beauty of the artwork and the fine detail, but I have to admit, I'm surprised as hell to see this on your body."

"You're surprised I have a tattoo?"

"I'm surprised you have two life-sized angel wings decorating your back that look so damn realistic I'm surprised they can't spread out and fly." She marveled at the tiny, intricate work that made up each feather. "This must have taken hours of work. The attention to detail is striking. They look *real*."

"I hate to disappoint you, but they're not, and I can't glamour them to life either. I wanted the symbolism. I'm the child of a demon yet am guided through life by an angel. I chose sides, Rafe. And though I'll never possess the real things, when I was eighteen, I decided I wanted the image marking my skin. It seems silly now, but I don't regret doing it."

Rafe caressed Ashley's naked back. She almost expected to feel the soft down of feathers as she touched each folded wing. The tattoos were incredibly lifelike with the stark white of the feathers shaded in soft grays and blacks. Rafe was tempted to lean in and blow on them just to see if the feathers ruffled from her breath. She was stunned by their beauty and realism.

"They suit you," she said finally, straddling Ashley's hips and kneading at her muscles. She started at Ashley's shoulders, rubbing her nape, then worked her way lower. She laid kisses along Ashley's spine, edging down until she could rub herself on Ashley's butt cheek. Ashley groaned as she felt Rafe move.

"Can you feel me?" Rafe rocked her hips, feeling her lips open and her clitoris nudge against Ashley's fleshy buttock.

"You're getting wet again," Ashley groaned, raising her butt to let Rafe ride.

"You do that to me." Rafe closed her eyes for a moment and took her own pleasure until the pressure became too urgent for her to hold in.

"Come on me," Ashley begged, arching her back to try to keep Rafe in place.

"I want to touch you." Rafe ran her hands up Ashley's spine. "Maybe ruffle these feathers of yours."

Laughing, Ashley turned and Rafe moved so they lay face-to-face. Ashley reached between Rafe's legs and spread her open, seeking where Rafe ached for her. Overwhelmed by sensation, Rafe clung to her, wrapping her arms around her and grabbing at Ashley's back. She could feel the wings beneath her palms and she held on tight as Ashley moved inside her. Rafe didn't need any more stimulation. She came with a shout and shuddered in Ashley's arms.

"Too damn quick," she complained, trying to get her breath back as she pulsed around Ashley's fingers.

"First you complain I tease you, now it's too fast." Ashley kissed Rafe soundly. "Guess we're just going to have to keep doing this until you're happy."

Rafe looked deep into Ashley's eyes. "It might take us forever to get everything perfect."

"I can do forever with you." Ashley brushed playfully at Rafe's hair. "Are you really not turned off by my angel wings?"

"They're beautiful like you are and one hell of a surprise, *exactly* like you are." Rafe planted a kiss on Ashley's smiling lips. "At least the only things you have pierced are your ears, so I'm grateful for small mercies."

"I know the wings aren't something a private investigator usually sports."

"I wouldn't know. You are the first PI I've had the pleasure of seeing naked."

"Met many pleasurable PIs, have you?" A touch of jealousy laced Ashley's tone.

"Not many, no. And only the one who's made me want to bare my own soul back to her."

"Rafe, you possess a beautiful soul."

"I think I could easily fall in love with you." She couldn't censure the words as they spilled from her lips. She liked how they sounded and loved how they made her feel. Unable to hold back any longer, Rafe had to give it voice, even though part of her felt crazy for feeling so much so soon. She watched sheer pleasure light up Ashley's face. The kiss she received made it worthwhile placing her heart on the line.

"I could fall in love with you too, Detective." Ashley spread Rafe's hand over her heart. "Can you feel that? It beats for you alone." She kissed Rafe again tenderly. "Show me how much you could love me."

Without hesitation, Rafe complied. She lowered her head to take Ashley's nipple between her lips when a loud ringing came from somewhere on the floor.

"Damn it all to hell! That's my phone." Ashley reluctantly peeled herself out of Rafe's arms and got out of bed. She searched through the jumbled mass of clothing littering the floor until she found the phone and answered it. Rafe knew by the look on her face it wasn't good news.

"Okay, we're on it." She snapped her phone closed then gathered up their clothing and threw it on the bed. "Get dressed, Detective. We have somewhere to be."

"We've run out of time, haven't we?" Rafe asked, pulling on her pants and threading her belt through the loops.

Nodding, Ashley handed her the gun from the bedside table. "That was Eli. We have another body."

CHAPTER TWENTY-THREE

The first thing Rafe noticed was that the location of this murder scene was entirely different than the previous three. It wasn't a run-down alley. It was a community garden with a paved area leading a trail through the many plants and small trees.

"Welcome to Eden," Ashley said as they walked to the address Eli had supplied them. Rafe had been instructed to park her car a few blocks away and for them to reach the murder scene by foot. She'd never walked so fast to get somewhere or kept to the shadows to not be seen.

"Eden?"

"That's the project's name, the Garden of Eden."

"Do you think the killer picked that on purpose?"

"Who knows what's going through this madman's mind?" Ashley directed Rafe to the apartment block overlooking the gardens, and they climbed up the fire escape. They passed darkened windows where the occupants slept inside, blissfully unaware of what lay outside their homes. Ashley pulled out her camera from her jacket.

"I didn't realize you carried that with you," Rafe said just above a whisper.

"I take it everywhere with me. I have to be prepared for every eventuality. I never thought to use it tonight. I could have had some marvelous candid shots of you to look at."

Rafe sniffed pointedly. "You don't need photos. We both still reek of sex."

Ashley lifted a hand to her face and breathed in deeply. "Yes, we do. Good thing I carry wet wipes on me too, just in case. Though not usually to wipe my lover's scent off." She eased up another few steps and stopped. "There she is." She leaned over the railing and Rafe instinctively held on to her to steady her. Looking down into the garden, Rafe could see a faint shadow in the darkness. Only solar-powered lights were lit among the plants, diffusing the area with little light. The moon played hide-and-seek with the clouds, so visibility was low. The street lamp glow didn't stretch far enough inside the garden to light where the woman lay dead. The almost blinding flash from Ashley's camera lit up the ground, and in that split second, Rafe could see the ruined body of yet another woman below.

Ashley held out her camera so Rafe could see the picture she had taken. "He laid her on pavement this time, a better canvas for him to paint his message on." Rafe was amazed by how accurate Blythe's input had been.

Ashley looked at the screen with her. Rafe knew by the soft exclamation beside her that Ashley had recognized what the killer had done. Only Rafe could say it out loud.

"She's been given wings."

❖

Rafe reached into her jacket for her cell phone.

"What are you doing?" Ashley asked, grabbing Rafe's arm to stall her movements.

"I'm calling Dean. He needs to get the crime scene guys down here before we lose any evidence to the night."

"You can't make that call, Rafe," Ashley said. "It has to be from an anonymous source. They can't ever link this back to either you or me." She patted Rafe's hand. "Put the phone away for now. We need to do something else."

Grumbling, Rafe did as she was asked, but Ashley could tell she wasn't happy with it. "Look around, please," Ashley said, searching the garden in the darkness.

"Care to let me in on what I'm looking for in the dark?" Rafe asked.

"Demon light," Ashley whispered. "We got here pretty damn

fast. Usually the bodies aren't discovered by anyone else until a little later. You need to check like I've had to every time I've come onto a scene."

"Search for the hiding demon in case he's still here getting his jollies at the scene." Rafe nodded once, looking into the night with a more purposeful air. "But if he's human, he won't be lit up like a Christmas tree, will he?"

"No, but that doesn't mean we can't look for him. It just means we have to be extra careful stepping from the fire escape and entering the kill site. If the killer is still in the area, we're as vulnerable as this woman was."

"I can't believe you've been at the crime scenes on your own." Rafe slipped her gun from its holster and kept it by her side. "That's just plain dangerous."

Ashley bit back a smile at the growing anger in Rafe's voice. She knew it was the cop talking as well as the lover. "I'm never truly alone, Rafe," she said.

"Eli comes with you?"

"Rest assured he is always watching over me and ready to lend a hand should I need him."

"And he could do what if you were attacked? Beat them to death with his wings?"

Ashley slapped at Rafe's stomach. "Do you know nothing of the weapons angels possess, *Raphael*?" She ignored Rafe's growl at her use of her full name. "You have the name of an angel and still have no clue. Angels are not defenseless beings of light. They are equipped with the Weapons of Truth."

"Weapons of Truth?" Rafe said. "I damn well want to know that if my girl is out sniffing around the body of a recent murder, she's protected by something more than just truth, justice, and the American way."

"Trust me, Rafe, Eli's more than ready to keep me safe."

"Is he here now?" Rafe scanned about her. "I can't see his white light."

"He's here, just not in a physical form or any you can see." Ashley knew exactly where he was. She could feel his presence near. She could always sense where he was.

"I need to go down into the garden. This woman needs me to find her killer." Rafe began edging toward the stairs.

"Go take a look, Detective, but you can't linger. You're going to need your people here to do their job."

Rafe led their way back down the fire escape. Ashley loved that for all her haste, Rafe was still thoughtful enough to guide Ashley's way down. Her gallantry didn't go unnoticed by Ashley and it just made her love her more.

The garden gate had been left open, as if inviting everyone in to witness the cruelty laid out inside. Rafe turned on the small flashlight she'd brought from her car. She let it play over the ground, marking a path where she and Ashley could step without contaminating the scene. They both looked at the body, and for a long moment neither spoke.

"Goddamn him. She's been killed exactly the same way as the others." Rafe knelt and shone her flashlight on the woman's face. "Christ," she said as the contorted face was caught in the harsh beam. "Her throat is cut. And I'd wager from the state of her clothing, her back has been ripped to shreds." Rafe took a step aside and waved Ashley forward. "Take your pictures, Sparky, then let's get out of here and start the investigation properly."

Ashley picked her way around the body, taking her photographs as swiftly as possible, recognizing the familiar pose once again filling her viewfinder. *How many more?* She wondered, deliberately trying not to look in the haunted eyes of the dead woman, knowing the terror left in place there.

"Ashley?"

Rafe's voice was soft in the silence. Ashley looked at her as she took her last snap.

"Are we looking for an *angel* killer here?"

Ashley glanced at the body on the ground as if seeing it with new eyes. "These women aren't angels, Rafe. They're entirely human."

"Are you sure?"

"I'm certain."

"I've seen it for myself. You have angels that hunt down demons. What if you've got a rogue element in the demon class who's taken it upon himself to even the score?"

Ashley considered this. She made certain Rafe was all done, at least until she could return in her official capacity. Then with a quick scan of the area, she had Rafe lead them back out of the garden. Once satisfied they were far enough away from the scene, she made a call.

"Have it called in, Eli." She ended the call and slipped her arm around Rafe's waist, grateful for Rafe pulling her in even closer. Ashley needed the physical reassurance; it had been desperately missing at all the other crime scenes she'd walked away from alone. She relished Rafe's presence now in every sense of the word. "This woman wasn't an angel and neither were the ones who died before her. His drawing wings in their blood isn't to show what they were."

Rafe stopped in her tracks. "What if it was to point out what they *weren't?*"

Iced blood ran through Ashley's veins at Rafe's hesitant question. "If you're right, then we really are looking for a demon. And one, it seems, whose taste for killing humans has escalated from weeks to just days. He's on a rampage."

❖

Dean hurried to Rafe's side the second she stepped from her car. He crowded her, keeping her hidden from the other officers who were starting to cordon off the area.

"Did Ashley get a call for this one too?" He gestured to the scene behind him.

"Yes, we got here just after one this morning."

"She called you?"

Rafe hesitated, not sure how much she wanted to reveal to him. She was still coming to terms herself with a relationship that had sprung out of nowhere and was developing at the speed of light. "Yes, I tagged along."

"Did you see anything?" Dean led her toward the murder site.

"Only what he wanted us to see." Rafe could see a small crowd already beginning to form. "Don't these people have anywhere better to be at this time of night?" She wished she was back in the comfort of her own bed with Ashley curled up beside her. She rubbed at her cold nose and caught the acrid scent of the lemon that had soaked the wet wipe Ashley had laughingly wiped her hands and face with. *Can't have*

everyone know what you were pulled away from, can we, Detective?
She had teased Rafe before kissing her softly and heading back to her
own apartment in a taxi.

"Didn't being on the scene so fresh after the kill give you the
chance to see anything?"

"His blood patterns form wings when painted on the right
surface."

"Shit," Dean exclaimed. "For real?"

Rafe cocked her head to the neighboring apartment. "From up
there you can't miss it. Down here we need to keep the foot patrol to
a minimum. I don't want the evidence disturbed." She caught sight of
Crime Scene Photographer Jim Pope getting out of his team's van. "Get
Pope to go up high. I want everyone to see what I saw." She waited
while her orders were carried out.

"Does it mean we've got a religious nut on our hands after all?"
Dean asked, returning with latex gloves and booties for the scene.

"He's a freak. I don't care what he wraps it up in." Rafe was
pleased to see only one person beside the body. Dr. Alan nodded to her
as she walked toward him.

"This killer is steadfast in his pattern, Detective. You've got to
give him credit for that."

"Show me what we've got, then we can get Pope to take her
picture. I want her either covered or removed by the time the kids in
that apartment block start waking up." She knelt beside the doctor, who
got down on one knee to lift up the long blond hair that was draped over
the massive wound in the dead woman's throat.

"It's the same initial attack, deep enough to incapacitate but not
enough to kill outright. It would appear he likes his ladies alive, at least
for a little while." He pointed to the woman's face. "Contorted in terror
again. I swear I'll see these women's faces in my nightmares for years
to come. To freeze them like that in the last seconds of their life. What
the hell do they see?"

Rafe kept quiet. She'd seen a man transform into a demon before
her very own eyes. *Would it have been written as clearly on my face too
if he'd killed me?* "Whatever they saw, I pray we never get to witness
it."

Dr. Alan ushered Rafe and Dean around the body. Rafe stopped him. "Don't step anywhere in the blood."

"That's a mighty big 'keep off' area," he said.

"I need the crime scene photographer to get a shot from above. I want to preserve the blood pattern enough before everyone has to walk through it to get this woman out of here."

Dr. Alan squinted at the blood spread high and around the body. "There something about the blood I should be seeing?"

"I believe it's part of his M.O. that he couldn't properly display in the alleys previous. But here, on the paved stones, it might yield some clues."

"What do you see here, Rafe?"

"He's painting wings with their blood, Doc. I need it undisturbed to prove it."

His eyes shot back to the blood pool. He shifted a few steps, stood back, and let out a gasp. "Damn, I can see it myself. Crudely done, but then blood isn't really the perfect medium in which to paint. What have we got here, Rafe?"

"Hopefully, answers this time. Four bodies are four too many." She walked around the woman's feet and watched closely as Dr. Alan eased the body up to reveal the butchered back.

"No doubt whatsoever in my mind this is the same killer," he said, laying the body back down at Rafe's nod.

She stood and waved a hand in the direction of the fire escapes "Doc, step back from the body. Pope needs to get a few aerial shots before he can get down to the scene." The bright flashes of the professional camera lit up the darkness. The smell of fresh blood permeated the air, and Rafe swallowed hard against the bile rising in her throat.

"Once the body has been transported, you and I are walking the scene," she told Dean. "Only us. Keep the other guys back for now. I don't want twenty pairs of feet trampling through this garden until we've cleared the area."

"That will piss the CSI team off. What are we looking for exactly?"

"A discarded weapon, a swatch of cloth, a footprint, even a drop of blood left away from the kill zone." Rafe blinked her eyes against the white lights seared into her retinas from the camera's constant flashing. "I want to check everywhere just in case he left something this time."

"Are we looking for occult stuff? Because, to be honest, we'd probably need the PI's eyes to spot stuff like that."

"Ms. Scott didn't see anything obvious while we were here before. I think the drawing of bloodied wings scrawled around the body gave us all we needed to know."

"And that is?"

"He's not going to stop if he thinks he's helping these women to *ascend* to a better place by giving them wings to aid on their journey."

"And he's accelerated his timeline. It's only been a few days since his last murder."

"He's eluding us every time, Dean, but tonight he left us more to his signature. That has to mean something."

"The wings?" Dean shoved his hands deep into his pockets. "I'd have settled for his name and address scribbled beside the art he's trying to portray."

"Let's hope this added detail is what leads us to him." Rafe waited as Jim Pope stepped into the crime scene and then she waved him on to start photographing the body.

"Another family to face," Dean murmured. "I hate doing that. I'd rather sit by the body all day than have to face their grieving loved ones."

Rafe agreed. She hoped they could identify this woman to spare the family any more trauma on top of what they were going to endure. The cool night air made her shiver and she tugged up her collar against the chill. She pulled her hat even further down over her ears and stood watching the painstaking process of everything being photographed and documented. When Pope was finished, he approached Rafe and Dean.

"Detective Douglas, why did you have me go up the fire escape?" he asked, fiddling with his camera lens.

"You saw her from up there; why do you think?" Rafe replied.

"The wings. I don't recall wings at the other murders. Damn, I wish I'd have thought to go above at those."

"The alley ground didn't exactly let him spread the blood how he wanted it to be seen. What we saw as scuffed areas was him trying to spread the blood out. We know better now," Dean said.

"My mother is very religious," Pope said, his eyes drifting back toward the body as Dr. Alan's men were carefully lifting her up and zipping the black bag shut. The harsh sound echoed through the garden. "She believes there are such things as angels."

Rafe watched the body be removed from the garden. *Another daughter of Eve removed from the Garden of Eden.* "Your mother is a wise woman, Pope. I guess we all need to believe in something." She gestured to the now empty space soaked in blood. "I know it's a gruesome request, but can you take some photos of the blood, please? Anything to show the pattern of the wings." He hastened to do her bidding.

"You ready to take that walk in the garden, Rafe?" Dean had borrowed a flashlight from one of the officers. He switched its bright beam on and shone it on the ground. "Do you really expect to find anything more than what we've found at the previous scenes?"

"I live in hope." Rafe wished she *felt* as confident. "I know we're chasing shadows here."

"There's a strange smell here. It's the damnedest thing," Dean said after a few steps. "Can you smell anything?"

Rafe sniffed at the air and shook her head. "What exactly are you smelling?"

"I swear I can smell lemons."

Rafe prayed her face didn't give her away. "Must be one of the bushes they have planted here." She unobtrusively took a step away from him.

"Probably. It's gone now." Dean shone his flashlight elsewhere.

I may never have sex again, Rafe thought, then thought better of it. *New rule of detective work: wash before leaving for a crime scene to remove all and any incriminating evidence.*

CHAPTER TWENTY-FOUR

It was daylight before Rafe and Dean returned to the Chicago Police Department. Alona ushered them toward the coffee and baked goodies left on a desk.

"You are a goddess," Dean said, gathering up three doughnuts in one hand and gulping down mouthfuls of his drink. Rafe headed straight to her desk.

"I didn't do anything. These goodies arrived three minutes before you probably pulled up in the parking lot." She brought up the photographs from the latest scene.

Frowning, Dean stared at the photos over the rim of his coffee cup. "How'd you get those so fast?"

Ashley walked into the office.

"Never mind," he muttered and greeted her. "Ms. Scott."

"Detective Jackson." Ashley picked up a coffee and held it out to Rafe. "Drink while you have a moment to breathe."

Rafe couldn't take her eyes off her. Ashley looked bright and well rested and surprisingly chipper. In comparison, Rafe felt like shit. She was bone-numbingly tired, she ached in curious places, and her eyes felt full of grit. She tugged her hat off and tossed it aside. She accepted the coffee gratefully and sipped it much slower than she wanted to.

"So you got a call last night saying that our killer had struck again?" Dean asked as he crammed a whole doughnut into his mouth.

Ashley nodded. "Please don't choke on that. There's plenty more left."

Rafe was already distracted by the photographs up on the screen.

She felt a hand tug at her jacket and she absently took it off, switching her coffee cup between hands and laying the jacket over her chair. Not once did her eyes leave the photos. Ashley's warm body brushed against her side, not too close to cause the other occupants in the room to wonder, but close enough for Rafe to feel the weight of a breast. "I'd say it's pretty clear what he's drawing in the blood from these photos." Alona traced the arching shapes with her finger. "Is he sending them to heaven, do you think?"

"I don't know what he's doing, but he left this woman in the usual state." Rafe asked Alona to bring up a street map alongside the photos. "The last three bodies were all in this area, left in alleys. Each of those killings gave us a gap of two weeks between them, regular as clockwork. Until last night. This time, he killed way over here." She circled an area on the map. "He killed earlier than his usual timeframe and he switched venue. But he got to leave behind what he'd been trying to show us from killing number one."

"Wonder what the trigger was that tripped his switch to bring this murder forward?" Dean polished off the last bit of his final doughnut at a more measured pace. "Do you think he chose the Garden of Eden as a punch line for his sick joke with the angel wings?"

Rafe wasn't certain. She studied the map, wondering what the geographical profile would make of it. "Three over here, one over here. This garden hasn't had much fanfare being built. It's just another in the city's improvement drive. The mayor thinks gardens will brighten up the areas and give people a place to go. This one is still being completed, so what does it mean to our killer? What's its importance to *him*? Is it the name? The location? Was it just an opportunistic moment as another blonde walked past him?"

Out of sight of her colleagues' eyes, Rafe brushed her hand over Ashley's and they linked fingers briefly. Her fatigue lessened at the touch of Ashley's skin on her own. She wished the caffeine would kick in soon, as lack of sleep was catching up with her. "God, I'll be glad when I'm over this damn beating." She spoke aloud and was surprised by the looks she got. She shrugged. "I'm tired of feeling like I'm only functioning at half-speed. It's driving me crazy."

Ashley steered her into a chair. "Don't worry, Samson," she said as she patted Rafe's head. "Your strength will return when your hair grows back."

Narrowing her eyes at her, Rafe huffed. She switched topics. "Dean, how long will it be before Doc Alan will have the autopsy written up, do you think?"

"Want me to go check on his progress?" he asked.

"Just don't make it look like I sent you to hurry him along."

"He knows you too well for me to get away with that." He picked up another coffee and left the office.

Alona returned to her computer screens. "Rafe, something came up this morning in the data stream. I'm not sure how much use it will be to you, but it's to do with the search you asked me to do. The one for incidents prior to the killings?"

Rafe wheeled her chair over. "What do you have?"

"I did as you requested, looked for incidents in and around our area. Then I widened the search. I thought I might as well put the data streams to the test, right? Well, four months before the first killing there were reports of women being stopped on the street by a man."

Ashley rested against the edge of Alona's desk to listen in.

"They said he grabbed them, stared at them for the longest time, then let them go. The general consensus was he was seriously creepy." She brought up a case file on the screen. "But he didn't stop there. He started restraining the next women, pinning them against walls and brandishing a knife. Some he roughed up more, cut their clothing, bruising their arms as he held them."

"Did they find out why?" Ashley asked, moving to look over Alona's shoulder.

"No, but the description of the women he stopped was all the same. They were all blondes. Enough of them filed complaints about it, and one even followed him home and got his address. The police paid him a visit to warn him off terrorizing the neighborhood. In the file it says his excuse was mistaken identity, he thought these women were the woman who'd wronged him. He said something about how she stole everything that was his. The cops who interviewed him said he was very convincing. They even offered to help him find the woman he was after so it could be sorted out legally."

"I wonder if he's still continuing in that trend. It could be worth checking out, if only to rule him out." Rafe watched the screen as Alona scrolled down it.

"I've got an address for him here in Chicago."

Rafe sat up straight in her chair. "Give me his name."

"Lucas Thorpe."

Ashley's body reacted as if she'd been shocked. Rafe gave her a puzzled look until the name sank in and she remembered. Lucas Thorpe, Ashley's half brother, born of demon parentage. Supposedly dead and buried.

"I need to go." Ashley hastily began gathering up her things.

"Give me the address, Alona." Rafe watched Ashley's frantic scrabbling for her jacket. She took the printouts from Alona and shoved them into Ashley's hands. "You're with me. Let's go pay this man a visit, shall we?"

"Shouldn't Dean go with you?" Alona said.

Rafe pulled on her jacket. "I doubt this will pan out to be much. Tell him I'll be back soon enough and we can go over the autopsy report together." She steered Ashley out of the office and toward the elevator.

Ashley began to speak. "Rafe…"

"Not here," Rafe said as they rode the elevator down in silence.

❖

Ashley sat stunned in the passenger seat of Rafe's car. She had no recollection of how she had even gotten to the vehicle in the first place; her mind was a blur. They hadn't left the parking lot, and Rafe had been unusually quiet reading over the reports.

"My brother's supposed to be in Boston, in their family plot, buried beside his mother," Ashley finally spoke. She willed her brain to remember the long-forgotten details of a family she'd had little contact with growing up and none at all since she'd moved away.

Rafe riffled through the pages. "It might not be him."

Ashley gawped at her. "You can't honestly believe that? The only Lucas Thorpe I know of is the son of a demon. He'd fit your profile."

"My profile fits a man who is your brother's age but is also a butcher or someone who knows how to handle a knife. It's *your* profile of these cases that says I should be looking for a demon." She looked over at Ashley. "Just because he's your father's son doesn't make him the bad guy. You're wonderful breathing proof of that fact, sweetheart."

"What if it is him? Alive and kicking and *killing*?"

"And what if it isn't?" Rafe took Ashley's hand in hers. "I didn't pull Dean in on this. If this is your half brother then we'll deal with the fallout if and when it comes. Your names aren't the same. You can't be linked with him unless someone digs deep and knows your father. I need you to come with me."

"I haven't seen him for years," Ashley said. "I couldn't pick him out of a lineup; it's been so long, and he was just a little boy when I last saw him."

"He's got a place on Washington Road."

Ashley's brain kicked in and she frowned. "Washington Road? That's only a few blocks east of last night's scene. We passed it driving to the scene this morning." She buried her head in her hands. "Tell me this is not happening." Her stomach churned at the realization and implications that suddenly opened up for these cases if indeed her half brother was involved.

"Let's discount him before you find him guilty."

"And what if he is guilty?"

"Then we bring him to justice."

Ashley laughed hollowly. "That's just it, Rafe. Whose justice? Yours or *mine*?" She held in the terrible wail that tore at her chest as she realized her true role in this case. *Damn you, Eli. Damn you to hell. You knew he was alive, you had to know. And you led me blindly along while he just kept on killing.* The sob tore out of her throat unbidden and she felt Rafe's arms wrap around her and hold her. She buried her face in Rafe's jacket, racking sobs escaping her in painful gasps.

"It could all be a coincidence," Rafe soothed her. "We just have to be sure."

Ashley nodded against her, listening to the steady rhythm of Rafe's heart, feeling the brush of Rafe's hand through her hair. "What if it is him? What does that mean for *us*?"

"It won't change how I feel about you. It won't alter the fact that I love you."

Ashley's chest hitched as another sob rattled through her at Rafe's gentle words.

"You said we were soul mates. I believe that is supposed to be for life," Rafe said.

"And beyond that?"

"There's nothing beyond that for me unless I have you beside me."

Ashley's heart broke at the sincerity in Rafe's voice. "What happened to my big bad detective who didn't believe in such things?"

"She's laid her badge aside for a moment to let the woman who loves you speak."

"I love you so much," Ashley whispered.

"And I love you. We'll leave only when you're ready."

"Can we just stay like this for a minute longer?" She tightened her grip around Rafe's waist.

"You can stay right here in my arms for as long as you like." Rafe laid her cheek on Ashley's hair.

"You should be going to interrogate this suspect, not having to hold me while I fall apart."

"He can wait for a moment. You need to know that I will always put you first when I can."

"God, Rafe, what did I ever do before you came into my life? Someone who sees me and isn't frightened by me or what I am. You've banished the darkness and the loneliness from my life. Soul mate or not, I'm never letting you go." She pulled away but leaned up to place a tremulous kiss on Rafe's lips. "Let me fix my face and then we can leave."

Rafe watched her silently. Ashley was intrigued by the lack of impatience she usually associated with her and which normally sent Rafe rushing into things unheeded. "You're remarkably patient for someone who might have found their killer."

"I'm waiting on you. Yes, I want to go grab this guy. Yes, I want to beat the truth out of him. Yes, it is seriously driving me seriously fucking insane just sitting here when I really just want to put the car in drive and peel out of the lot. But I'm doing it for you. We'll go when you are ready to face him because I think this is going to be harder for you than it ever will be for me if it does turn out to be your supposedly dead brother."

"Who made you so wonderful?" Ashley caressed Rafe's cheek and held her breath when Rafe laid a kiss in her palm.

"Ask your angel friend. I'm sure he knows more about it than I do."

I'm sure he knows more than he ever let on. Ashley resisted the urge to call Eli forth because at this moment she didn't know if she wanted to question him or rip his wings off. *Please let my half brother be somewhere else today, anywhere but at this address that's home to a possible murderer. I'd even wish him to be six foot under if it meant it wasn't his cruel signature being scrawled in Chicago's alleys.*

"You might want to fasten yourself in," Rafe said as she started the engine.

Ashley didn't begrudge her the screeching of rubber as Rafe reversed the car out of her space and shot them out of the lot. The flashing light in the windshield provided a steady rhythm for Ashley to watch as they drove through the busy morning traffic.

"You going to call Eli?" Rafe asked.

"No, I really don't want him involved at the moment." Ashley took a deep breath, and for the first time in a long time, couldn't feel the presence of the guardian who watched over her in life.

CHAPTER TWENTY-FIVE

Ashley stayed belted in long after Rafe had pulled up outside the duplex listed as the Thorpes' residence. *I really don't want to do this.*

"Ready?" Rafe unfastened her jacket and removed her gun from its holster.

Ashley stared at it. "Do you really need that?"

"Four murders say I might. Just stay behind me, okay?"

"I'll just follow your lead."

"If he starts growing horns, I'm deferring to your expertise, and whether you have a problem with Eli or not, I'd be happier to know he was backup for us." She got out of the car and waited until Ashley joined her.

Casting an eye up and down the street, Ashley couldn't see any sign of anything remotely demonic. "The street is clear."

"Glad to hear it. Let's go see if he's in." Rafe led the way up the cracked pavement and opened the screen door. Ashley winced as the squeal of its hinges set her teeth on edge.

Why do I suddenly feel frightened? I've faced demons before; what makes this one so scary? If it is my half brother then surely I shouldn't feel so apprehensive. We're family. She chewed on her lip while Rafe banged on the door. *It's bad enough being linked to a cast-out angel, but a killer was something my father never was. Oh please, don't let this be little Lucas.*

An angry voice shouted from inside. "I'm coming, I'm coming! Quit your banging!"

Rafe looked over her shoulder at Ashley. "He has his dead mother here with him?"

The door opened fractionally and a red-rimmed eye appeared in the crack. "What do you want? I ain't buying anything." The voice was scratchy and gruff. Ashley recognized it as belonging to Marion Thorpe, her father's last mistress.

Rafe held up her badge. "Detective Douglas, ma'am. I'm looking for Lucas Thorpe."

"What's he done now?" Marion looked suspiciously at Rafe, then opened the door a touch wider.

"Is he here?"

"No."

"Do you know when he's expected to return?"

The door opened even wider. "No, I don't because the little bastard never tells me anything. He just leaves me alone for hours at a time and expects me to cope." She stepped out onto the porch and looked Rafe up and down. "Looks like someone beat the shit out of you." She looked behind Rafe and shock was clear on her face. "Oh my God," she gasped. "Ashley?"

Whatever hope Ashley had of this being unconnected to her had vanished the second Marion opened the door reeking of whiskey and cigarettes. She'd aged but was still recognizable as the woman who didn't want Ashley as any part of her family.

"Marion," Ashley acknowledged her. "I was told you and Lucas were dead."

Marion laughed harshly. "I might as well been. I swear that bastard son of mine aimed for that other car on purpose and slammed his truck into it. How we got out alive I'll never know. Lucas dragged me out of there before the whole mess just blew up before us. I read reports that everyone died in the crash and there wasn't much left of the bodies to be identified. But I'm still breathing, girl. Bet that just about has ruined your day, hasn't it?" She smiled unpleasantly and revealed smoke-stained teeth. "Now what the fuck brings you to my doorstep?"

Ashley clenched her teeth to stop from responding in the same tone as Marion. *Still as charming as ever, I see.* "Where's Lucas?"

"Well, he's not here. And what do you care? Are you police too?"

"I'm a private investigator."

"Same difference," Marion spat. She glared at Rafe again. "You going to put that gun away or are you going to shoot me with it?"

The corner of Rafe's mouth twitched as she obviously considered her options. She holstered the weapon but left her coat open.

"May we come in?" Rafe brushed past Marion and stepped inside the house.

"Like I could stop you anyway." She limped back to her chair, sat down with a thump, and reached for another cigarette.

Rafe was checking out the various doors that led from the living area. "I need to check the other rooms to make sure they're empty." She gave Marion a look. She was waved away.

"Go ahead. Knock yourself out. Just don't steal anything."

Ashley didn't know where to look. She desperately wanted to trail after Rafe and get out of the sight of Marion, who was staring holes through her with those penetrating hate-filled eyes of hers.

"You've still got your father's eyes," Marion said.

"They're not something I could grow out of."

"When I saw you, I thought you'd come after him. But then you'd know more about where he is than I would, wouldn't you? He always kept you close. Any time he spent with us he was only half there. You were always on his mind."

"You had him more than I did growing up, Marion. He left me on my own. I was a child."

"I had a child too!"

"And you made it very clear you didn't want another one in the way."

"He needed to be a proper father to his son. He couldn't do that with another kid in the way."

"I was his firstborn."

"Your mother was gone. He was *mine*." Forcefully stubbing out her half-smoked cigarette, Marion immediately shook out another from her packet. "So where is the bastard? Did he find some other woman to fuck around with once he'd left my bed?"

Ashley frowned. "You think Dad *left* you?"

"He just up and went and never came back. Broke my Lucas's heart, and what was I supposed to tell him? That his daddy's a cheating demon who can't keep it in his pants?"

"Didn't Dad tell you what was going to happen to him?" Ashley couldn't believe Marion didn't know the truth. *No wonder she's so bitter.*

"He left me for someone else. That much I gathered."

"Surely he explained that he could be captured and banished?" She was surprised when Marion shook her head.

"Banished? Banished where?"

"Dad was banished years ago to hell for daring to come to earth and take on human form."

Marion took a long drag from her cigarette. "So he didn't leave me for some slut?"

"No, he's in hell for all eternity because he fell from grace."

"I'll give him hell when I catch up with him! Bastard left me with his damn kid to raise all on my own."

Rafe called Ashley's name from another room. "I think you might want to come see this."

Ashley hastily located which room Rafe was in and saw immediately what she had found. Hanging on the wall of what was undoubtedly Lucas Thorpe's bedroom was a painting. A woman adorned with huge white wings lay naked on the ground. Beneath her raged hell in vibrant reds and blacks, demons grabbing for her feet. Her one arm was stretched out above her as she reached toward the heavens. A beam of light lit up her blond hair like a halo as she pleaded for entry.

"Dad painted it," Ashley said. "I knew I recognized the damn pose." She clenched her fists to stop herself from punching something. "Mom hated it and I remember her making Dad put it away. It hung in the hallway of our home, and I was always frightened by it. I was only tiny, and when it was hidden away I forgot all about it."

"Looks like Lucas had inspiration for his own works of art." Rafe reached over the bed to remove the painting from the wall. "It needs to come with us. This is evidence."

Rafe carried the painting back into the living room and confronted Marion. "We have reason to believe your son is behind four murders that have occurred in the city."

Marion snorted with laughter. "You have got to be joking. That boy can't do anything without being pushed into it first. He's spineless."

"Marion, did Lucas ever display any powers?" Ashley caught

Marion's flash of fear and how she glanced at Rafe nervously. "It's okay. Detective Douglas knows all about demons and their powers. You can speak in front of her."

"*Powers*. All we ever heard from your father was how smart you were. How talented you were. How you could be anyone you wanted to be."

"You know I can alter my appearance."

"Why didn't you today so I wouldn't have to see *you*?"

Ashley reeled back under the venom spat at her. "Because I have nothing to hide where you're concerned. And my dad, for some reason, loved you, so I granted you the courtesy of that knowledge and came as myself."

"You say this cop knows what you can do?"

"Yes, she's aware."

"You're some kind of disgusting shape-shifter. Christ, your father was just so proud of that fact. My boy tried so hard to live up to that, but he didn't stand a chance. He couldn't match up to Daddy's Little Angel. So what does he get from me being impregnated by a demon? Something he could do easily enough on his own. He's not handsome. In fact, he's just as plain as they come. You wouldn't pay him the time of day. He might as well be invisible. Stick him in a room and he just blends into the background."

Ashley's jaw dropped. "You're talking literally? He's a *chameleon*?"

"Just slips right into the shadows. What fucking use is that for a boy? So I dragged him straight out of school right into a job. Might as well get some use out of him, I thought. I got him a trade he could be proud of. Got him a good one too. There's always work in a slaughterhouse."

Ashley felt the floor tilt beneath her feet. A moan rumbled in her chest and nausea rose to her throat.

"He's a butcher?" Rafe asked, flipping open her phone and dialing.

"He's that and more. He's a master at the trade. It's about the only thing he ever did right."

"Where is he now?" Rafe asked while simultaneously speaking to Alona.

"Probably out skulking around. His new boss has been nasty with him about the amount of time off he's had to take." She lifted up her skirt to reveal her knee; the stitches and bruises spoke of a recent operation. "I need him here to look after me. I can't look after myself so soon after coming out of the hospital, can I? I have to keep having surgeries because of that fucking accident he caused. Makes me dependent on him."

"So he's been off work while you've been convalescing. How long has that been?" Rafe still had Alona on the other end of her phone.

"About six weeks, I guess. I've been in so much pain one day has blended into the next." She picked up her glass of whiskey and drank from it. "At first his company was okay with it, but when he started missing his shifts because I was so dependent, his boss started to get nasty."

Ashley looked pointedly at the half-empty wine and liquor bottles littering the coffee table.

"Don't you judge me, girl. My son tried to do that and I told him straight: you've got the blood of a demon running through you and you're still pathetic. It's no wonder his father left him and never came back. He had his daughter to be with. Lucas was worthless."

Ashley only half heard what Rafe was talking to Alona about. She dimly heard work sheets mentioned. She was too flabbergasted by Marion's vitriol. She wondered how it could be that she had been kept separate from this other family of her father's and yet still be the center of attention in it.

"He's on the list," Rafe told her and Ashley forced herself to nod back and acknowledge her. She had a terrible feeling that was clawing at her guts and threatening to engulf her.

"Ashley? What's wrong? What have I missed here?"

"The blond hair? The wings? Lucas isn't killing these women to send them on as angels. He's killing them to get rid of *me*."

CHAPTER TWENTY-SIX

Rafe slammed her fist into the steering wheel to vent her anger. She grunted at the pain, then immediately did it again.

"Shit!" She'd just let Ashley go into a store to get provisions on her own. Rafe had argued that Ashley wasn't safe alone now that they knew that she was the target. Ashley had informed her that demons didn't hunt during the day, so she figured she was pretty safe getting sandwiches and doughnuts without Rafe glued to her side. Her tone had brooked no argument, so now Rafe was left sitting in the car feeling impotent. She drew back her fist to punch again. Her hand was stopped midair. Startled, she looked up to find Eli in the passenger seat of her car, his hand holding hers still.

"Tell me you didn't know who this killer was, Eli," she said.

"I didn't, but that doesn't mean someone higher up was also unaware."

"Damn it, Eli, four women are dead and Ashley thinks it's because of some damned sibling rivalry that stupid lush of a stepmother cooked up."

"One word can shape a person's entire perception of themselves. Being told you're not as good as another can wear a soul down."

"Even one that's demon marked?"

Eli nodded. "Ashley's father was an unusual angel. When he fell to earth he fathered two children. One who was all his goodness and light, the other who apparently inherited the evil."

"He's going to go after her, isn't he? I think he's been substituting these women for Ashley because the last time he saw her he was just a child. He wouldn't know what she looks like now, so any blonde would be a target for him. Or maybe he was hoping to call her out with the killings because he knew she'd be brought in as an investigator?" Rafe's head swam with the terrible possibilities that all led to the same conclusion: Lucas Thorpe wanted Ashley dead. "Why now? What's triggered his killing spree?"

"Maybe being forced to hear his shortcomings daily from his bitter mother. Since the accident, they have been in closer contact. He's her primary caretaker now. And Marion has never been one to curb her tongue about her thoughts on someone else's inadequacies. Perhaps he decided to seek out and destroy all he could never be."

"How is Ashley supposed to live with that knowledge?" She looked toward the store where she'd sent Ashley to retrieve food for the evening.

"You're here to help her."

Rafe fixed him with a stare. "You saved me, didn't you? That night in the alley? You came and banished Armitage and stopped him from killing me. Why? What makes you think I was worth saving?"

"Because you're her One, the one she turns to, the one she seeks comfort from, the one who makes her life worth living. The *One* she loves."

"We've barely even met," Rafe said weakly.

"But you know *her*. You know that your own life is nothing without her in it. You love her."

Rafe nodded.

"Then it's only right you were saved so she wouldn't go through this trial alone."

Rafe watched Eli's bright light shift and sparkle before her, thankful he was now muted to her vision but still in awe of the power that shone from him. "She's angry with you."

"I didn't know they were alive. Sometimes even angelic information can be erroneous. And I am told only what I need to know. I had a job to do here. I brought her in as part of it."

"Your boss needs to redefine his rules a little."

Eli smiled. "I'll be sure to pass your comments on through the appropriate channels."

"Do you know where Thorpe is?" Rafe had to know the reason why Ashley's guardian angel had sought her out alone.

"Not yet, but now that we know who to look for it makes it easier."

"And you're going to get him, right?"

Eli shook his head. "It's not my call. Ashley needs to be the one to confront him."

"Why, for fuck's sake?" Rafe's voice was loud in the confines of the car. "You're the ones who can send him to hell. Do your own fucking dirty work!" It riled her no end to have Eli just sit there and regard her so passively while she was shouting. "What?"

"He's not entirely demon. I can't do anything to him. I'd be killing a human. It's different when it's a demon pretending to be human."

"So you're telling me it's Ashley's job to hunt down the offspring of demons? You've got her killing her own kind?"

"She's not like them. She has a pure heart."

Rafe couldn't argue with that. "Are you saying Ashley is an angel?" She didn't know how she could reconcile that with the woman she loved.

"No, angels are created, whereas a demon can be born from lust or greed. She is neither, but she has all the best her father could give her before he was corrupted completely. She's human, Rafe, but she possesses special powers. Powers for good. That's her gift."

Rafe felt the constriction in her chest ease. "So what do you expect to happen now?"

"Now that we know who he is, we can watch for him."

"Can we expect a call when you find him?"

"You have my word on it."

"I'm not letting her face him alone." Rafe felt the weight of her gun sitting snugly against her side.

"I wouldn't expect you to. Your place is by her side. We acknowledge that."

"We?"

"You've been watched too, Rafe Douglas."

"Watched for what reason exactly?"

"To see if you were worthy."

Could this get any weirder? She stared out the windshield and wondered if the people on the street could see her talking to the angel in her passenger seat. Or was she alone in their eyes and looking like a lunatic shouting at thin air? Finally, she said, "Worthy of what?"

"Not what; *who.*" Eli spoke as if explaining it to a child.

"Worthy of Ashley?" Rafe shook her head. "Damn it, Eli. I could live a thousand lifetimes and never be worthy of her."

"She loves you. That's the price of your worthiness, Rafe."

"I hope it's worth it." Rafe began to wonder why she was talking about her love life to an angel.

"She believes so."

"And what do you believe?"

"I believe in everything and all things. But I believe, in the end, love conquers all."

On that profound note, Eli vanished. Rafe sat staring at the empty seat until Ashley got back in the car and filled it.

"You look like you've just seen a ghost," Ashley said.

"I've just had a visitation."

Ashley settled the grocery bag in her lap. "Anyone we know?"

"Just your usual friendly neighborhood guardian angel."

"I guess that means we can expect a call."

Rafe was amazed at how calm Ashley was.

"It's just another day in Demon Central, Detective." Ashley waved a hand for Rafe to start the car.

"But it's not," Rafe said. The killer turning out to be Ashley's half brother only made the case even harder to deal with.

"I have to believe it is, Rafe. Otherwise I can't do my job."

Rafe understood that reasoning. She slipped out into the traffic and kept a watchful eye out for Thorpe all the way back to the station.

❖

"You're going to have to let me out of your sight sooner or later, Detective."

Rafe looked up from the paperwork that had failed to keep her attention all afternoon. "Not in this lifetime if I can help it."

Ashley leaned back in her seat with a sigh. "You can't keep me locked up in the DDU office until one of your men or mine spots Lucas out on the street either."

"I wouldn't dream of it. I'm just enjoying the pleasure of your company."

"You've got Dean camped outside their home with sniper rifles trained on every entrance and exit. There are eyes on every street within two blocks. You know he won't go home. His mother will have tipped him off."

"She wasn't very receptive to us telling her that her son was a murderer. Surely she wouldn't be so stupid as to cover for him?"

"You met her, Rafe. There's only one person who can berate her son, and that's her. She'll protect him like she no doubt always has in everything else he's done that we don't know about."

Rafe thought back to their meeting with Thorpe's mother. "You called him a chameleon?"

"It's a variation on my own talent. I can take on full forms with my glamour. It sounds like he takes on the environment. It just shows our differences. My glamour is used for protection. His is used to hunt. He blends into the shadows."

"That fits Blythe's profile of him. She said he wouldn't stand out in a crowd. If he blends in, those women wouldn't have stood a chance in seeing him coming."

"Dean has no idea you've sent him out on a worthless waiting game, has he?"

"What was I supposed to tell him? This Lucas Thorpe is definitely our killer, but I'm sorry, our people can't take him in because he needs to be banished to hell instead." Rafe reached over the desk toward Ashley. "And, oh! How fortunate! I just happen to know the exact someone who could do that for us." She eased back into her seat. "It's not that simple. I can't tell him what needs to be kept hidden for your safety and my supposed sanity."

"Nothing's simple in my life, Rafe. I certainly wasn't expecting this outcome when I took on the case."

"Me neither." She reached out to hold Ashley's hand. "Least of all you."

Ashley tightened her grip on Rafe's hand and squeezed it. "So what excuse did you give Dean for not joining him on the stakeout? Seeing as you two are usually joined at the hip."

"I played the fatigue card." Rafe hated to admit it. She had felt like a complete and utter shit for deceiving him.

"You actually used your injuries as an excuse?"

"I had no choice." She knew technically she was still supposed to be on strict desk duty, but she'd paid no attention to the doctor's instructions so far. "I told him I felt rough after not getting much sleep and the pain was really bad. So I'd be forever indebted if he did the arrest and I'd prepare for the interview." She rested her forehead in her palm. "Lame, so lame."

"I guess you never mentioned some of those sleepless hours were taken up with us making love quite energetically?"

"No, for some reason I left that part out. What makes it worse is how easily he believed me and was so caring and solicitous. I'm a lousy friend and an even worse lead on this case."

"We'll take him out for dinner after this is all sorted to make up for it."

"And tell him what? That we were sneaking behind his back looking for a demon and also dating on the quiet at the same time?"

Ashley smiled at Rafe's exasperation. She stood and stretched, affording Rafe a tantalizing glimpse of flesh. Rafe was caught looking but felt no guilt. Ashley moved behind her and draped herself over Rafe's shoulders, hugging her.

"How long before Alona returns?"

"We have about forty minutes. She likes to linger in the presence of Detective Powell."

"Can you bring up the map of the locations of the murders for me?"

Rafe did so, staying seated while Ashley commandeered the giant screen.

"Any idea how he knew about your tattoo, Ashley?" Ashley's shoulder's visibly stiffened at her question.

"I guess he must have seen it once. I remember going to see my dad one summer at Marion's house. Lucas must have been there. I know I had a summer top that left my back exposed and showed off the artwork. Dad was a little spooked by it as I recall." She smiled at what was obviously a happy memory. "'Guess you really are Daddy's little angel,' my dad said as he waved me off." Rafe caught the shiver that ran through Ashley's whole body. "Was he really cutting these women open searching for my wings?"

"I think he's a sick bastard who would have found some excuse or another to kill. You were the impetus he chose. It probably didn't help that his mommy dearest fed his mind with lies about why his father walked out on them. Both you and your father were used as scapegoats."

"Dad really should have told them the truth. He knew he had to be banished once the angels found him."

"How did he manage to stay hidden for so long?"

"He didn't show up on their radar. When angels fall, they don't look the same when they reach the ground. Dad became someone else, *something* else, and he lost his angelic sparkle. As a demon he was extra careful about drawing attention to himself. He wasn't like the other demons that roamed the streets. He was an ex-angel. He lost his wings but gained the knack for subterfuge."

"What finally tipped the angels off to him?"

Ashley was quiet for a moment. "Me. My powers were growing and they could see me as clearly as a beacon shining in the night. Didn't take them long to come seek me out to see where I had sprung from. Eli found me and, consequently, Dad."

"You say Eli didn't rat your dad out for years?"

"Angels have a totally different concept of time. He merely bided it until he couldn't hide Dad any longer. I think Eli really liked Dad and it hurt him to have to banish him. They were brothers in heaven, after all. Add to that I'd have been left all alone at such a young age. I don't think Eli liked that idea."

"It's not your fault, Ashley. None of this is."

"Really? They found my dad because of me not being able to control my glamour."

"He would have been found eventually anyway. He wasn't supposed to have free rein on the earth. He was a fallen angel. It was just a matter of time before they wanted him back."

"And Lucas?"

"He's demon born and sadly twisted by his human excuse for a mother who could probably put most of the minions of hell to shame."

"Maybe I could have stopped Lucas."

"How? As a child, you weren't allowed to be around him. Again, that wasn't your fault. Bad decisions made by bad people set the course that led Lucas to do what he did."

"Well, I have to stop him now."

"Do you have to kill him?"

"I don't know. I've never had to face down a crossbreed. I just know he can't continue and I have to stop him."

"Can I just shoot him?"

"I'd rather you didn't."

"I know from firsthand experience that a well-aimed bullet can save your life from a demon."

"I want him banished. He isn't a demon in a human form; he's human with demon in him. That's a big difference. Shooting would probably kill him."

Rafe couldn't see her point. "I don't really see that as a loss, Ashley."

"Can I please do it my way before you take aim, Detective? I've been doing this job a long time. The circumstances may be a little screwed this time, but I need to see it through."

"Why can't you just be a normal PI so I don't have to worry about you?"

Ashley wrapped her arms about Rafe's neck and hugged her tightly. "I don't want you to have to worry, but I'll let you in on a secret." She tugged Rafe's head lower and her breath whispering in Rafe's ear made her shiver. "I'm glad you have my back." She kissed Rafe tenderly. Rafe closed her eyes as soft lips promised so much more. Her eyes only flickered open when Ashley drew back. "Now, Detective, I believe we have time to go home and feed that cat of yours. Demon activity rarely takes place in daylight. *My* team is searching for Lucas using genetic markers they recognize me with. He stands very little chance of eluding them now."

"So the second he steps out from the shadows?"

"He's visible to all on high," Ashley said.

CHAPTER TWENTY-SEVEN

The call came at midnight.
"He's hiding in the Garden of Eden." Ashley grabbed for her jacket and rifled through a pocket inside. She withdrew a small handgun.

Rafe gaped at her. "Since when do you carry a weapon?"

Ashley checked that the chamber was full, slipped on her jacket, and put the gun back out of sight. "I always carry a gun, Detective. I work the streets at night. I need some kind of protection against the crazies. It's licensed; I am a PI after all."

"You have a guardian angel for protection," Rafe said.

"That doesn't mean I don't need to still be able to look after myself. I know martial arts too. Remind me to show you sometime when you're not so banged up and I can pin you down." She pushed Rafe out the front door. "We can compare caliber sizes later. The Garden of Eden obviously means more to him than the first scenes."

Rafe hastened beside her, tugging on her hat. "You know this is probably a setup? He's got to be aware that you're watching for him just like we are." She opened the car door for Ashley to get in then rushed around to get in the driver's side. She started the engine and pulled away from the curb at high speed.

"Would it be any easier if I say I have right on my side?" Ashley understood Rafe's trepidation. After all, she was deliberately going to confront a serial killer who was also demonic. She knew Rafe had already faced down a demon personally. So she knew intimately the strength they possessed and the damage they could inflict.

"I'd feel better if I could call my people in to cover us. It's just the whole demon element that fucks up that plan of action."

"This is my job, Rafe. I have you here. That's all the backup I need."

"And the angels, right? There will be angels?"

"The angels are always there."

"Why don't I feel like we have everything covered?"

"Because this is my realm you're stepping into and you have no idea what that entails. I need you to do as I say and just trust me."

"I really don't take orders very well. I'm more used to giving them out."

"I'm asking you as my lover as well as a cop. I need you to let me lead in this."

"If he even thinks of touching you I'm blowing his head off. We'll deal with the banishing crap after."

Ashley watched the streets as they drew closer to the block that the Garden of Eden was on. "Park where we did the night we came to view the body. I need to go in on foot and alone." Rafe pulled the car over as directed and parked. Ashley got out and spoke into the darkness. "Eli, I know you're here; I can sense you."

Eli appeared instantly beside her.

"You had no idea, did you?" Ashley's faith was justified when he shook his head.

"You wouldn't have been called in had I known," he said.

"Is he still in the garden?"

"He hasn't moved since he glamoured to hide in the shadows. We could read his signature immediately. We've just kept watch on him until it got late into the night and the city started to sleep. He's got your father's coloring; he glows a golden orange."

Ashley tucked her gun securely into the back of her jeans and made sure her jacket covered it. "Will you find somewhere safe for Rafe to hide please?"

"I'd rather be beside you," Rafe said. Her own gun was out and in her hand.

"What did I say about trusting me?" Ashley loved how focused Rafe was on her safety, but she needed to have her step back. This wasn't a police matter. Not anymore.

"And what did I say about my not being good at taking orders?" Ashley looked to Eli. "Rafe is in your charge." She took a step away but was pulled back gently by Rafe's hand on her arm.

"Don't take any chances. He may be family, but he's still a killer. Don't let sentiment blind you to his agenda. He wants *you*." Rafe moved closer still. "I'm not prepared to lose you."

Ashley placed a kiss on Rafe's lips. "I'll be careful, I promise. You and I have a lifetime to explore together." She took a deep breath to prepare herself. "God, I'm not usually so nervous."

"Family reunions will do that."

❖

Ashley was grateful that there were no police guarding the crime scene. Rafe had told her that with the scene processed so thoroughly it had been decided to leave it yellow taped but unguarded. The police were needed to look for the killer, not guard where he'd already been. Ashley had asked who had decided that. Rafe had admitted she had, in the hopes that Lucas would return to the garden to relive where his art had been displayed as he'd intended. Ashley wasn't surprised Rafe had proved to be correct. She slipped under the yellow tape and opened the garden gate. There was an eerie silence that put Ashley's already heightened senses into overdrive. She knew that the angels would have secured the area themselves. No one would witness what happened in the garden; human eyes would never see a banishment take place. A Shroud of Secrecy would have been placed over the area. She stared into the darkness, searching for the glimmer. He lit up the darkness like a flame to her sight.

"Come out of the shadows, Lucas. It's Ashley."

A voice spoke out almost hesitantly. "Is it really you?"

"Come see for yourself." Ashley looked over to where his voice was coming from. His shimmering pulsated amid the shadows, effectively marking his hiding place.

"How do I know it's really you? So many have been you until I looked closer and found they were just meat."

Ashley could barely contain her revulsion at his choice of words. "I haven't changed that much from the last time you saw me. Let me see you. I'm sure you've changed a great deal from the little boy I last saw."

He emerged from the darkness. The shadows seemed to fall from him like he was shedding a cloak. His glamour dimmed, then winked out and Ashley finally got to see him. He was not much taller than she was. His hair was a mousy blond kept short but unkempt and his face strongly resembled his mother's. Ashley could see the demon in him, though, the legacy from their father. It was starting to alter his human features as it struggled against his humanity.

"Is that the face you showed your victims before the throat wound you inflicted made them mercifully bleed to death?"

"No one ever really looked at me. No one sees *me*. But *they* did; they saw exactly what I am."

"And what are you, Lucas? A murderer without conscience?"

He straightened his shoulders and stood proud before her. "I am my father's son."

Ashley shook her head at the arrogance in his voice. She laughed at him and watched his face fall at her derision. "Your father was no killer. You defile his memory by claiming to be something he'd be proud of."

Anger erupted across his face, contorting it even more. His true nature became even clearer to see. "No, but then he was always so proud of you, wasn't he? Daddy's Little Angel. Fuck! That's all I ever heard about."

"That's not my fault. You can't honestly expect me to believe you killed innocent women because of that? That you were pissed because Daddy loved me more? Grow a set, Lucas! Take responsibility for your actions."

He stormed forward and Ashley reached a hand back for her gun, praying Rafe wasn't already taking aim to fire. He stopped, his breathing sounding harsh in the silence.

"I grew up in your damned shadow and then found I could hide easily in them for real. Who would have thought little Lucas Thorpe would finally get a gift all his own? Of course, it was nothing compared to yours." He bowed mockingly at her. "You can become anyone you choose to be. Anyone at all. Yet you've become what? A private investigator. You're out saving the world when you could be ruling it."

"I don't want the responsibility of the world, Lucas. I just want a normal life."

"But you're not normal! You're the daughter of a demon. A very powerful demon. One that used to be an angel." He looked around them, scanning the garden excitedly. "Did you bring him with you?"

Ashley frowned. "I beg your pardon?"

He stomped like a petulant child. "Did you bring Dad with you so he can see what I've done?"

Ashley shook her head at him. "Dad hasn't been around for years, Lucas. He got banished."

"No!" Face contorting, Lucas screamed and his skin began to mottle with bright red patches. "No. You took him away to live with you."

"No, I didn't. The angels came and banished him to hell because he wasn't supposed to be here. He didn't leave you and your mother willingly. He was taken before he could tell you he had to go."

"You're a liar." Lucas's voice growled as the demon inside him grew.

"Why would I lie? I lost him too."

"But I wanted him to see," Lucas whined, rubbing at his face and tugging at the horns that were starting to sprout from his forehead.

"See what?"

"I wanted him to see me when I cut your wings off and get to wear them for myself."

❖

Rafe was surprised by how strong an angel could be. With just one finger pushing downward, Eli had stopped Rafe from raising her gun when Lucas had taken his threatening steps forward.

"Just let me take a shot. I just need one. I can nail him from here."

"Your weapon won't be much use, Rafe, and Ashley could get caught in its path."

"He's going to kill her and you're going to stand by and let him do it?" She struggled against his pressure until she could fight no more and lowered her weapon. Hoping to catch him off guard, she stepped forward to sprint, but he blocked her way like a solid wall. "Goddamn it, Eli! Let me past."

"No. I am going to wait until the time is right and then I will give you the weapon you require."

Rafe stopped struggling. "You have a bigger gun?"

He gave her a withering look. "Our might is so much more than bullets, Detective." He held out a small silver pen. "Here."

Rafe took the item and examined it critically. "What? I'm supposed to *Bic* him to death?"

Eli sighed and directed her attention to a small button. "Press here."

Rafe did so and the small instrument became a much larger spear. "Holy Christ!" she gasped as she felt the weight of the object in her hand.

"Exactly," Eli said.

"It's a Spear of Light." Rafe recognized the weapon. She balanced it on her palm, testing its weight, then gripped it tightly. "Where are the angels this belongs to so they can run that bastard through with it?"

"There are no angels for this killer, Rafe. He's half human. He needs a different form of capturing."

Rafe considered this. "He has to be taken by humans?"

"He has to be banished by ones like him."

"I'm not demon born, though, for all my mother would argue otherwise."

"You've been marked by a demon. You can see what he truly is."

"He's an ugly mother—"

Eli hastened to interrupt. "And you were healed by a pure heart. The same pure heart who faces him now."

"So I do what? Try to creep up on the guy and wield this like a javelin at him? He'll see me coming."

Eli put his arm around her. "No, he won't. You will let me hide you from his sight and then you can run him through and ground him."

Rafe recognized the blinding white light when it enveloped her. For the first time, she embraced it. "Guide me, Eli."

"You learn fast."

"He's threatening Ashley. I want to rip him apart."

"That's an outdated form of punishment, Rafe. We find banishment so much more civilized now. Tonight, Detective, you'll get to mete out justice of a different kind."

❖

Ashley saw the flames start sparking in Lucas's eyes. She forced herself not to take a step back and show him she was afraid.

"I looked for you. I looked everywhere for you. Then I started to see you and I just wanted to talk, but you would get frightened and start shouting. Then the glamour faded and it wasn't you after all. So I just followed the lights and found more women all pretending to be you." He stared at her critically. "I still can't see your lights."

"My glamour is only visible when I take on the form of someone else. I don't shimmer all the time. I'm like you; I can turn it on and off."

"It's because you're more human, though, isn't it? You didn't get the full undiluted demon blood like I did." His sneer was intimidating and Ashley began to feel unnerved. "Did Dad know you weren't a true child of his? That you got more of your weak mother's humanity?"

"You're half human too, Lucas. Don't forget that."

"Not enough to save me, though. I got the best parts of my father. The brute strength to cut those women open and the face to have them stare into as they died right before me. I liked that part. I'd lie down beside them on the ground and watch the light go out in their eyes. I was looking to see if I could find you in there. I never did, but I figured I still needed to double-check if it really was you. So I looked for your wings."

"My wings are tattoos; you didn't need to dig deeper. You didn't need to cut them, Lucas."

"They're real! I saw them myself. You have angel wings growing from your back. That's why I had to cut through to the bone."

"They're just pictures inked into my skin."

His teeth audibly ground as he clenched his jaw. "I saw them. I want them for myself. Then I can be Daddy's Little Angel and he'll love me more than he ever loved you. Then on dark wings descending, I will wreak havoc on the earth and can finally be the demon my father expected of me."

"He wouldn't want you to be like this. He wouldn't have wanted you to kill women because you were pissed off at me."

"I thought they were you. I could see you everywhere. You wouldn't leave me alone! So many glamours; all of them calling to me." He tore at his hair and ripped a piece out. Ashley finally realized his madness went deeper than she had ever imagined. Demon dementia. His human DNA was at war with the demon blood in his veins.

"The women you killed weren't me, though. They were innocents."

"I made them into angels. I gave them wings of their own so they could fly away to heaven and be redeemed."

"You painted wings in their blood that you had just butchered them in. You copied Dad's painting to pose them. Why?"

He shrugged. "I thought Dad would see it and like it. I brought his picture to life. I made it real for him."

"You killed innocents."

"They were supposed to be you."

"And what if they had been? What if one of the women you slaughtered had really been me, Lucas? What then? Would you have slit my throat as well to stop me from crying out to ask why my own brother wanted me dead?"

"I didn't want you dead. I just want what you've always had. You got Dad's angel wings when he fell to earth. I want them."

"I got no such thing. I got the ability to shape-shift. That's all I got from Dad."

"I want the wings. I want Dad to see I have them now."

"Dad got banished to hell. He hasn't seen a thing you've done since the last second he laid eyes on you."

"You *lie*!"

"He was sent to spend eternity in hell because he broke the rules. He gave up his angel status to come to earth. He fell from grace."

"He ran off with another woman."

"No, that's what your mother thought. No one told her Dad was going to be punished for his sins. So knowing of his wandering eye, she figured he'd found someone new. He hadn't. He didn't leave you on purpose. The angels came for him."

"You all took my father away!" He turned his head to the sky to bellow out his words. "I can get him back. If I have your wings, I can get him back." He removed a long, lethal tipped blade from his jacket. "Now that I have the real you, I can end this." He took a step toward her. "I promise this won't hurt a bit. I'm a professional. I know how to put animals out of their misery." He raised the blade. "You're going to help me see my dad again."

CHAPTER TWENTY-EIGHT

Give him his wish."
Eli's voice echoed in Rafe's head as she stood poised behind Lucas, the spear raised in her hands. She'd been in the garden a while and had been able to hear every word the deranged young man had said. Rafe had seen Ashley's face lose some of its fear when the unmistakable light that Eli emitted had come into her view. Rafe remembered Ashley telling her that demons couldn't see an angel's light until the Spear of Light captured them and their eyes were opened.

What Ashley wasn't expecting was to see Rafe step out of the light wielding her weapon. Bathed in the brilliance shining from Eli, Rafe hefted the heavy spear and slammed it down into Lucas's shoulder. It slipped through his body as if it were weightless. Rafe almost fell forward on her face with the ease the spear cut through his torso. There was a satisfying thud as the spear dug into the ground and Lucas Thorpe was left pinned. He flailed his arm out, but Ashley was nowhere near the knife. His screams were earsplitting as he fought to get at her.

Rafe felt Eli remove himself from around her. It was a curious feeling and she was left oddly bereft. A cold chill shivered through her as the white light retreated. She stepped forward to Ashley and clutched her to her chest.

"You okay?"

Ashley buried her face in Rafe's shoulder. "I am now. Since when do you get to play with angel toys?"

"Since Eli reckoned only you and I could bring this killer to justice." She spared Lucas Thorpe a glance. "He really doesn't look like anything special, does he?" She deliberately baited him, watching as his face grew into a form she was familiar with. "Oh, put your monster face away. I've faced uglier demons than you, and quite frankly, you are lacking in the horn department."

He swung the knife out at her, furiously slashing at the air. His body twisted on the spear but he was effectively trapped. "You bitch. I'll cut your heart out. Who the fuck are you anyway?"

"I'm your sister's lover, and that makes me the scariest thing you'll ever face, demon boy."

He flipped the knife over in his hand with a swift move and was about to throw it when a hand appeared and very gently removed the weapon from him. Lucas looked over his shoulder, his eyes widening.

"You have wings," he whispered.

"And they are not for the taking," Eli told him as he carefully handed the knife over to Rafe for safekeeping. "Your time here is done."

"But I need her." Lucas stared at Eli, then whipped his head around to look accusingly at Ashley. "I always lose out to you."

"No, Lucas. This time you win. You get to spend eternity with our father. Be sure to tell him hi from me."

Eli restrained Lucas's hands with his own and called Ashley forward. "Touch him. Draw forth his demon, then the angels can come and take care of him. Until they are certain he's unredeemable they won't interfere."

Ashley slipped from Rafe's hold and took a tentative step forward. "Could I heal him?"

"I fear he's beyond what your power can do."

Ashley placed her hand on Lucas's chest and gasped as if burned. Rafe took a step forward, but was kept back by Eli's silent command.

"What do you sense, Ashley?" Eli asked.

"That there's very little human left inside him."

"Then he's ours for the taking. Only someone with a pure heart could have seen into the human soul and found it missing."

Ashley stepped back and into Rafe's arms, her body visibly shivering. Rafe held on to her tightly, sensing her pain at all that had transpired. Eli looked up and Rafe followed his line of sight. "Finally, backup," she said gratefully.

"She has a pure heart?" Spit dripped from the sharp needle-pointed teeth that erupted from Lucas's mouth. He snapped at her like an animal. "I should have ripped their fucking hearts out too!"

Two angels descended from the sky and took hold of Lucas's arms. Being this close, Rafe got to witness Lucas's demon soul being forcibly removed from his human body. It was as if the angels skinned him alive. A snarling, demonic creature was dragged free from the human form. Lucas now sported cloven feet and his eyes burned with the brightness of sulfur ablaze. His human body slumped to the ground intact and the Spear of Light clattered beside it. In a flash, the angels disappeared and Lucas was gone with them.

Rafe looked at the body on the ground. "So what is this we're left with?"

"Lucas Thorpe's human shell." Eli retrieved the Spear from beside it. "I would suggest you leave now and expect a call much later. We'll deal with this from here."

Rafe held out a hand to still Eli's activity. "You can't make him disappear. The families of those women need closure. I want a killer caught."

"And so you shall have it, Rafe," Eli said. "He'll leave a suicide note and everything to close this case to your satisfaction."

"What about his mother?" Rafe was worried she would incriminate Ashley, and she wasn't going to stand for that. She couldn't have Ashley in any way implicated in her case.

"She's being dealt with. The rerouting of the brain can be used for many things, Rafe Douglas. She won't remember her son's father or anything, or *anyone* for that matter, connected to him. She'll be as much an innocent victim as the women her son killed."

Rafe considered Eli closely. "You mean to tell me you could have wiped out memories while you were messing in my head?"

"I didn't have cause to. I was merely turning down the lights for you."

Rafe felt Ashley shift at her side. "I'm taking Ashley home with me. You know where to find her."

"You'll be called to a scene back here in the morning, Detective. I figure you could do with some rest before you bring this investigation to a close." Eli held out his hand for the knife and Rafe grudgingly handed the murder weapon over.

"Don't lose that," she ordered. Eli favored her with a look that made her feel decidedly uncomfortable. Rafe tugged Ashley aside. "Come on. We need to get you home. You've had more than enough fun for tonight." Ashley didn't make a protest as she was guided out of the garden with Rafe's hand on her arm.

"Oh, Rafe? You forgot this." Eli held out the Spear of Light to her. He pressed the tiny button and it reverted back to its innocuous pen guise.

Rafe wouldn't take it. "I don't need it."

"But there might come a day when you do."

"I already have a job, Eli. I'm a cop, not a demon hunter."

"But you could be both. You could help Ashley should the need arise again."

"It won't." Rafe tried to ignore the soft laughter she could feel shaking Ashley's body.

"This is Chicago, Detective, remember? Demon Central? You might want to take the gift offered you," Ashley said. "They're not given out lightly."

"But I don't want to fight any more demons. Haven't I fulfilled my quota for this lifetime?" Rafe knew she was close to whining but didn't really care.

Eli pushed the pen into her hand. "Just keep it beside you anyway. I'm sure it will make a nice writing implement if you choose to just keep it that way." He shooed them out of the garden, leaving Rafe wondering just what he was going to set up where Lucas Thorpe's body was concerned. She risked a look back over her shoulder. Ashley's hand caught her chin and directed her eyes forward again.

"Let Eli sort it. Your job is done for now. Let's go get some sleep before you're called out again to deal with whatever he has set up."

Rafe took Ashley back to her car, settled her in, and hurried around to get in herself. "Does Eli stage many crime scenes?"

Ashley laid her head against the headrest and closed her eyes. "Only the ones involving demons."

"How do you feel?" Rafe could see the strain of the night's events on Ashley's face.

"I've just watched the last tangible link I had to family be ripped away from me. For the second time now, seeing as the first reports of his death were a little erroneous. You just don't expect him to be killing in your name when you finally do meet up after all that."

"It doesn't seem fair he gets what he's always wanted."

"But he has to be in hell to get it. And something tells me Dad won't be too happy to see his only son dropped into the pit to spend eternity with him labeled a murderer."

"Will your dad know that Lucas tried to kill you?"

Ashley smiled humorlessly. "Oh believe me, he'll know *exactly* what put Lucas in hell."

Rafe pondered this a moment. "I can't see it being a happy reunion for them. In fact, it does seem rather fitting, now that I think about it."

"You should always be careful what you wish for. One man's idea of heaven is another man's hell."

❖

It was a call from Dean that finally roused Rafe from her sleep. She had been sprawled out on the couch with Ashley wrapped in her arms and Trinity curled around them. Dean wasted no time once Rafe answered her cell.

"The stakeout was a complete and utter bust, but we've just gotten a call in. A body has been found."

Disoriented from her slumber, Rafe feared the worst and spoke before her brain kicked into gear. "Another woman?"

"No, it's a male. They think it might be Thorpe. I'm on my way to pick you up."

Rafe managed to untangle herself from Ashley's hold without waking her. She covered her up with a blanket, tucking her in tenderly. Trinity moved to take up Rafe's spot. "Watch over her, please." Rafe fussed at the cat, who yawned, revealing sharp white teeth and a very pink tongue. The cat kneaded at the blanket, then managed to cover herself in it. Rafe could hear the steady purring start up again. "Make yourself comfy, why don't you, Trin."

Rafe grabbed her jacket and was out waiting on the sidewalk when Dean pulled up in his car. He handed her a coffee the second she got into the passenger seat.

"You'll need this. It's frosty this morning. I know the weather has been getting steadily cooler, but I swear I've seen snow in some places as I've driven through. That's freaky even for us. There's been no mention of a snowfall on the weather reports all week."

Rafe sipped her coffee gratefully and rummaged in the paper sack Dean had dumped in her lap. "Coffee and doughnuts?"

"I figured you hadn't eaten, and I'm still buzzing from all the caffeine I drank on the stakeout. I need something to soak it all up."

"You said it's a male body. What makes you think it's Thorpe?"

"The lady who found it works at the Garden of Eden, the same place the last woman was found killed. She recognized Thorpe when she found the body this morning. According to her, he used to hang around the garden. She said he was creepy, kept saying something about how he was going to take the garden back for the snake." Dean pulled away from the curb and turned onto the main road. "She reckoned he was just another drunk looking to bunk down on the bench in there. But seeing as he mostly kept out of her way, she didn't feel the need to get the police involved. She found him this morning when she came to see what damage had been done to her patch with all our feet trampling through the scene. She figured if she came in early enough she could slip under the tape and just have a look. She found more than she bargained for." He cast Rafe a critical look. "You don't look any more rested."

Rafe purposely kept her eyes forward. She didn't dare meet his concerned gaze. "I'm rested enough. I was working out the strategy for our interrogation, but I didn't expect you to tell me he wasn't going to talk…indefinitely."

"I froze my ass off watching his house in the hope he would slink back there to hide. Instead, the sneaky bastard was back at the last scene leaving us another dead body."

Rafe was thankful that this time she was driven directly to the scene. She was tired of having to park blocks away and sneak in like a member of the special ops squad. The previous crime scene tape was still in place, but there was a heavy presence of officers guarding the area. Rafe followed Dean, curious as to what she would find left behind by Eli. There was something strange about stepping onto a murder scene where you'd already seen the murder happen hours ago but had yet to see it staged. She forced herself to remain professional and not look around for any signs of angels watching.

Lucas Thorpe lay in a smattering of snow. He was spread out on his back, eyes wide open staring sightless at the sky above. Rafe stepped toward him. His wrists had been cut and the blood was spread out above his head and down to his sides. For a moment, the significance escaped her, but when it registered she hastily stifled a snort of laughter. She coughed to cover it.

"You okay there, Rafe?" Dean asked, putting a hand on her arm.

"I'm fine. Must have swallowed a snowflake." She walked around the body to make sure she was seeing what she thought. "Am I the only one to see a snow angel here?"

Dean's head whipped up at her then back down at the body. "Fuck, you're right."

Dr. Alan picked his way across the light snow to join them. "Makes a change for one of these to do the right thing and take himself out."

"Saves taxpayers too." She knelt beside the body. "So what do you think, Doc? He slit his wrists, then lay down to make a snow angel?"

"I've seen stranger things, Rafe, but I'd say that pretty much sums it up. He left a note stabbed to a tree with a huge knife that I would guess was the one he used."

Rafe looked over to where he pointed. Sure enough, there was a piece of paper with a message scrawled upon it. It was held in place by the murder weapon he had brandished at her and Ashley earlier.

"That really is a big fucking knife." Dean padded over to retrieve the evidence. Jim Pope was already on hand with his camera documenting the scene so Dean could remove both the knife and the note.

Dr. Alan edged over to Rafe and bumped her gently from her musings. "I…I checked him for you."

"Checked him for what?"

Dr. Alan brushed at his forehead. "Horns. If ever there was one I'd expect to have them, it would be this guy."

Rafe couldn't agree more. "Any sign?"

Dr. Alan shook his head. "Not on my initial examination, but I'll take great pleasure in sawing open his skull to take a deeper look."

"Keep me posted on your findings, horns or not."

Dr. Alan nodded, then edged closer still. "Do you want to bring your PI friend down to see this body?"

"I don't think there'll be any need for her to do that. Ms. Scott's involvement is finished now that the killer is dead. This case is mercifully closed."

"Did she help your case, Rafe?"

"I don't think we could have solved it without her."

CHAPTER TWENTY-NINE

Rafe studied the photographs taken at Lucas Thorpe's suicide scene and laughed silently at the irony on display. *You got your wings after all, Lucas, laid out in the snow and painted with your own blood this time.*

Dean stood beside her all but breathing down her neck.

"Damn creepy, if you ask me," he said.

"I want to know why he killed himself." Alona enlarged the photo and Lucas Thorpe's dead eyes stared out at them. "I mean, he seemed to be a man on a mission."

"I think us closing in on him tipped his hand. He had to have come to the realization he wouldn't be able to spread his wings in a cell on death row."

"He was an angel maker." Dean picked up the painting that they had kept on display in the office.

Rafe found the artwork curiously beautiful in its rendition of a fallen angel seeking to return to former glories. Yet it was equally disturbing knowing it had been used for deadly inspiration. She was of two minds whether to have it valued by her brother for its artistry or to set fire to it. She hoped it got lost somewhere in the evidence locker and would remain forever unseen.

"So all along he was delusional and killing women because he thought they were angels and he could steal their wings." Alona held the bagged suicide note in her grasp. "Explains the ripping open of their backs." She waved the note at Rafe. "Have you spoken to Ashley about this?"

Rafe nodded. "I called her from the scene. She said she'd drop by later."

"Was this anything to do with the occult?" Dean turned the picture in his hands to another angle. "Because this picture depicts a weird way of looking at the world."

It's truer than you'll ever know. "That painting isn't much different from the religious frescoes you find in certain cultures. Everything is angels and demons. I think the only occult thing we'll find is that he was chased by his own set of demons."

"Well, his mother was no use whatsoever. She couldn't shed any further light on him at all." Dean put the painting down in exasperation. "She was a weird one too. Just kept on about how she had to raise him all on her own."

"I told you her view of the world was pretty much observed from the bottom of a whiskey bottle." Rafe wondered how much Eli had removed from Marion's memory. She marveled at how easy it could have been for him to have done the same to her. *Would I want to forget Armitage and that alley?* Rafe fingered her scar reflectively. *It brought Ashley to me; I want to remember it all.*

"It was strange how she kept assuring me he was a good boy and how much he looked after his mother. It was obvious he hadn't been home for a while."

"Some kids can do no wrong in their mother's eyes," Rafe said.

Alona patted her computer. "Well, I for one was just glad we had the data stream up and running and his previous brushes with the cops were documented here."

Rafe was pleased with that good fortune. Thorpe's previous dealings with the police had given them the basis to build their case on and pursue him before he killed again. "Guess all this tech just made itself invaluable," she teased Alona. "And we're only just starting. Imagine what we can find out when all the DDUs are set up around the country. We'll have information at our fingertips within hours instead of days or weeks."

"Without the interference of jurisdiction rearing its ugly head," Dean said.

"That was the final hurdle. Law enforcement officers do tend to clutch their territory to their chests like a precious commodity. With these units we can open up the world of investigation." She caught Alona checking her watch for the second time. "Got a date, Officer Wilson?"

Laughing, Alona shook her head. "No. I'm making sure you make your appointment with Detective Powell so she can break the case on tonight's news."

Rafe waved a hand dismissively. "Yeah, yeah. I'll go see her shortly and she can go tell the city how wonderful we are and that they can all sleep soundly in their beds for another night."

"She'll be surprised to get you instead of me."

Rafe shot Alona a sly glance. "I'm sure she'll find another way to get you alone." Rafe gathered up her files and patted Alona on her shoulder as she walked past her. "I'll be back in a little while. Just need to go feed the media its sound bites for the evening."

"Paint us in a good light," Dean called after her.

"Of course I will. We chased down the bad guy and cornered him until his only way out was to take his own life. Case closed; the city rejoices. Justice is seen to be served."

"And Thorpe can rot in hell," Dean added.

No truer words had been spoken.

❖

Rafe wasn't surprised that Ashley came into the office much later in the day. Dean was down in the morgue trying to speed up Dr. Alan's autopsy report and Alona was out getting food since none of them had eaten for hours. When Ashley's blond head appeared around the office door, Rafe's pulse soared at the sight of her.

"Hey," she called, suddenly aware that the screen behind her displayed the photos of Lucas Thorpe's suicide scene. She wanted to wipe the screen clean or at least reduce the size of the photos that were boldly emblazoned for all to see.

"Don't hide them on my account," Ashley said as she slipped into the room and headed straight into Rafe's arms. "God, it feels good to be near you again." She buried her face in Rafe's neck. "I woke up to a furry alarm clock purring in my face. I'd have rather had you to wake up to."

"I got called out by Dean bright and early. I didn't want to wake you. How are you doing?" Rafe held her and became aware of just how slight Ashley was in her arms. She nuzzled her face in Ashley's hair, delighting in the familiar scent.

"I've had better lifetimes, but finding that the killer I was brought in to take down was my own brother was a bit of a shock."

"I can't imagine what you're feeling." Rafe deliberately kept Ashley turned away from the screen. Ashley gazed up at her with a knowing look.

"You can't hide the screen from me forever. I need to know the last scene so I can put it all to rest."

Rafe loosened her hold and let Ashley turn around.

"So, officially, you caught the guy?"

"The reports read that he killed himself at the scene of his last crime because we were closing in on him."

Ashley took a step toward the screen. She was silent for a moment, then peered over her shoulder at Rafe. "Who says angels don't have a sense of humor?" She studied the photo again. "I did wonder at the early snowfall we experienced this morning. I didn't expect it to be for artistic license courtesy of Eli."

"I'm finding it hard to get my head around the fact I saw Lucas dragged off by two guys with wings and yet I'm also seeing him here obviously dead."

"Have you been down to the morgue?"

Rafe shook her head. "I sent Dean. I was honestly too creeped out by it. I keep expecting his eyes to pop open or something."

"You've watched too many scary movies."

"I just never realized they could come true." Rafe handed Ashley the suicide note in its plastic evidence bag. "Signed, sealed, and stuck to a tree with the murder weapon. Eli left nothing to chance."

"He's thorough." Ashley read the note. "Case closed, Detective?"

"Thankfully, yes, but I can't help but wonder what comes next." She sat back against the desk and her restless hands caught at the silver pen she had kept beside her all day. She didn't want to acknowledge its presence, but she couldn't let it out of her sight either. It was a dilemma that tore at her.

Ashley's eyes fell on the pen. "Next?"

"There's suddenly more to my policing than just humans out to do wrong. I've got demons invading our territory and the occasional half blood to make matters even more precarious." Rafe brandished the seemingly innocuous pen at Ashley. "And then there's the little matter of this thing."

"It's just a pen."

"You and I both know it's a whole lot more than that."

"Only if you want it to be."

Rafe whispered even though she didn't need to. "It's an angel's weapon, and I'm not an angel. Why would Eli entrust it to me?"

"Maybe because he sees in you something that goes beyond your innate sense of justice and right."

"So I'm supposed to do what? Go out at night and ram it through every person I see glittering?"

Ashley laughed. "Not all of us. Some of us aren't meant to be banished. Myself included, I hope."

"See? How could I ever know?" Rafe shoved the pen into Ashley's hands.

"You'll know because you'll see the demon in the shimmering, like you're able to."

"It's a responsibility I can't handle."

"And I think it's a responsibility you've been chosen for."

"Don't I get any say in it?" Not for the first time did Rafe wish her hair was grown back in so she could have something to tug at in frustration. The soft bristles of her crew cut just tickled her palm.

"Of course you do. It all comes down to free will, remember? You reminded me of that. We are free to make our own choices in life."

After a quiet moment, Rafe gently plucked the pen out of Ashley's fingers. "And this is what? My agreement with a higher power that I'll help chase down the bad guys who escape hell?"

"Look at it this way; you're just expanding your jurisdiction," Ashley replied with a grin.

Rafe stared at the floor as if searching for the answers she needed there. "And what does this mean for us?"

Ashley's finger caught Rafe under her chin and lifted her head up. "It means we start our own family business, if you want to."

"I'm not quitting my day job."

"I'm not quitting mine either. It just means that sometimes the regular nine-to-five work will include some nighttime investigations. I doubt we'll come across any more human-demons for a while, but we can always help out with the more common garden variety."

Rafe caught Ashley's hand in her own. "Now that this case is solved, do you have to move on?" The fear of Ashley's departure tore a gaping hole in Rafe's chest. She was surprised Ashley couldn't see it.

"I've asked to stay. I'd like to see what Chicago has to offer a girl with a glamour." She ran her hand through Rafe's blunt hair, tickling her scalp. "I'm sure I can find something to keep me busy here. If nothing else, there's the demon hub by my building."

"Do you have to live there in order to protect it?"

Ashley's face creased into a sly smile. "Why, Detective, are you proposing I rent out a U-Haul already?"

"I've seen your place. Trinity could carry out what you have to live with." Rafe tugged Ashley toward her, settling her between her legs. "If I'm to become a hunter by your side, I want you by *mine*."

"You're a fast worker."

"I've lived a lifetime in the last few days, Ashley. I don't intend to let time go to waste for propriety's sake. It's too short and unstable not to cling on to what is dear."

Ashley caressed Rafe's cheek. "You're such a romantic behind that badge. I like that a lot." She kissed Rafe softly and tenderly until Rafe took over and the kiss became more heated and raw. Rafe tugged Ashley tight against her center. The pressure of her pants seam against her clitoris was enough to rip a moan from her throat and she quickly forgot where they were.

"There are cameras in this room," Ashley mumbled against Rafe's hungry lips.

"Let them see." Rafe cupped Ashley's buttocks and pulled her in even closer.

"You keep that up and they'll see more than either of us would wish!" Ashley placed a restraining hand on Rafe's chest and pushed back. Rafe groaned at the loss of Ashley's warmth against her.

"You're right. I know you're right, but just once I'd like to remember something nice in this office instead of the death we're surrounded by."

"You keep kissing me like that and your desk will bear witness to something you would have a hard time forgetting!" Ashley took a step back and straightened her shirt. "You do amazing things to me, Rafe."

"Can we continue this tonight?" Rafe couldn't help herself. She ran her fingertips over Ashley's swollen lips and shivered when Ashley licked at them with a quick flash of a warm tongue.

"It's a date." Ashley turned to leave but halted once more at the photos displayed behind them.

Rafe rested a hand on Ashley's shoulder. "I'm really sorry about your brother. Truly I am."

"We're in a constant fight on this planet. Good versus evil. Good won out last night where he was concerned. It's the side I've chosen to fight on."

"It's not that simple, though, is it?" Rafe knew how hard it must be for Ashley to live with what had transpired. Killer or not, demon or not, Lucas Thorpe had still been family. He had been the last link to a father who had already been taken away from them. And he was her brother, one whose sibling rivalry had proved deadly.

"It will take time to reconcile it. For now, a killer has been stopped in his tracks. Any comfort I need I draw from that."

"You really are an angel."

Ashley smiled wryly. "Hardly," she drawled, placing a kiss on Rafe's lips. "My thoughts concerning you aren't in the slightest bit angelic."

"Can I thank God for that?"

"You can thank whoever you like, my love. But I'll expect you to thank me later when I'm done with you."

EPILOGUE

Rafe flipped the valuable silver pen over the backs of her knuckles one way then another in a nervous gesture. She sat atop the roof of Ashley's former building with her attention fixed firmly on the street below.

"Are you sure we're expecting visitors tonight?" she asked Ashley, who was sitting back in her chair ripping open a large bag of chips.

"Yes."

"Shouldn't we be down on the street?" Rafe stopped her movement with the pen and waited for an answer. "Unless you're expecting me to throw this like a streak of lightning from up here."

Ashley shook the bag vigorously and got to her feet. She tipped out a line of chips along the edge of the parapet and then trailed a line across the roof of the building, dumping the remainder of the chips in a pile. "This demon is said to have wings."

Rafe moved further forward in her seat. "So you're laying a food trap for him?"

"He'll be drawn to the smell. Winged demons are voracious eaters. He'll come straight to us. We grab him while he's busy stuffing his face."

"And then?"

"Then the cleanup squad comes. They can take him back to where he belongs, and you and I can go home."

"I like the sound of that last part. It's the whole luring the winged demon straight to us I have a problem with."

"It will make for a nice change from the lesser demons that you capture."

Rafe made a face. "Yeah, let's hear it for variety." She winked at Ashley to take the sting out of her sarcasm. Rafe had never been happier since Ashley had moved in with her. It gave her a sense of peace she'd never experienced before. Ashley had brought so much into her world, not least of all love. Rafe wouldn't swap a second of it, even the hours spent on top of a run-down building waiting for demon bait to fly by.

"Heads up; I smell sulfur," Ashley said.

"I don't know how you can smell anything over the smell coming from the chips." Rafe strained to see if she could spot anything escaping from the sidewalk below.

"Would you care to step back into the shadows with me and get your spear ready?" Ashley reached for Rafe's hand and helped her up from her chair.

"I'd feel happier with my gun."

"I know, sweetheart, but bullets just don't cut it."

"I only need the Spear of Light," Rafe said, reciting what was drilled into her brain. She'd heard it often enough from Ashley every time she brought up the fact that, sometimes, she'd really just like to stick a bullet in a demon and have it count. She stepped back into the shadows of the doorway and readied her weapon with a press of the button. The spear appeared with its regular speed.

"That's my girl." Ashley cuddled against Rafe's back as they waited.

Rafe heard an ominous sound. It was the heavy, labored flap of wings unlike any bird she had ever heard fly. Accompanied by a rasping breathing noise, the air suddenly began to vibrate around them. Rafe looked over her shoulder at Ashley. "Just how big is this thing going to be?"

"Nothing you can't handle. I have the utmost faith in you." Ashley smiled up at Rafe, her love shining from her eyes brighter than any glamour she could employ.

That faith spurred Rafe forward with Ashley by her side, confident that, together, they could face anything hell threw at them.

About the Author

Lesley Davis lives in the West Midlands of England. She is a die-hard science fiction/fantasy fan in all its forms and an extremely passionate gamer. When her Nintendo DSi is out of her grasp, Lesley is to be found seated before the computer writing.

Visit her online at www.lesleydavisauthor.co.uk.

Books Available From Bold Strokes Books

Dark Wings Descending by Lesley Davis. What if the demons you face in life are real? Chicago detective Rafe Douglas is about to find out. (978-1-60282-660-1)

sunfall by Nell Stark and Trinity Tam. The final installment of the everafter series. Valentine Darrow and Alexa Newland work to rebuild their relationship even as they find themselves at the heart of the struggle that will determine a new world order for vampires and wereshifters. (978-1-60282-661-8)

Mission of Desire by Terri Richards. Nicole Kennedy finds herself in Africa at the center of an international conspiracy and is rescued by the beautiful but arrogant government agent Kira Anthony—but can Nicole trust Kira, or is she blinded by desire? (978-1-60282-662-5)

Boys of Summer, edited by Steve Berman. Stories of young love and adventure, when the sky's ceiling is a bright blue marvel, when another boy's laughter at the beach can distract from dull summer jobs. (978-1-60282-663-2)

The Locket and the Flintlock by Rebecca S. Buck. When Regency gentlewoman Lucia Foxe is robbed on the highway, will the masked outlaw who stole Lucia's precious locket also claim her heart? (978-1-60282-664-9)

Calendar Boys by Zachary Logan. A man a month will keep you excited year-round. (978-1-60282-665-6)

Burgundy Betrayal by Sheri Lewis Wohl. Park Ranger Kara Lynch has no idea she's a witch until dead bodies begin to pile up in her park, forcing her to turn to beautiful and sexy shape-shifter Camille Black Wolf for help in stopping a rogue werewolf. (978-1-60282-654-0)

LoveLife by Rachel Spangler. When Joey Lang unintentionally becomes a client of life coach Elaine Raitt, the relationship becomes complicated as they develop feelings that make them question their purpose in love and life. (978-1-60282-655-7)

The Fling by Rebekah Weatherspoon. When the ultimate fantasy of a one-night stand with her trainer, Oksana Gorinkov, suddenly turns into more, reality show producer Annie Collins opens her life to a new type of love she's never imagined. (978-1-60282-656-4)

Ill Will by J.M. Redmann. New Orleans PI Micky Knight must untangle a twisted web of healthcare fraud that leads to murder—and puts those closest to her most at risk. (978-1-60282-657-1)

Buccaneer Island by J.P. Beausejour. In the rough world of Caribbean piracy, a man is what he makes of himself—or what a stronger man makes of him. (978-1-60282-658-8)

Twelve O'Clock Tales by Felice Picano. The fourth collection of short fiction by legendary novelist and memoirist Felice Picano. Thirteen dark tales that will thrill and disturb, discomfort and titillate, enthrall and leave you wondering. (978-1-60282-659-5)

Words to Die By by William Holden. Sixteen answers to the question: What causes a mind to curdle? (978-1-60282-653-3)

Tyger, Tyger, Burning Bright by Justine Saracen. Love does not conquer all, but when all of Europe is on fire, it's better than going to hell alone. (978-1-60282-652-6)

Night Hunt by L.L. Raand. When dormant powers ignite, the wolf Were pack is thrown into violent upheaval, and Sylvan's pregnant mate is at the center of the turmoil. A Midnight Hunters novel. (978-1-60282-647-2)

Demons are Forever by Kim Baldwin and Xenia Alexiou. Elite Operative Landis "Chase" Coolidge enlists the help of high-class call girl Heather Snyder to track down a kidnapped colleague embroiled in a global black market organ-harvesting ring. (978-1-60282-648-9)

Runaway by Anne Laughlin. When Jan Roberts is hired to find a teenager who has run away to live with a group of antigovernment survivalists, she's forced to return to the life she escaped when she was a teenager herself. (978-1-60282-649-6)

Street Dreams by Tama Wise. Tyson Rua has more than his fair share of problems growing up in New Zealand—he's gay, he's falling in love, and he's run afoul of the local hip-hop crew leader just as he's trying to make it as a graffiti artist. (978-1-60282-650-2)

Women of the Dark Streets: Lesbian Paranormal by Radclyffe and Stacia Seaman, eds. Erotic tales of the supernatural—a world of vampires, werewolves, witches, ghosts, and demons—by the authors of Bold Strokes Books. (978-1-60282-651-9)

Derrick Steele: Private Dick—The Case of the Hollywood Hustlers by Zavo. Derrick Steele, a hard-drinking, lusty private detective, is being framed for the murder of a hustler in downtown Los Angeles. When his brother's friend Daniel McAllister joins the investigation, their growing attraction might prove to be more explosive than the case. (978-1-60282-596-3)

Nice Butt: Gay Anal Eroticism edited by Shane Allison. From toys to teasing, spanking to sporting, some of the best gay erotic scribes celebrate the hottest and most creative in new erotica. (978-1-60282-635-9)

Murder in the Irish Channel by Greg Herren. Chanse MacLeod investigates the disappearance of a female activist fighting the Archdiocese of New Orleans and a powerful real estate syndicate. (978-1-60282-584-0)